MISTER'S MISS

C. ROBINS

PAGE PUBLISHING, INC.
New York, NY

First originally published by Page Publishing, Inc. 2018

ISBN 978-1-64214-174-0 (Paperback)
ISBN 978-1-64214-175-7 (Digital)

Printed in the United States of America

• • • • • • • ● • • • • • •

Mister Revealed

Winter months sprung into spring, carrying with it a frigid arctic breeze that would soon be replaced by a much warmer zephyr that could accurately be described as chilly air microwaved on medium. Even the melting morning dew that encompassed the faded blades of grass helped polish up the lackluster green right in front of the man known as Mister. This fabulous spring morning lent Mister a view into beauty that he had not seen in all his existence. Mister's once closed soul would soon be open wide, helping him to see where he had once been and was going. His plight had been long and turbulent, but now, hope was finally springing eternal. The expected seasonal changes happening all around Mister were as transparent as transparent could be, yet the unexpected ones directly happening to him went unnoticed. While Mister could not yet feel the formulating changes, they would soon plot him a new course.

Mister is a thirty-something man living in a sad existence. Throughout the years of his ever-increasing age, his struggles were constantly being thrown into a blender and mixed up with ice, alcohol, and negativity, sinking him deeper into the darkness. Mister's compassionate kindness was still there, but now, his once-bold gestures were ever so subtle. As his undying spirit of yesterday kept growing blurrier by the day, he felt more like a one-hundred-thirty-something-year-old lost soul roaming a battlefield laden with landmines than a man in the prime of his life. Although the older and wiser Mister was not yet panicking, he surely felt the walls closing in. All four walls were about to intersect, and he had no clue on how to react. Loss, loneliness, and civil unrest kept Mister locked down in his own emotionally made solitary confinement, yet the only thing he wanted to have was a normal life. He could not handle any more misadventures, period; his psyche was too fragile to go through anything else alone. While Mister lusted after change, all he found was status quo. He was sick and tired of wading through the same old shit, but day after day, he reluctantly pushed through it all on his own.

Overall Mister's life was good; not perfect, but it was better than the majority. For the first twelve years, he cruised through life with melting butter sticks attached to his feet. His childhood was filled with riding bikes and playing with the neighborhood kids in a new housing subdivision on the edge of suburbia. Mister's parents passed down to him the knowledge of life rather than the green, gold, and silver world currency. The knowledge he was taught greatly made his inbred emotions more sensitive than most boys his age, forever compounding his every feeling. His strong religious upbringing kept his morality in-check even when he did not want it to.

From an early age, Mister physically, emotionally, and financially gave himself without expectations of a return. He must have been five years old when he bashfully walked up to the fluffy red-and-white Christmas dressed bell ringer with a mature agenda for a five-year-old. This Christmastime, Mister passed up the vending machine gumballs and cheap plastic-made toys. Instead, he gracefully smiled at the Salvation Army volunteer while dropping in the handful of change that his mom just gave him, then skipped away with his eyes and heart wide open to faith without even knowing what it was. Even though he did not know anything about faith, he felt joyful feelings far deeper in his spirit than a young man his age could ever feel. None of his other siblings were given that kind of ability, making Mister the shy family donor. Mister learned what to do and what not to do through the eyes of his older siblings. He was the baby of the family, two brothers and one sister. He saw the good and the bad at the same time while vicariously living through his older siblings. He saw them stay out late, break all the household rules, and pick the wrong friends to hang out with. He even sometimes saw the police at the front door because of one of his older brothers was in trouble again. He had the opportunity to be the good one, and that is what Mister became.

As he grew, Mister developed into a shy young man that took his gentlemanlike presence wherever he went. He was always cordial, compassionate, and went after everything he wanted with strong passion. Mister's astrology sign gave him strong leading qualities that helped him endure all his trials with resounding strength. From the age of eight, Mister was involved with sports, keeping focused on being the best player that he could be. He played baseball and soccer for many years. Sports kept him naive to the world's negativity while thrusting his hope and positivity forward. Mister kept to himself and grew into the best sports star he could be. He pushed himself hard without ever knowing what a perfectionist was; for hours on end, he practiced kicking the soccer ball around or throwing a tennis ball up against the garage door while pretending to be a pitcher in the World Series. Although Mister was too young then to conceptually grasp pride, he felt it while helping lead his teams to countless victories. He quickly became the star of the team, humbly accepting the spotlight. Mister won several trophies for first-and-second-place finishes in tournaments and league play, but those early victories were soon lost forever. His early dream aspirations of being a professional baseball player lasted until adulthood began. His sudden lost interest in sports gave way to needs of being laid.

He was a shy guy then, but he already knew what he wanted out of life—success. Even though Mister was socially laidback and too reserved to go out and take whatever he wanted, his pumping testosterone demanded different. While his lack of social interaction kept his "hanging out with the right crowd" a steady constant, he immensely struggled to tame his raging hormones. Although he managed them well enough, he was jealous of how his friends went out and fucked, sucked, and kissed whomever they wanted to without feeling any guilt. It was Mister's proper upbringing that forced him to feel the guilt from doing wrong, and because of that, he kept his friends at a certain distance, not ever letting any of them get close enough to cause hurt. He had certain reasons why he did that; one of those reasons came from seeing his older siblings emotionally scarred by their friend's actions. Mister did not want that for himself, which forced him to keep all his friends at a two-foot distance.

Despite all his lonely sadness, Mister was a man full of sexual tease that could melt anyone's numbness to pleasure. The plethora of erotic fantasies stored up in his head and heart laid dormant waiting for the right woman to come along and breathe life into them. However, finding the woman in his erotic dreams would not matter if he could not break out of his emotionally sentenced self-made prison cell. There were many times that Mister found himself standing at the edge, not sure if he should jump headfirst over the gnarly cliff right into the dark awaiting abyss or keep on waiting to find the end of the tunnel. Every day's hesitance left him standing all alone on the cliff edge, teeter-tottering back and forth, when all he wanted to do was get off the ride.

While his personal life was an epic disaster, his professional life was much better, although the last year had been a real struggle. Over the years, his strong work ethic excelled him to the top of his job scale. But as of late, his work performance had been on a sloping downward spiral. Part of it was the crappy economy, and the other part of it was a lack of enthusiasm for life. For months now, Mister had been faking his once-genuine enthusiasm. Even when he felt something good starting to happen, he stayed stuck playing the zero-sum game, bound to a path leading nowhere good.

Then two months ago, an unsuspecting person pulled out the rug right from under where Mister stood. His boss, Mr. Tsar, set up a one-month ten-thousand-dollar sales contest. The money would be awarded to the salesperson that reached that ludicrous sales total by month's end. The total number that Mr. Tsar set was an obscene goal to meet, meant to challenge both of their skill sets. When his coworker D met the sales goal and won the contest, it devastated Mister in many ways. D won it by flaunting her curvaceous thick hips, voluptuous breasts, and short skirts to ogling CEOs to win their attention and make more sales than he did. Sure, Mister was happy for D that she had won the contest, but he would have rather have had a fair fight. He knew right from the start of the contest that he might be doomed by her mega-sassy appearance if she played her flaunt-the-assets game. D used her looks to cheat herself to victory. But once D realized how much the loss stung Mister due to her unprofessional tactics, she tried to make it up to him, but the damage was already done. It made him realize he was not the MVP star of the team anymore. Instead, the loss made him feel like he was expendable. The company and the world could revolve without a Mister in it.

When D cheated and won the contest, it left all of Mister's raw nerves exposed. Even though Mister got along with his boss well enough to not worry for his job, his own perfectionist ways still conjured up fear. His life had not changed much over the years. Positive progressive change is what he needed most. That recent sales competition loss to D brought up deep emotional pain that had been festering inside Mister for a long time. Regardless of D's method she used to make her sales, her monthly sales numbers did not falter or waver. For a week after the loss, Mister kept himself busy to avoid thinking about his life's dysfunctionality. D exposed his insecurities more than he ever thought possible. Despite the sales contest loss, Mister kept trying to push through the negative rhetoric one day at a time, not ever recovering from last month's fallout.

It was three years ago since Mister's last vacation. It was not so much a vacation, more than it was a three-week sabbatical to put himself back together from the heartbreak that his ex-fiancée left him with. He thought she was the one. They met at his previous company, having had a strong working friendship that quickly turned into a relationship. Mister had been missing a soulful connection in his life ever since his parents departed the world. He sought out that emotional connectivity in his ex-fiancée, but she turned out to be one of those unpredictable things not worth having. Some friendships should stay friendly, and theirs was one of those. The dynamics became overly complicated way too fast for both of their likings. Intimacy was once okay but not ever earth-shattering. Good sex turned boring and repetitive, and to Mister, that was devastating. He liked intimacy more than anything else; a hot erotic connection with an equally matched partner was his thing. He knew his ex-fiancée was not prepared to give him that as she was more focused on her career than him. Their friendship that quickly turned into a relationship was doomed from the start, but his familiarity with her idiosyncrasies made him stay. Mister was the last one to know what was happening when their relationship unexpectedly ended. He went from being a comfortably taken fiancé to an uncomfortable bachelor in the brevity of a few hours on an idle February Thursday some three years ago. She abruptly walked out of his life, severely blindsiding him. The aftermath of her devastation caused Mister to extend and reinforce his fifty-five-foot-tall wall of emotional solace.

During those dark weeks of an extended sabbatical three years ago, he contemplated suicide on several occasions but never went through with it. He loved life too much to end it over a woman. Instead, he broke down and rebuilt himself back up. He dealt with his parents' tragic death and the loss of his fiancée simultaneously. Ever since that three-week soul-searching journey, Mister put his nose to the grindstone, working three years with unwavering determination. Though the last eleven months was a rough patch. All past insecurities slowly crept back in, seriously affecting his professional existence more than ever before. A lot of sleepless nights took their toll on his emotional fragility, always sending him back down to his self-inflicted dungeon of sad loneliness, making Mister feel the stinging pain of failed relationships, lost loves, and bad investments repeatedly. No matter what Mister did or did not do, bad luck and disappointment always lingered around the next corner.

Ever since the onset of adulthood began for Mister, he developed a second personality out of survival. He did not have multiple personalities, but instead, he learned to always let his compassionate gentleness be shown, never showing his inward turmoil. The one good thing about his detached personality was that it allowed him to have overwhelming desires to flirt with life. Flirt with life, he did. From wearing stylish outfits to using his eyes to make every woman wet with the "what if" possibility, Mister's bold outward appearance showed off a mystique that was far from who the real Mister was. His outer appearance projected a strong man in control of everything, but his inner emotions were bound up with vulnerable complexities that made him uncomfortable to be himself. He was born a sexual god, yet life's circumstances mostly kept his talented tongue and sweltering charm held captive. Although his subdued charisma unintentionally made everyone stand up and take notice, the best part of him was locked away. Where the world expected a cocky loudmouth know-it-all, Mister was anything but. The quietness and depth of his moral character left people wanting to know more. His mystique and mystery made everyone near and far intrigued.

For the last nine months, he put on a show for everyone to see. No one knew about his fake façade but Mister. It was something he chose to keep to himself. Not even D, his closest friend and coworker, knew how he had been feeling. To make matters worse, he occasionally felt the weight of the world's pain resting squarely on his shoulders. Feelings of overwhelming helplessness came and came again. Multiple failed attempts made him want to quit trying to seek out a joyful ending. He hid behind infrequent meaningless relationships well. The one sure thing Mister knew about himself was his convincing intensity. He hated to break hearts, but sometimes it happened that way. He knew what he was looking for in a companion, but the one he wanted was already spoken for. It stung to not be able to have the one he wanted, but he kept on going. He vowed to himself that his next relationship would not end up like the last one did, so the empty time in between doomed friendships were spent going on frequent out-of-town blackjack trips. While the monotony bored him sad, the blackjack losses devastated his bottom-line. All the losses kept adding up in his disappointments column, never putting a W in the win column. He was only a few wins away from achieving victory, yet the losses kept coming.

Unintentionally, Mister kept torturing himself by continually playing the unwinnable game of life. He knew he could not win the game if he did not play it right. Unfortunately, Mister was never taught how to win the emotional game of life. He did not know how to play it to win, at least not yet. Every time he played another round of the unwinnable game, he lost. The losses kept Mister a shackled-up prisoner in his own penal institution. Not even the people closest to him could break him out of his self-made prison. Despite it all, Mister kept waking up to put on his shoes so that he could traipse through the same motions and emotions one day at a time. He lived his life with diminishing expectations that one day all his self-induced torture and emotional sadness would end, but the wait was taking countless years off his life.

Mister's once-positive attitude was now buried deep underneath the brick-and-mortar foundation of his self-created cell. Not even a sunroof or a window could be found. Just cold pebble-like concrete surrounded his jail cell. Day after day, his emotional disconnect from the world grew. Until he could resolve his conflicted personal life, total isolation was exactly how Mister needed it to be.

He sought out and tried everything under the sun to get out from under his emotional debacle, from meaningless three-month relationships to counseling to years of trying to make a married woman his. All his futile attempts to find the right one miserably failed. So Mister sat, laid, and stayed in his cold emotional prison cell anchored to the foundation with thick steel-forged chains that wrapped around his bare-naked soul. Those same steel chains weakened his once-strong self-made confidence. His strong childhood confidence of yesterday was gone, squelched by all his misadventures. He spent years trying to fight off the emotional pain, but in the end, it was loneliness and sadness that trickled out of his unsealable wounds. The constant pain was unbearable, but so were the intense sexual thoughts that constantly monopolized his brilliant mind. A grown man in appearance yet a teenage boy in thought kept fueling his sexually perverted frustrations. The only thing Mister truly wanted was happiness so that he could live free and die hard.

He needed to be touched, teased, pleased, and appreciated more than he needed to be left alone wallowing in self-pity. He waited and waited and waited. Something. Anything had to happen before he succumbed to his inevitable fate. When something simple was all it would take for Mister to win his emotionally fought civil war, not one glimmer of hope had come. Maybe a dream or a nervous breakdown would relinquish his past pain. Even finding a woman with muse-like qualities to raise up his ego while stroking down on his cock with superior mastery could inspire change. Mister needed an intimate bond with the opposite sex to bring out his sensualistic personality deeper into the unknown world of erotica. He needed a Miss to make him have withdrawals while physically separated yet, while together, soothing his charm with her strong ladylike character anywhere they were at.

Everyone close to Mister sensed his sadness, but he would not ever talk to anyone about it. Something had to give. He did not know if a break from life would truly lend him fresh perspective or not, although it was well worth the shot. Just last night, D told Mister to take a vacation. It was rare he listened to anyone, but since D was more than a coworker, he told Mr. Tsar, his boss, that he needed a break. Without any further questioning, Mr. Tsar gave him what he wanted, a break.

Mister planned to be back the day of the quarterly meeting in two weeks. Plans to strengthen his core and rebuild lost enthusiasm were the only things he had on his agenda. As he began his second sabbatical in three years, he detoxed alone and secluded himself in his big bedroom suite with Rocket by his side. He spent the thirteen days off reconstructing his past and planning his future.

CHAPTER 2

• • • • • • • • • ● • • • • • •

Swirling Change All Around

On his last day off, just when Mister thought he had it all figured out, change rapped once on the door. It was one of those silent inter-ruptions that you feel more than hear. He dreamed a dream that forever changed him. He only needed to pick himself up and get over to the bright lights of possibility to will his new future into existence. As vivid and as real as life itself, he woke up dazed and confused to everything he once knew.

As his eyes opened to the weirdness of a wild one-night stand with an extra splash of serendipity, Mister did not know if he was dreaming or awake. However, Rocket's sharp obnoxious bark star-tled Mister fully awake, and he knew he was not dreaming anymore. He laid fully sprawled out on his California king-size bed with all his stark-naked emotions exposed for the entire world to see. He woke up a sweaty mess with his heart nearly thumping out of his chest. With a confused mind and a heavy heart, he took up a deep lung-filling breath and paused after he could not take in any more air. He held his breath for eighteen seconds to allow the fresh o2 purity to help him catch his breath from the wild ride he just stepped off. Mister then exhaled all the bad emotional shit that he had been carrying around for decades. It was that small morning moment of spectacular that gave Mister back his lost confidence and renewed his once-lost feelings of victory. He smelt money and pleasure in the same room conjugating with the powerful aromas of fresh budding flowers growing yards outside of his bedroom windows. As the aromas filled up Mister's bedchamber, he felt more alive than he had in all his years of existence. The slightest breeze blew in sweet fragrances of life while the soft morning rays of sunlight warmed up the satin sheets he laid on. Mindful clarity nudged life forward on a day that Mister never thought would ever come.

Eventually, his morning euphoria was broken. As he begrudgingly picked up his phone to see what time it was, he felt instant relief knowing that he woke up earlier than his alarm clock did. His pulse raced, and the sting in his eyes uncomfortably burned from the sweat that had seeped in. Although the burn was not wanted, it kept him strongly aware of what just happened. Mister was in a hazy fog of disbelief as he moved around in his all but empty bed while contemplating his next move. He rolled over and sat up, being careful not to accidentally kick Rocket off the end of the bed. He treated Rocket like his best friend, probably because he was his only close confidant. That part of Mister's life was a cliché, whereas the rest of it wasn't so much. Rocket was all he had left. His best friend was there before and after his fiancée yo-yoed in and out of his life. At least Rocket was the one love in Mister's life that could not walk out on him.

He used his pillows to prop himself up against the headboard. The sheets and comforter were mostly on the floor from all the bucking around he did while sleeping through his naughty dream of euphoria. Even his satin matched pillowcases were damp to the touch. Mister liked the feel of satin; it was slick and smooth, and it always matched his body's temperature within minutes of being draped over his manly skin. Satin always brought out the naughty in Mister. Anytime he wanted to get frisky with the sheets, he could seduce them with subtle thrusts from his powerful hips. Without any resistance, Mister always took from them what he wanted. The submissive satin never said no to his convincing charms. Though this morning Mister would not be a need to make a move on sassy Miss Satin due to her specialized midnight attention that coaxed the semen out of his big shaft as he dreamed a wet dream that was more real than he anticipated. The glimmering satin blue sheets lying beneath his masculine sculpted body made the good morning great.

He went to bed buzzed on whiskey with his emotions bleeding out all over his king-size bed. Yet when he awoke, he had peace in his heart and found desire in his once-lost soul. Where once sat a dark heavy rain cloud that followed him everywhere, there was none. Yet it was the morning breeze whisking in through the slightly opened window that made his blue cotton tank top and style matched button-fly boxer brilliantly cling to his clammy skin, outlining his flaccid member with exquisite visual acuity. As the reality of his lucid wet dream set in, Mister finally awoke. Standing up on the heated tile floors, he made his way to the bathroom, stumbling along the way. While the room spun around, he thought that he might have drank too much alcohol last night when he did not. For the most part, Mister drank only to be buzzed, not incoherently smashed, so his off-balanced state was curiously annoying.

Around and around, the walls slowly jogged by. The music from the night before still played subtly in the background. To Mister, the room was uncontrollably spinning, yet he rode the spun, spinning high above it all. Despite it being morning, Mister's body was already physically exhausted from having the night dream. He was absolutely confused but, at the same time, overjoyed with stiff energy. He needed a sedative and a pick-me-up all at the same time. The sedative to tame his amped-up energy and a pick-me-up to revive his physically drained body. For being his first day back to work in thirteen days, Mister's mind was overstimulated as if he drank two pots of coffee in a fifteen-minute span of time.

Even while being jittery and off-balance, he made it into the bathroom without falling. He stopped at the sink to visually check himself out in the mirror. He needed to make sure he looked just as he had looked the previous morning. He saw the same manly sculpted curves of his European ancestry beaming back, although his hair was more salt and peppered with silver than he remembered. He stood just under six feet tall, with hazel-colored eyes standing out best. Then when he saw morning whiskers, he knew he was the same Mister, though his face was a little bit swollen and pale from night sweats. His entire face was covered in sweat. Mister splashed some cold tap water onto his face, then looked at himself in the mirror again to see what changed. Something changed, but he did not know what. The more he stared at a three-quarter naked man posing in the pale blue morning light, the more he noticed a very snazzy shimmering silhouetted glow all around him that told him much more than he visually saw. Sure, it was only a silly dreamed-up fantasy, but Mister somehow knew any kind of emotional episode like that could get him out of solitary confinement. Just one breakthrough was all it took for Mister to get back into the unwinnable game and win. This he knew.

Is this it? Is this really the end of my self-imposed jail sentence? It cannot be. Can it?

His lucid wet dream literally left him speechless with cottonmouth. He could not take the dryness anymore, so he grabbed for the glass of water sitting on the bedside table and swallowed it down. The big gulp of water immediately soothed his parchedness. As the morning minutes ticktocked by, he remained dazed and confused to all that just happened. Mister's perfect impression of his steamy dream was subtly losing its sharpness. If it were not for the smell of sweat and drying ejaculated semen, he might not have remembered his nocturnal wet dream as perfectly as he did.

With fading memories, Mister remembered stuffing a faded-blue notebook in his bedside table drawer for times just like this. He put the notebook there well over two years ago just in case he had another déjà-vu-like dream worth writing down. He reached over to the dark cherry-pine-stained table, opened the drawer, and took out the faded-blue notebook. He closed his eyes and zoomed in on as many of the details as he possibly could. Before Mister picked up the cheap plastic green ballpoint pen, he flipped open the notebook to the first blank page and scribbled down anything and everything he could remember about the dream. No matter how insignificant it was, he wrote it down. From experience, he knew that he could not rush to any foredrawn conclusions. Everything he wrote down would later on help him make sense of its tangled and untangled meanings. He saved deciphering it for later.

CHAPTER 3

● ● ● ● ● ● ● ● ● ● ● ● ● ● ●

Lucid Wet Dream

Mister was standing in a mid-length line of passengers that were all waiting to board the pristine mirage. The line snaked around several orange-and-black pylons that kept everyone neatly spaced out in an orderly line while they nervously waited their turn to board the big vessel. She was grand and beautiful. Tall and stacked with sensualistic curves that stretched the full length of her 404 feet of chivalrous magnificence. All he could do was stare at her in complete awe.

The tranquil sounds of exotic island rhythms played throughout the ship's intercom while secretly seducing her entire passenger list. Mister saw many others around him patiently waiting to board the same pristine virgin ship that he was about to board. Everyone appeared to be complete strangers to each other. Type A and B personalities were making friends while the type Cs kept to themselves. Every type was mystified in their own way about what was about to happen. There was an overwhelming sense of mystique that Mister felt swirling all around. Its mystique intrigued his fancy.

Mister got the impression that everyone boarding the splendid megaship was clueless as to where they were going and why they were there. All the lost souls boarding the cruise ship were being laid with fresh-cut flowers while listening to body-grinding music echoing everywhere. The exotic mixtures of yellow, red, and green petals were proof that paradise exists. He recalled seeing the dwindling line of beautiful men and gorgeous women unable to contain their bubbly anticipation, but that did not change the mysterious confusion.

Mister sought out answers to unknown questions that he had no knowledge of yet.

The gawking line of eager passengers had to watch hundreds pass through the ship's threshold before they did, being patient as patiently patient could be. As Mister approached the ten-story-high hull, he was immediately seduced by her bright white-and-blue paint job with striking logo decaled over her vast beauty just above the one-ton dangling-down anchor. Nearing the front of the line, Mister looked behind him to see how many others remained unboarded. Then all visual acuity went black as if someone blindfolded him without his consent. The echoes from the water lapping up against her thick body and the squawks coming from the nearby seagulls let Mister see what he could not. He was severely seduced by the smells and island beats playing in the background. He soaked up the erotic sounds all around him, lulling him into the exact place he needed to be. His eyes were closed, yet his mind was wide open, taking it all in.

A small pause in his writing let him build up the complete dreamland already laid out in his perverted subconscious. He drew up a deep breath to take the whole confusing cruise into his psyche. Remembering all those finer details helped Mister recall the vividness with incredible accuracy.

The scent was the purest he ever breathed in. The mixture of salty sea air and fresh exotic passion petals sunk him deep into a catatonic subconscious state of tonic immobility. When the boarding attendant reminded him to have his ticket and identification out, it startled him alert to everything with strong visual acuity. He noticed everyone around seemed wickedly excited with growing anticipation of things to come. He sensed a peculiar, nervous undertone which threw him off. Mister felt as though everyone that was boarding the ship was meant to be there on his or her own terms and his or her own reasons even though it was his dream. That confused him more than anything else did. It was as if others dreamed up the same cruise ship dream with different planned agendas on the same ship heading for the same place.

Mister found out that his own path and stateroom were pre-bought and determined even before he fell asleep. The things he saw and felt made him feel like it was another bout of déjà vu happening all over again. From time to time, Mister had dreams of something specific, then months or even years later, that exact dream played itself out in living color. He always thought it was weird how it happened that way, but over the years, he let those déjà vu dreams be comforting reminders that he was supposed to be there at that exact place and time. With many levels of mystery to his lucid wet dream, Mister felt confused and lost, yet he kept filling up the blank pages with scribbled down verbiage. He noted his lost feelings in the side column in small quotations. He placed a question mark with a circle next to it for a strong reminder to figure it out later. He needed to put his lucid dream in perspective before making any definitive conclusions.

He felt a sinister perversion all around him as he was the next in line to board the ship. As he crossed over the noisy clanking metal platform, his entire personality changed. He became sexually aggressive with the echoing sounds and pure sea air penetrating deep into his locked-up subconscious. The sounds and smells turned him on to romance of the naughty kind, leaving him with strong impressions that his dream was more than just another wet dream. It was a life-altering journey on a cruise ship bound for somewhere special.

Mister's once-sharp kinetic impressions were beginning to fade away without his permission. He wrote faster and thought harder just so he would not leave anything out of his written-down memories.

He could not remember checking in at the registration desk, but the memory of his dream picked back up with him standing outside of his brilliant turquoise grandiose stateroom door. He looked up and down the hallways, admiring her rich splendor. He caught the ship's larger-than-life logo again, but he still could not make out her name as it was blurred in his dreamlike peripherals. He did not see the bellhop unlock the door, but instead, he heard the bellhop inserting the key into the door lock; they were over-amplified in his psychedelic mind-set. Three clicks of the stateroom door were heard before the bellhop led him all the way in. As he walked over the silver-accented threshold, he was in awestruck disbelief from the first impressions of his magnificent stateroom. He knew it was out of his feasibility range, but then again, it was just a rich dream in his middle-classed mind. The room looked and smelled new and was spectacular in every probable way. The carpet was a medium-dark earth tone that over time would blend in any future stains with subtlety while preserving her sex symbol swagger. The walls were painted in an erotic red, accented with light-blue trim throughout. The stateroom also had a separate sitting area with a private wet bar that was dressed up with crystal bling and a sparkly black-and-red-specked granite countertop. There were no TVs to speak of, but there was an electric fireplace that could be turned on with the press of a button. Even the bathroom had magnificent matching decorations from the hard marble floors to the same red-and-blue-swirled colors in the hard granite tiles that dressed up the sink and shower. The shower was big enough for a five-person orgy, with three massaging showerheads overtop and clear glass all the way to the ceiling. What particularly caught his fancy was the bed. It sat low to the ground with a virgin-white veil all around it. The comforter was deep burgundy red with speckles of white all over it, and the satin sheets were dyed a warm passion red that spoke the language of lust. In the corner of the room was an oversized chair specifically made for sex. It was big and fluffy with sweeping curves of enjoyment. It was the perfect height for deep sexual penetration unless you wanted more than two participants. However, the best part of the entire room had to be the sliding glass door that led out to the stateroom's very own private balcony area. Luckily, every stateroom had its own secluded balcony designed for outdoor high-sea romance.

After the bell servant finished hanging his dress shirts in the closet, he reached down into his bag of goodies and pulled out a special treat for the man of the hour. It was the sexiest bottle of Gentleman Jack Mister ever saw. After setting down the big bottle of whiskey, the bell servant quickly turned magician and vanished into thin air. Immediately, Mister became puzzled on how the bell staff could have known that Gentleman Jack was his favorite branded whiskey. Even while being mystified with the staff's knowledge of his drinking preferences, he grabbed the logo-imprinted shot glass and poured himself a double shot of delicious heaven. The rich golden whiskey fell perfectly into the dark-blue see-through glass, not spilling one drop, almost as if he planned it. After he began to sip on the omnipotent whiskey, his mind meticulously tried to figure out what was going on in his subconscious. In between sips, Mister's eyes were drawn to the glass's striking logo that was emblazoned on it. Its vivacious colors jumped off the shot glass three-dimensionally. The same logo that he saw on the ship's hull and throughout the hallway was of a yellowish-red-painted sun peering over a big wave that was painted in light blue. The ship's white-painted bow was placed under a wave that was about to break against the hull. His interests were piqued to know its name. He gave the glass a 360-degree turn around in the palm of his hand until he saw the ship's name for the very first time ever. *Lucid Wet Dream* was her name. Most of his dreams were in black and white, yet this dream was filled with colors galore. The name was etched into the thick blue glass with a rich gold color outlined in red touting the ship's richness.

Right then was when everything started to make some sort of sense. Although he was still confused about where he was at or where he was going, he knew that the break he had been waiting for had come.

The unknowns mixed with confusion caused him to toss back the rest of the first double shot of guilty pleasure, immediately filling it up again for a second go-around. He felt the bold oak and faint fruity flavors tease his taste buds good and hard as the second round of liquid courage slid down the back of his throat without any delay. With the finest whiskey trickling into his bloodstream, Mister meandered over to the sun deck to take in the picture-perfect view. He stared out into the ocean for a few minutes before discovering the handle to his very own sliding glass door. The view of the wild ocean seas made Mister know that he was staying in one of the best staterooms that *Lucid Wet Dream* had to offer.

He looked outwardly, spying on everything that he could see. While on his self-guided tour, he noticed that the deck was made of dark-stained teakwood. Even the outer metal ship wall had a top layer of exposed teakwood. The freshly stained teak could still be smelt, but it was not the aroma that caught his attention next. He spotted two loungers neatly folded up and pinned against the ship's exterior with bright white bungee cords keeping them in place. The loungers and balcony were unexpected treats, but then again, his entire lucid wet dream was an unexpected spectacle that he needed to experience. With the twist of the gold-plated handle, he unlocked the door and slid it open. Curiosity led Mister over to the edge of the balcony where he bathed in the mind-seducing ultra-picturesque ambience of the open ocean and sunset. As the shots of whiskey began intoxicating him, the fresh sea air worked on freeing his tormented soul. With the ship rocking back and forth and the potently smooth Gentleman Jack comingling, it made Mister feel lightheaded and drowsy. Before he fell to the ground, he reached for the closest bungee-corded lounger and unsnapped it free. At this point, Mister was on his knees from all the lightheadedness so much so that he was barely able to unfold the lounger from his knees, but somehow, he climbed onto the lounger and passed out under the orange Creamsicle-colored sunset.

The next thing he remembered was sensing a shadow passing over the top of him. He opened his eyes and saw the bright morning sun shining down on him and his unexpected company. Someone was on his private balcony with him, and he could not believe who she was. An impeccably dressed island beauty was lying beside him on the other lounger, only clad in a shiny bling-covered watermelon thong. She was within touching distance, yet he did not know who she was, how she got there, or who let her in. The longer he was awake, the more confused he was. Mister began to wonder if he had drunk too much or died and was in heaven. Whichever it was, he refused to leave the euphoria behind.

Mister's dream and waking reality infused into one elaborate concoction of pleasure. He was fully engaged and totally aroused while recalling his freshly dreamed dream.

The warm sun teased his less-than-perfect body to life as he lay in the lounger next to her. They basked together under the tropical island sun of temptation. At least she had on a thong to protect her most prevalent assets, whereas Mister was completely naked. Mister did not exactly know how he got naked, but maybe he wasn't supposed to know the hows or whys of it.

He lay under the erotic glow of the hot morning sun for a while longer, pretending to be asleep. With squinting eyes, he kept strict watch on his dish of deliciousness. His mind spun a million miles per hour. He was completely seduced by the sweet coconut scent permeating from the tanning lotion that was mysteriously rubbed into his untanned skin. Even hours after his drinking binge of the night before had come and gone, the bold aftertaste of whiskey still clung to his flavor pallet. However, seeing his semi-erect cock glistening from the suntan lotion and sweat made Mister want to get off right in front of her.

As the minutes passed by, Mister's body subtly shifted around to let his new friend know that he was awake. Their first eye-to-eye contact was completed with smiles and nods. He tried to make conversation with her, but she only looked at him and kept smiling. He was shocked to discover she did not want to talk. His babbling only distracted her for a few seconds before she regained control over him. She leaned over into his personal space while using her index finger to trace the outline of his desirable lips. He relaxed in his lounger as she took complete control. She used her unmanicured index finger as a pleasure toy, vertically pushing it up against his lips as if suggesting him not to say one more word. While her right index finger hushed him up, her left index finger enforced her no-words policy as she pressed it up against her glittery red-painted lips.

Surrendering control was all new to Mister. He never really had a powerful woman in his life to take the reins like that before. So when she took control over him in his dream, he was completely turned on as he wrote it down.

When his island beauty stood up from her lounger, so did his uncovered erection. She looked at him and saw his eyes saying yes. He was drawn to her presence like metal to a magnet. She prominently stood next to her lounger, showing off her vibrant watermelon-colored thong that augmented the rest of her naked curves for his viewing pleasure.

That was when he realized there were too many symbols and suggestive meanings for this to be another sexually repressed wet dream. Her control over Mister tweaked his nipples with an exuberant amount of sexual energy that ran right through him.

Her dark-golden tanned hips glistened from the small beads of sweat that mixed well together with her coconut suntan lotion. Besides the obvious scent of coconuts, the sunning lotion also protected and enhanced her delicate olive-colored skin. In all her enormous presence, she used scent, visual stimulation, and the natural sea backdrop to keep his attraction hard and steady while gracefully making her way over to his lounger. Her curvy hips stood out to his erotic delights. Mister was dumbfounded as he admired her potent sex appeal. Then his island beauty visitor swayed her thick hips back and forth on a short hop over to his lounger. She saw from his erection that his attention was solely focused on her. His seductive bedroom eyes were what she indulged in first, followed by his naughty smirk. As her eyes scanned over his every visible inch, she unequivocally knew he wanted to be deep inside of her due to his staring back.

She then lifted her left leg high enough so that she could get it up and over his lounger all in one fluid motion. As she stood over the top of him, her striking beauty penetrated his shaved balls with precision aptitude. She was serious; that was clear from the get-go. She knew he wanted to speak, but she would not have any of that. The only way that the two of them could effectively communicate was through eye and facial gestures. Mister was not going to let that stop him from telling her exactly what was on his mind.

Their eyes began to make slow love to each other's souls while they silently shared hot intimate truths about each other. Her provocative smile kept him hypnotized with her bright pearl-white-colored teeth, yet it was her elusive glittery red lip gloss that made him think naughty thoughts about her lips sliding up and down his meaty shaft. No words out of the English language could define his unspoken feelings for her. But then again, no audible words were ever allowed to be spoken at her request. She kept his words sequestered with her hypnotic power of seduction. He abruptly ended their naughty eye conversation just so he could fall harder into her web of pleasure. Her innie belly button was at the perfect eye level to make him entranced. Mister's new vision focused on what was right in front of him. He noticed that her cute belly button had a puddle of salty sweat and coconut lotion built up from all the lounging she had done before they had officially met. The view was the icing on his cake. He visually liked seeing her topless with only a sequenced thong covering her up. While he admired her accentuated belly button more, she checked him out, admiring his strong baby-soft face and his light coat of manly hair on his upper chest and lower belly. Her lingering eyes got hungrily turned on by seeing his broad shoulders that once were regularly worked out on a lat machine. Mister's thighs were naturally thick from all the running he had to do for sports. His small nipples were made just for her to suck on, yet she never had the chance to put them in her mouth nor bite them like he wanted.

On that balcony under the hot sun on that day, Mister only slightly cared about having control.

While trying to figure her out, his island beauty's lingering effects kept his cock throbbing for attention. Despite his subconscious psyche creating her character, he could not figure out how to get her close enough to steal a taste. While he tried to plan his suave moves to get a taste of her, he remained baffled on how he could have given up all his control to a woman that he subconsciously created.

Mister wrote all this down as fast as he could. In fact, so fast that his hand cramped, but he knew that he had to keep writing it all down before his fading impressions were forever lost. His dream left him wanting much more than he could handle. What the man of the hour really wanted to do was release his sticky orgasm all over the place. Nevertheless, he endured his horny excitement despite his better judgment.

Mister would gladly give up any kind of control in exchange for a taste of her moist sex. With every advancement that he made, she applied more resistance. He kept trying; she kept batting. Yet still she did not let him have one single touch of her silky-smooth skin. While planning her next move, she suddenly stopped everything while holding both of his hands in hers. As she shook her head signifying no, she purposely took control of the situation to postpone his explicit wants to lay her down on his lounger and overpower her missionary style. That would not happen while she was his self-created dreamlike dominatrix because she was more than a fuck; she was his lucid wet dream girl. Their passion melted them both from the inside out. Mister's body felt like a lightning rod that had just been struck by three bolts of lightning that were heaven-sent. Sexual electricity flowed through them both, and the bountiful surges made them dizzy with passionate delight.

The sounds of wind blowing by at top cruising speed combined with the omnipotent ocean swells repetitively lapping against the side of *Lucid Wet Dream* naughtily seduced them in every way possible. Neither of them was perfect in appearance, but to each other, they were perfect. Her curvaceous lines were more than Mister ever sought out in a companion, yet it was her attention and personality that he wanted to experience more than anything else. Her goddess-like appearance kept him hard.

Seeing her standing over his pure-white covered canvas lounger made him ache all over. He wanted to be deep inside of her. With her sultry stomach inches from his eyes, he took the opportunity to insert his velvety soft tongue into her glistening belly button. She grabbed onto his head helping him to finally get what he had wanted all along. While tasting her for the very first time, she embraced him in her arms. He whimpered in ecstasy, and she purred from his tickly touch. She kept him in the embrace for a long while before letting him up for a breath. She still was not going to let his feisty hands touch her; that much was evident.

With every grain of sand that passed through the hourglass, her horny horns exponentially grew. His wet tongue was not teasing her erogenously-zoned belly button anymore; instead, he curiously paused. His pause gave her opportunity to refresh her sexually aggressive control over him as she slowly lowered herself onto his chest. She let him get a whiff of her sex while maintaining strict control. When his mystery island beauty wiggled and grinded her butt cheeks into his chest to make herself more comfortable, he was made to smell the sweet coconut lotion and her tangy womanhood without being allowed to say no.

Slowly their sweat mixed, causing her butt to slip and slide all around his naked chest with amazing ease. At first, she did not do it on purpose, but when she saw how much he liked it, she gave him more slippage. With huge smiles and giggly laughs, his island beauty purposely tortured him to the brink of orgasm.

His subconsciously concocted island beauty reached out and grabbed both of his hands for the second time. Yet this time she bound them together at the wrists. She positively needed to know that he was not going to touch her at all during her bump and grind show on his well-lubricated chest. He was too sexually frustrated to react, so he let her proudly sit on his chest without disturbing her intentions. Soft and slow his island treat teased him with her dream like charm. Just when she started to trust him, she let his wrists go. He knew better than to touch her right away, so he grabbed the lounger rails and let her ride around his chest in slow motion as she saw fit. With her hands now free, she fondled her own exposed breasts. Pinching and playing with her slick nipples made Mister squirm out of his skin. All her temptress ways kept him as hard as he could get. Throughout all the intense foreplay, their eyes stayed intimately connected. Even their hot sweat began to fornicate. Their DNA-laden secretion mix made up a highly addictive cocktail that deserved to be sipped on, not swallowed. He soon saw her dime-sized nipples up close and personal. They were erect and on display for him to see. She only let him appreciate their enticing view for so long before softly laying herself down on top of him. He still planned on stealing control back so that he could lay his thick cock into her, but was waiting for the perfect time to do it. For now, he was content being pussy-whipped.

She peeled herself off him for the brevity of a minute to compose herself from almost having her own spontaneous combustion all over his chest. As their skin separated, feelings of love, lust, and fornication brought her ever closer to climax. She sat upright and looked at her man. He lay there with impatience overtaking his emotions. They both felt the eroticism pass between then while her bountiful breasts were completely covered with their well-mixed DNA cocktail.

The dreams impression showed Mister that both of their souls were now connected as one.

His horniness took over, and he selfishly grabbed for her plentiful butt cheeks. This time, she let him get away with it. Immediately he seized the opportunity to steal back his lost control even if it was only temporary. He took her exposed cheeks of slick sin into the palms of his hands and fondled them with naughty intentions. He spent several minutes caressing and rubbing on them with his well-moisturized hands. He massaged her overflowing flesh with tantric delight. When she tilted her head back and moaned, Mister knew he was back in control. Her moans of pleasure kept his erection in perfect form. He looked deep into her soul through her squinting eyes while he watched her body lose complete control. In that split second of change, his island beauty knew she was not his dominatrix anymore; she loved his soft caresses too much to care anymore. With her lips only inches away from his ears, her ever-increasing breaths sounded like a symphony playing in a beautiful concerto. It was her whimpering moans that pushed his oversexed dream into overdrive. She rolled her sweaty breasts into his chest some more, helping her to relaminate their bodies back together. They were no longer two horny strangers fooling around. Instead, they were now one soul connected from the inside out.

Their moist lips kissed for the very first time. The kisses were tender and soft, leaving a strong intoxicating aftertaste on their fornicating lips. That kiss scored Mister a lifetime memory worth remembering. The unforced kisses were slow and unrushed, allowing their lost souls to deeply climax together. Their moist lips slowly danced naked together with hot precision. Mister felt a strong impression that something more momentous than kissing just occurred.

He wrote down more dream impressions, specifically ones about the kisses. In the dream, he felt and saw the thick negativity lift off him and disappear high up into the atmosphere, whereas in dreaming reality, he ejaculated his hot semen into his boxers as he laid facedown in his bed. The nocturnal release was more than just an orgasm. It was his self-inflicted torment and emotional confinement being set free. He strongly felt that, and that is exactly what he wrote down in his faded-blue notebook. From the kiss onward, Mister knew that his lucid wet dream was the breakthrough he had waited for ever since he became a man. He also knew that dreams were not always what they seemed. So as he sat on the edge of his bed, Mister knew he had to decode its subliminal meanings sooner than later. He needed more than a few days of reflection to fully grasp its complete subconscious complexity. He kept capturing as many of the details that he could in his bedside journal before they completely faded out.

The last thing he remembered was his stateroom door opening and his sultry island beauty walking out on him. No hellos, and no goodbyes. At least she left him with a lasting view of her thick, lusciously shaped butt covered only by a narrowing T-shaped watermelon-colored thong. Then she was gone. Her fast departure left him speechless. He could not even remember if they did anything sexual, but from the semen soaked into his satin boxers, he could only assume something sinful went down.

There was a long pause that separated him from thoughts of anything at all. It was excruciating for him to sit there in silent peace, but he did it. A complex dream like that could not just be interpreted in the physical sense. It had to be decoded in the spiritual sense too. Maybe he was not supposed to remember the lost details at all. Maybe he was supposed to remember exactly what he remembered for certain unknown reasons. The dream, now vague in remembrance, would soon have a lasting impact on Mister forever.

Unfortunately, Mister could not stay raptured up in his lucid wet dreamlike bliss for very much longer; he still had a career and life to live. He looked over at his bedside phone acting as his alarm clock to see how late he was going to be for work. When he saw that he was only behind his normal wake-up time by eight minutes, it considerably mellowed him out. Mister was one of those men of the world that was extremely anal when it came to his appointment schedule. The slightest change of schedule caused his sphincter to clench up good and tight. A tight sphincter was one thing he hated more than he hated the word *hate*. Before it tightened up for the rest of the day, he quickly got back on track, starting off with his usual morning cup of java. Coffee always helped him wake up just as much as a hot shower did. He had both on his morning agenda. Standing straight up, he stretched his hands upward just as he normally did. He then made his way into the kitchen to get his morning wake-up drug of choice. Since the house only housed bachelors, they treated coffee differently than most. Mister always made a full pot of coffee at the start of the week and kept it refrigerated so that they could draw upon it over the week as they needed it. They mostly brewed the more expensive coffee beans that were already infused with different flavors so that they did not have to use coffee additives. Both Mister and Alex liked tasting the flavored bitterness of the black brew. As he poured the cold coffee into a mug, he put it into the microwave on high for a minute. While waiting for the coffee to warm up, bits and pieces of his dream kept popping in and out of his buzzing sub-conscious. The last of the pieces did not exactly add to its overall profoundness, but it kept him concentrated on the dream more than waking life. The sounds of the microwave bell abruptly sounding snapped him back into reality.

After he got his coffee, he took it with him down the hallway and into the bathroom, all the while sipping on it. He usually drank three or four swigs before stepping into the steamy hot shower. Although this morning, Mister might have gone for one of those coffee enemas, straight up the tight sphincter and directly into his bloodstream. Fortunately, he was not into any sort of enemas at all. He settled on drinking it down fast. The fourth gulp of coffee had to wait until after he was out of the shower.

As he soaped up his middle-aged body, he was a man on a mission. Starting from his chest, working his way down. He hardly ever mixed pleasure with cleanliness, but this morning would be an exception. He did not realize he was molesting his cock at first, but in fact, he was being perverted with it. With the lucid wet dream still in his memory, and his hands on his cock, he became erect. Mister disliked squandering erections, so whenever the opportunity popped up, he always made sure to get it off. Even if it happened to be at work or in the middle of the day somewhere, he made it a point to end its hardness. So when he snatched up the liquid tea-tree-fra-granced soap and drizzled it over the palms of his hands, he had a plan. The tea tree soap gave off a minty tingle all over his body that he specifically liked feeling. As he mixed the tingly sensation with gentle hand squeezes and long fast strokes over the head of his penis, it caused sexual chaos.

He looked down to admire his thick erection moving fluently in and out of his hand. He pushed Play on his locked-up fantasies of D. Once his queued-up video clips started to play, that was all the stimulation he needed to climax. A little soap, hot water, and naughty thoughts about D's first day on the job was all it took for Mister to orgasm. Much of his wasted naughty shower-time escapade was squandered by an intense red-hot selfish jerk-off session that resulted in one hell of a knee-buckling release that made every stroke worth it. His release was so climatic that when he came, he almost fell out of the shower. Fortunately, the glass shower walls kept him safely inside. That one hot hand-job gave Mister his most intense orgasm in years.

The afterglow was felt several minutes afterward. It only took him six minutes to squirt his warm love juice all over the steam-covered glass shower wall but twenty-six minutes to recover. He finished the shower basking in the luxurious steam encapsulated bathroom while regaining his faculties. He squirted more liquid soap in his hands to wash away the smell of ejaculated semen and night sweats. The minty smell pulled him out of his sexual coma and delivered him into a new reality. The entire morning made Mister feel powerful and sexy and worth it. It gave him back lost control of his future destiny, making him feel like a superhero sitting on top of the world with growing invincibility. He felt strong enough to take on the world.

Mister stepped out of the shower and reappeared back into the big bad world full of anything possible. He pushed forward onto his new path of unknowns. There were only a very few people left in this world to really know what true inner peace felt like, and for now, that perfect utopia was his to own.

CHAPTER 4

Seeking to Find

Mister walked in through the glass double doors with positive swagger to his step. Not what it once was, but he now had something to look forward too. His short sabbatical was the best thing he could have done with the prevailing circumstances. He walked into his dark office, turned on the lights, and sat down, resuming his role as the company's top salesperson. Since he had done well over the years, they gave him a roomy office to use. He really did not spend a whole lot of time in it though, only when his monthly sales reports were due. He would rather be given other rewards that would benefit his home office, but he just went with it. Since Mister was the third official employee of the company when it was new four years back. He knew everyone, but his outside-of-work friendships with the Tsars afforded him a comfortable situation no one else in the company had. He worked with Mr. Tsar at his previous job, which was how Mr. Tsar knew about Mister's incredible salesmanship talents. For the first two years, Mister was the only outside sales representative, but his sole salesperson position would not last long. He was given a lot of freedom throughout his tenure, yet he never took advantage of it. He had always been a man on a mission. He treated the company as his own. Even though it was a privately held corporation, Mister was given company stock certificates for his help to kick start the company to greatness, which was exactly what he did.

While reacquainting himself to the job from his time off, Mister noticed a plain white envelope tucked under his keyboard, with just the top edge visible. Strong curiosity made him lift the keyboard and retrieve the envelope. After he ripped open the envelope, a strong perfume-scented note from D welcomed him back in style.

"Welcome back, Mister! I missed your cute face, naughty teases, and commanding salesmanship. Let US own the competition together."

D signed it with a kiss from her very own lip-gloss-covered lips. The note made him feel wanted, needed, and appreciated. It was not what she said so much as it was the genuine thought behind it that Mister appreciated. The combination of her note and his last night's lucid wet dream gave Mister an unexpected ego boost. Seeing her silk-screened kiss made Mister reminisce back to many memories of amazing times they shared together outside of work. He went as far as kissing her note-stained lips with his. Memories of how sweet D's sugarcoated lips tasted triggered more unremembered lucid wet dream details.

He remembered hearing the boarding gate attendant reveal her name and more.

"Hello, Mister. I am Jennifer. I want to welcome you aboard LWD. We are so glad to have you aboard."

Jennifer greeted Mister with an energetic bounce and a cheery smile. Her white-and-blue-striped polo shirt prominently displayed the ship's logo. However, it was her lower attire that dominated his view; snug-fitting zipper-closed blue-and-white striped neoprene shorts with black fishnet stockings properly focused his attention. Jennifer sat him down in the ship's boarding lounge before disappearing. Mister first noticed three odd-shaped leather couches that others were sitting on. The stylized couches were nothing he had ever seen before; their appearance looked sinfully sexy. Still puzzled by their uniqueness, he scanned the rest of the boarding lounge, paying attention to the vessels sensualistic lines of creative elegance throughout.

He did not remember the entire boarding procedures, but then Jennifer reappeared, smiled, and grabbed Mister's hand to escort him to the bellhop station. She introduced him to Bob; he was the same black-and-white tuxedo-clad bellhop that escorted him down the hallways, up the elevator, right into his stateroom. It turned out that Bob was the same guy that placed the Gentleman Jack whiskey on the bar top.

As Mister sat comfortably in his fine black leather swivel and tilting office chair, he was completely zoned out to the outside world. He stared out of his office window, physically fixated on the drizzling-down rain while mentally he was back in his lucid wet dream. His emotional mentality was somewhere deep inside of his stirring soul. He felt that the entire lucid wet dream happened for very specific reasons. Acting under autopilot, he stood up and walked over to the window to get a better view of the hypnotizing rain. In his illusion-entranced mind, the raindrops appeared to him as magnified visions of wonder. The droplets were blown-up images appearing to him just as if he was on a psychedelic high. They were slow and purposeful. And as they hit the ground, the epicenter spread out like a slow-erupting volcano. Every other raindrop that splattered against the hard concrete walkway sunk him deeper into a hypnotic state that he should not have been while at work. After what seemed like hours, Mister stopped seeing raindrops and started seeing all kinds of past, present, and future memory clips playing in a monotone black-and-white theater. He thought it might be his déjà vu abilities hard at work again.

The first few times that déjà vu happened to Mister, he dismissed it. However, after a few more times of his dreams coming true, those exposed premonitions could not be explained away. Sometimes the déjà vu results would not happen for years, and other times it happened only months after he dreamed them. Déjà vu always put Mister on edge, but as he grew older, the premonitions comforted him to know that he was supposed to have been at that specific place at that specific time. He kept holding out hope for more déjà vu dreams to foretell his next checkpoint, but they never came. Then finally that hope was delivered to him with a gold VIP stamp on it by the way of his lucid wet dream.

Just when Mister began decoding his lucid wet dream, it came to a shuttering stop. Somehow his coworkers infiltrated his daydream with their useless hallway talk. Their high-pitched girly voices and clacking heels flowed in through his doorway like nails on a chalkboard. Few things frustrated Mister, but the interruption bothered him more than expected. It made him walk over to the door and abruptly close it shut. He was melancholy, borderline pissed, that his daydream was over. At least he was closer to figuring out the meaning behind his subconsciously made-up lucid wet dream. Despite his angst, he got back to work, concentrating on the monthly sales reports that needed to be turned in before their morning quarterly meeting at 10:00 AM. He kept working right up until he finished it before 9:30 AM, then delivered the reports to Mr. Tsar. They chatted about life for a few minutes before they walked into the conference room together. Mr. Tsar led the way into the conference room with monthly, quarterly, and yearly reports in hand.

The conference-room vibe made Mister feel like it was D's first day on the job all over again. Just like that day, Mister and company was dressed down while D dressed up. D took up Mister's usual spot while Mister made a new spot situated directly across from D. That was the "new" normal seating arrangement ever since D showed up on scene. D always liked receiving attention from anyone that would pay it to her. So she made it a point to dress up for every company event after the first one; no matter how mundane or spectacular the event, she cloaked herself in professionalism. D's three-piece skirt suit was a hit. Although the one she wore on that day was not pinstriped, it still was a sweet visual delight for anyone to see, especially a single man returning from a thirteen-day sabbatical. Mister walked into the conference room with smiles and renewed confidence that D recognized. Then Mrs. Tsar began to speak.

"Welcome to another quarterly meeting. Thank you for everyone's hard work and determination. We are rapidly growing better than expected. Last quarter was great, and I am expecting this coming quarter to be even better. You should be proud of yourselves for positioning us number one in the local market."

With all of Mister's morning emotions flayed open and exposed, the meeting and morning antics left him starving. He felt the urge to do lunch alone, going out for a bite to eat at one of his favorite lunchtime hangouts. Early on, Mister found a place close by that gave him exactly what he wanted out of lunch, a good meal with lots of choices. The sandwich place quickly became his favorite indulgence. They made their sandwiches bigger than big and never skimped out on the sides. With every sandwich, they included a large dill pickle on the side with extra potato salad. Their potato salad was the best. It was almost as good as his mom's, but not quite. It did not have his mom's tender loving care that she put into it to make it fabulous.

Sometimes he took D out to lunch, but that was only when they both could afford the spare time. Their tight working friendship bordered being intimate, but sales incentives and spiffs for sales performance kept their personal friendship on an up-and-down saga brought on by work-induced competition. They were both competitors always playing to win. Neither one of them knew how to stop competing where work was concerned. For both, work was an escape from their lonely realities. They internally used the workaholic syndrome method to their advantage, shedding off personal life drama. However, that day, Mister wanted to dine alone. He moxie-upped a five-dollar tip, putting it in their clear glass tip jar before taking his food to go. He drove over to his favorite parking lot spot of wonderment to enjoy a solemn lunch in secluded peace and serenity.

The day was filled with scattered rain with occasional sunspots forcing their way through the dark rain clouds. God could not decide if he wanted to make it rain hard or have it mist, so Mister had to keep the sunroof and windows rolled up. Despite the roadways wetness, he pulled right into the empty parking spot like a driving pro lapping the competition on the final home stretch. His lunch would be spent under the tall oak tree that shaded nothing at all. He loved that park because it had a river that ran through it. The local river was always tame, yet its babbling sounds lulled him into deep thoughts of life outside of work on more than one occasion. Whenever he could afford the time to take a break, that was his spot of choice. He sometimes went there on the weekends just to calm his chaotic soul. That was his chicken soup.

He inhaled the lunch, then tilted the seat back and pondered his dream while being serenaded from songs off his big digital music playlist. Normally, the music relaxed him, except for today, when the music amplified new thoughts of hot desire. He reclined the seat and looked up through the moonroof, taking advantage of his hour-long lunchtime break. Mister was fortunate that he never had a set time for lunch; he took breaks whenever he wanted to, provided he never overbooked his sales appointments. However, right then, Mister needed an extended absence to figure out the true meaning behind the lucid wet dream and all its symbolic meanings. So when he closed his eyes, he drifted out of anything real. The first five minutes worked well, not thinking about anything else except the melodic river seduction. Then Mister drifted off into another daydream.

Two daydreams in the same day for Mister to have were unheard of, yet he found himself in a delirious state of mind while daydreaming about love and lust, friendships and futures, and erotic adventures. With his eyes shut, he daydreamed that his island beauty reappeared.

She was sitting in the Humvee alongside him. She looked over at him, smiled, opened the car door, and got out. He daydreamed that she walked around to the front of his Humvee and motioned for him to follow her. Still daydreaming, Mister opened his door and was immediately blinded by the bright sunlight glaring in. Before he could see again, his daydream was interrupted by a nearby car door slamming closed. The distraction abruptly ended his lucid wet dream sequel.

Then this gorgeous woman dressed in tight yoga pants, zip-up sweatshirt, bright-green running shoes, and a bouncy ponytail reemerged where his island beauty was standing; Mister sinisterly cackled with a great seventies hit song in mind, "Afternoon Delight." The runner was not looking her best, but Mister saw beauty beyond makeup and heels. It was her youth and unmolested glamor that inspired him to think back to overheard water-cooler conversations that the younger office interns had about their exaggerated sex lives. Things like having multiple girlfriends and late-night booty calls for spontaneous sexual liaisons that were made to order dominated the interns' cooler talk. Mister was lucky to get away with an occasional three-month stand, but nothing like the kinds of things those twenty-something-year-old interns talked about. His youth was not even remotely close to what they gossiped about.

"Wow, how times have changed."

Overhearing his coworkers' sexual trysts of depravity flooded Mister's mind with "what if" scenarios. However, as an older, wiser man, he knew that most of their stories were probably embellished mockeries of being denied anything good. Mister knew that the dating game had changed a lot since he was their age, but he still knew many of the established rules of engagement had to exist. Mister considered himself a true gentleman that obviously walked in rarified air when compared to future generations. You would not catch a real gentleman kissing and telling. Nevertheless, Mister was slightly turned on by hearing all about his coworkers' ungentlemanlike liaisons. Stories of sexting and wicked webcam girls doing dirty things blew Mister's mind. When he realized that he had the digital age at his feet, he knew that finding his Miss could just be a few sentences and lots of charm away.

For minutes, Mister sat with the Humvee door wide open while watching the runner jog away. The new Mister wanted to run after her, but old Mister's insecurities crept back in. His midday epiphany made him consider doing something he never thought he would do.

Could I really meet the woman of my fantasies through the internet? What would others think of me if I told them of my plans? Could I really be an internet Romeo? Will I be able to find a woman meant just for me? Could I be the confident stud in the lucid wet dream, or will I still be the tormented man of fucking failure?

Mister's insecurities held him back even though he knew where he had to go. The one thing that he could not handle anymore was finding the wrong one. Somehow, he had to put a kibosh on his past insecurities and grow his newfound confidence.

If I find her, could I give her my best, or will I hesitate and hold back out of fear?

With his lucid wet dream still fresh in memory, he somehow needed to will his dream into a tangible existence. The island beauty that reappeared in his Humvee triggered him to want to seek out and find his Miss more than ever before. The more Mister sifted through his lucid dream and daydreams, the more inspired he became to post his very own ad for the world to see.

Someone must have ordered up my island beauty treat. She was that perfect. But who? Did I order up one hot Miss to go and didn't even know it? How do I find her, get her, and make her mine?

Too many triggers made Mister want to do it. His own personals ad had to exist. With all his delicate panache, he started out completely speechless.

What could I possibly say to an all-female worldwide audience to entice the Miss of my dreams to come and find me? He sighed.

Mister knew he had to be charming enough to be intriguing yet naughty enough to be a mysterious pleasure. He needed to earn a wet stain on her panties but still be charming enough to be philosophically desirable. While being all alone in his mellow music-infused Humvee, Mister grabbed for the yellow-paged notepad out of his computer bag and started making notes of his intentions.

As the pouring down rain banged off his well-protected suit of armor, his subconscious was powerfully being seduced by nature's rain. More questions than statements flooded his psyche like fast bullets shooting out of a fully automatic Uzi gun. Just then was when Mister truly woke up from all his past self-inflicted torment.

Can I really find my Miss this way? I hope she lives closer than further away. Will she be able to have the same kind of relationship that I want to have without regret? She must tease me and keep me solely focused on her one-of-a-kind personality? I want her to smile more than frown, and hug more than not. I need her to soothe my every burning desire no matter how hot it is. Her eyes need to always lure me into her deep aching soul even if it is from across the room or across the world. And our kisses, no matter how soft or how wet or how long they might be, they always must mean something. I want her to be able to wear leather and lace and everything in between. Smarts! She must have them and use them to keep me in check. Tease! She would always, always know how to tease me and turn me on because she would just know. Oh, and she had better know how to earn and keep the title Miss with every ounce of fiber of her being.

All of Mister's chaotic thoughts and unanswered questions made him want to get back to the office and write out his own personals ad. Without hesitation, he pulled the seat upright, turned on the Humvee, and peeled out of the parking lot. His oversized tires gripped the asphalt hard enough to jolt his head back into the headrest as he headed down Main Street. He was back to work in less than eight minutes, walking into work through the back door just because he needed to do to avoid any possible distractions. He made it past D and the bosses just as planned. No one really used the back door, yet it was Mister's favorite entrance to get in and out of the office without detection. He frequently used the back door when he did not want to be bothered by any office distractions.

He purposely left his office door slightly open while leaving the lights off and the blinds closed. He hoped that his dark office would discourage any would-be visitors from entering. However, the office was friendly enough that a closed door was not exactly a closed door at all. While he did not want any distractions, he was still on the clock, so the occasional interruption had to be tolerated. For now, Mister hoped the lights off would be a strong-enough sign that he did not want to be bothered. And with newfound clarity, Mister began writing out his personals ad.

"Call me Mister. I am looking for my Miss. Are you her? If you think you could be her, you need to keep reading along. But only keep reading if you think you can keep me tuned in and turned on with your flirty sassiness. All men love that, especially this one. If you think that you can get and keep my attention, we need to talk."

At first, he struggled to find the right words to write down, but then after the first twenty minutes and two sentences later, he jumped right into the meat of it without skirting about. Mister allowed his suave charm to come out and take over.

"You will know you are my Miss *if* you can close your eyes right now and feel my every sensualistic word making love to your soul repeatedly."

The way Mister came up with innuendoes to grab his future Miss's attention was a slow stroke of genius. He did not want to come off as being cocky or arrogant, but confident enough to win her over.

He was unsure if he could pull it off, but his gentlemanlike words of tease had to do just that.

"Let us walk hand in hand to the bedroom and tuck each other in with a lingering wet good-night kiss."

Mister's ad read off just as he intended it to—calm, cool, and seductively collected. Yet less than a week ago, he would not have been able to write what he just wrote, let alone publish it on the internet. His lucid wet dream gave him a big boost of emotional confidence that he had not ever felt before. It was his gentlemanlike ways being infused with sinful perversion. He played up his superb salesman skills with every intriguing word he wrote.

"I dare you to take my hand and come with me. Let me show you what it would feel like to be my one and only Miss. Challenge me, tease me, tempt me if you dare."

Just when he found his writing stride, the ringing phone stalled him mid-stride. To top that, his office door squeaked open in perfect unison, throwing his groove right down the shitter. That was the fourth fucking interruption in just as many minutes, and there would not be a fifth fucking time. He could not take any more interruptions, but he could not react to them either. At least a familiar feminine voice preceded the last interruption.

"Is everything okay, Mister?"

Like music to his ears, D's voice came from the partially open door. She was a beautiful, sassy, well-grounded, middle-aged woman that was already spoken for. Her looks and attitude could stop any man's heartbeat, especially Mister's. From her fine red hairs to pale freckled skin, from her sassy smart-assed smile, to her pouty light-pink lips, even her green eyes screamed fiery redhead all the way. She earned the rest of her sassy attitude from a salty marriage, yet she always maintained class no matter what mood she was in or day it was. Her high heels, silk stockings, and borderline appropriate business attire got her the attention she did not get at home. From day one, Mister gave her the attention she starved for, and that swelled both of their beaten-down egos higher than they should have been. D and Mister had an on-and-off friendship for all the years that they knew each other. From the first moment Mister saw D three years ago, her sassy elegance turned him on. He kept fantasizing about her ever since they met on that fateful June day.

In Mister's private moments of weakness, he always thought back to D's first day on the job; it was that memorable. D's alluring dominant voice caused Mister to look up and pay attention. Where Mister worked, they did not condone employee fraternizations ever since Mr. Tsar was caught cheating on Mrs. Tsar with his secretary. It was a real-life cliché that ruined the good old boys' office environment it once was. Mister was not into judging other people's infidelities, especially someone that signed his paychecks. However, when the Tsar's affair became company knowledge and his wife took over everything including Mr. Tsar's pecker, it tidal-waved the entire office right into the undertow. Mrs. Tsar was friendly enough just as long as you did not cross the line she drew in the sand. It was her way or the highway, and that made the office and everyone in it her domain.

So when D interrupted Mister's deep thoughts in his office, he felt a little hidden guilty pleasure and a bit embarrassed that he was caught off guard.

"Mister, I can see you're a million miles away. Did you find any answers on your sabbatical?" Humph! D sighed between sentences. "I know that when my mind is far away, it's usually trying to escape from reality." A flirty smile followed by a brief pause between her words was evident.

Mister was aloof. No words in his vocabulary came out. Just a blank stare and silence. Despite his nonresponse, D kept being friendly.

"Is everything okay with you?"

As of late, they were redeveloping a friendly working friendship that had been beat up by work competition. Their friendship was almost romantic, but D would not let it ever cross that line. However, the line was definitely blurred. Even though they were not romantic, there was still a mutually connected sexual magnetism that existed. That strong sexual magnetism was what kept them coming back to each other for comfort. For unknown reasons, they were naturally drawn to each other. They straddled the border of being lovers, yet they remained great friends. When D wore her skirt and tight pant outfits, she was unstoppable. That same attention-seeking sex appeal D sought after also damaged their friendship.

Throughout their entire working friendship, he fantasized about her something terrible. In his private moments of weakness, Mister always thought back to D's first day on the job. He never told D exactly how he felt about her, but he was certain that she knew about his secret desires to have her in his bed.

"I'm okay, I just needed a break to stretch my neck and mind, is all."

He was not in the right frame of mind to converse with D as his thoughts were solely focused on his personals ad. It showed in their brief question-and-answer period.

D coyly sassed back.

"I don't buy that! You blushed when I startled you. I bet you were probably dreaming about something steamy. Huh? Who is she?"

He turned around to look at her in her eyes, and with his mis-chievous chuckle, he let go of his fantasized horny thoughts of D climbing on top of his cock and riding it for everything it was worth.

"Well, D, if you must know, last night I had a crazy dream. It has me all fucked up."

She playfully giggled, catching him off guard. She wanted to know what made him blush, but he was not letting on. That was just one of the fun games they both liked to play with each other. Their games kept were what kept the sexual tension fresh and intact.

"Was it one of those naughty wet dreams about me?" A sinful smile took D over. "You know I am just joking around with you, silly man. Don't you?"

She went on to extend him an innocent invitation.

"I don't know if you can remember that far back or not, but I am a good listener. If you ever need someone to talk with, I could lend you my ears and whatever else you might need to borrow."

Mister's friendly answer to her invitation was simple.

"Thank you for that offer, but I do not know if I should burden you with my drama. Tell you what, if I do change my mind, you will be the first one that I will seek out. Fair?"

The room got silent, and they both felt chills shoot right through them as their eyes stayed bonded together.

"I do miss our friendship we used to have. It was flirty and fun, and it took my mind off everything that mattered. Don't you miss it, D?"

D seductively glanced over at him with the biggest smile on her pale-complexioned face reaffirming Mister's sentiments.

"I miss that too! More than you know. But seriously, Mister, I mean it! I won't bug you anymore. I will let you get back to your deep thoughts in peace. But I don't recommend daydreaming about me too much more, otherwise you might make me wet."

Mister blushed as D smiled, turned around, and walked right out of his office on a buzzy high. For seconds, D's spectacular ass was on display for Mister to see. He saw her button-down blouse and erect nipples poking through the soft fabric, causing Mister's mind to wander off to a place it should not have been while on the work clock. He could not help but vision D in a watermelon-colored thong. He hoped she would come back into his office with her pomp and sass and say something clever, but she never did. Instead, D let him squirm in his own puddle of sexual chaos.

What Mister really wanted to do was go home and make mini Mister squirt hot creamy semen all over the place more than a few times. Instead of succumbing to his sexual desires, he chose to leave his erection alone. He sat there behind his desk with a hard-on looking like a schoolboy salivating over his first schoolgirl crush. He hoped that she did not see his flushed face, but it was a blatantly inevitable discovery.

D's sexy appearance helped Mister pick up right where he left off. But now his creativity flowed better than it had been as his words leapt out of his head and onto the screen with precision. From time to time, he threw in some comedy to keep the ad lightheartedly charming and funny. All his chosen words meshed well enough to charm the panties off anyone reading it. However, it would take the right woman, on the right day to truly "get him."

Mister's self-doubt made him reread it several times over to make sure it was exactly how he wanted it to be. He went for something dramatic to leave something to his future Miss's imagination. He did not want to give out too many details but share enough to earn her undivided attention. He hoped his mysterious approach would not scare her away, but then again, his Miss, the one he sought out, would like a good mystery. While Mister wanted his Miss to respond yesterday, he would have to wait it out.

Finally, the heart of the ad was finished, and now, he only needed to write out the ending, and give it a catchy headline title. The ending had to be just as alluring as the rest of it was. Fortunately for Mister, he did not fuck about in getting out what he had to say. Thanks to his recent lucid wet dream, he knew exactly what he wanted to get out of the ad. He engrossed himself in becoming the new charming gentleman with a side of tease, not exactly sure about what kind of friendship his ad would get, but nothing as serious as a fiancée would be perfectly perfect.

Something with a deep emotional-connection barring soul mate qualities and lots of eroticism oozing out of every twisted curve. Mister made sure to say that in his personals ad. That and many other confirming notions of going on an open-minded adventure were mentioned several times in the four-paragraph ad. Mister's impeccable choice of words summed it up best.

"I dare you to come and find me wherever I am at. Grab my attention with your gorgeous eyes and steal the entire show with your sassy elegance. Take my hand in yours and guide me over to the bed. Lay me down and hold me tight. And when the sunlight appears, wake me up with sweet erotic whispers of 'Good morning, Mister', as you kiss me on the lips with naughty intentions in mind."

Now it was down to the eye-catching, heart-stopping headline. It had to sincerely mean something to the "one" while pulling her in. The title had to be a bright enough beacon to beckon "the one" over to it. After many minutes of thought, he came up with the perfect title, officially titling it "Gentleman Seeking a Vixen for an Ongoing Lucid Wet Dream."

Just as Mister typed out the headliner, he heard another pair of heels clacking down the tiled hallway. From the sounds of the stride, he knew it was D.

CHAPTER 5

• • • • • • • • ● ● ● ● ● ● • • • •

Office Tease

The alluring sound of heels tapping on the tiled hallway grew louder and louder, and then the clickety-clack stopped. Stopped clack-et-y-clicking heels made Mister look up and see D standing outside of his partially opened wood-and-glass-made door with her hands on her hips in perfect sassy-mode character. Immediately Mister noticed D's "I have something to say" look even before she spoke a word. Mister did not waste any time to give her the causal "come on in" nod.

Concernedly, D walked over to the front of his desk to let him get a better look at her sincerity while she peeked at his handsome smile before letting business words fly.

"Did you do the newly required sales forecast report for next month yet? Because I was not exactly clear on what Mr. Tsar is looking for. Why does he want forecasts now anyway? Can you show me your report so that I know what to put in mine?"

D had been a little bit nervous and a lot bit curious as to what Mister's dream was about.

Why won't he tell me anything about his dream? Just months ago, he would have told me everything. Why nothing now? What a dick. That is so not fair. He must still be mad at me for winning the contest? Why can't he accept my apology and move on? Sheesh!

D kept trying to reposition herself back into Mister's life ever since the contest debacle went down. She preferred playing the "nagging nanny" game to get her way more than the "acting out and respond to me because I deserve it" sport. Through the years, D got good at perfecting that skill. So when D asked Mister that silly question about the new forecast reports during one of the busiest mornings of the month for Mister, he gave her a flippant but truthful answer.

"Mr. Tsar wants to get a better handle on our future sales just in case he needs to hire another salesperson to help us grow."

D purposely walked around to the side of his desk and position herself in between the desk and the credenza to be squarely in his line of sight. She staunchly stood up next to his commander's chair and coyly demanded his attention.

"Come on, D! I know you better than that, Miss Smarty-Pants. You just want to find out what my dream was about, don't you? I already know you want to know. It is that obvious. Remember, I know you better than anyone. I know your deepest, darkest secrets. You cannot fool me D. It's okay to admit it. I will not hold it against you. I swear."

"Okay, fine. Yes, Mister, you caught me. I admit I am checking up on you. You have me worried. You have not been yourself for months. Sure, I get that I hurt your feelings by winning the sales competition in the manner that I did, but to my defense, I have said sorry many times over already. I even took you out to three expensive dinners and paid to get you that naughty one-hour massage with a two-handed hand-job finish. You remember that, don't you? That should earn me some forgiveness, shouldn't it? I truly am your friend, Mister, despite your popular off-balanced beliefs. I know that you have helped me through many difficult times in my life, and for that, I can only repay you in spades, although if you do not accept my apology and repayment methods, we will not ever be close again. I do not want that. But no matter what you choose, I will not stop trying to be your friend. And as your friend, I want to make sure you are better than okay. Is that all right with you, Mister?"

"Of course, it is okay with me, D. I thought you were tired of me, and that was why I left you alone. I really am doing okay! 'I had an interesting two weeks' is all I can say. Let me rephrase that, I had an interesting last day off that put my entire life in a different kind of perspective. It was one intense dream that is changing me from the inside out. But I need some time to try and figure it out before I say anything to anyone about it. But when I figure it out, you will be the second to know, me being the first. I really do appreciate your concern."

Mister knew she was trying to be a good friend, but right at that moment, he was not ready to talk about it, though seeing D's freshly coated lip gloss and dangerous sex-infused wedge-styled heels made his mind wander right into the dirty gutter. Mister would rather like a meeting redo where D gets to prance back into his office and be his submissive play toy for the day. He knew exactly how he would take her too. Lots of positions, lots of ways, but one stuck out far more than any other one did.

Mister's winning fantasy had D strutting back into his office wearing the exact same outfit, but now, her catlike strut was more pronounced by her tail swishing back and forth with a flair of arrogant commandership. D would read his every thought while following his every uncommunicated direction. She would be standing in the same place, but this time, she would use her heels to push his chair backward with her abrupt authority, making his manhood grow to its maximum potential. This time, D would hop up onto his desk and sit right on the edge of it while scooting herself into the perfect "look up my skirt" position. Neither of them would speak a work, letting their actions rule the outcome.

D's dramatic fuck-me grin and inner-thigh exposure would give Mister a midday steamy office sex show. She would "just" know what to do next, teasing him with the possibility of seeing her glistening wet pearl of pleasure for the first time ever. Mister wanted D to dominantly grab his chair's armrests and pull him in to her perfect V-shaped apex in a gesture of surrendering the one thing she has yet to give to him. While enjoying her sexualized scent from a foot away, Mister would expect D to run her hands through his hair. By giving his head a dominant pull into her steamy delight, she forced him to smell her sex through her Lycra-and-lace-covered panty. He wanted so much for it to end with him grabbing her around the waist, pulling her off his desk and sitting D down on top of his throbbing cock for a fast hot fuck.

But since that exact fantasy could not happen anytime soon, Mister looked up at D and mumbled something back to the effect of "he would e-mail over the sample reports in a few" to satisfy his colleagues wants.

"Thank you, Mister. I appreciate all the things you do. You are a good man, so don't you forget that. But Mister, I couldn't help but notice that you locked yourself in the office all morning. What is up with that? That is not like you. Are you writing me a juicy love letter or something?"

D's eyes bled with erotic desire, which kept Mister's semi-erect penis on the border of being fully hard. He turned her innocent guessing into a flirtatious opportunity to lay on some more of his seductively smooth charm.

"In fact, buttercup, I was just writing you a hot sex story about what I want to do to you in my office. How badly I want to take advantage of you. Heck, I would push all my paperwork and pens onto the floor just so I could lay you down on my desk and put my big dick inside of your tight pussy. I could go on about the details, but they would only make us want to rush right home to my empty place and do it everywhere we can."

Mister clearly wanted to share his feelings with D in another attempt to get her into his bed.

"My, my, Mister! You keep thinking that for the both of us, okay? Right now, I need to go home to my kids and cook for my cock-sucking prick of a husband because it is getting way too hot in here for me to stay."

D's sassy attitude helped her make a grand exit from his office. She swiftly pivoted on the heels of her wedge-shaped shoes and walked out, disappearing down the hallway for the second time that welcome-back Friday.

Their late workday afternoon private meeting emphatically turned him on even more than he had been. The dream and the flirting with D, mixed with writing out his personals ad, all contributed to his erection. He was sexually overloaded. Mister could have exploded in his pants if anyone or anything came remotely close to touching him there. He was just that excited.

His instincts told him to follow her down the hallway. And that was exactly what he did. He followed her back down the hallway into her office. He found D standing behind her office desk chair putting on her black suede jacket to go home. He did not know if she was ignoring him or if she really did not see him standing there. No matter which it was, he walked into her office unnoticed and stood there until he was. Mister had not considered that D had already tuned him and the office out while getting ready to go. So when D did not pay any attention to Mister's arrival, he cleared his throat to announce his presence.

D acknowledged him with her sultry eyes and freshly touched-up lips.

"Are you following me, Mister? You better not be stalking me, sir, unless you intend to do something about it."

D was not smiling when she spoke, yet Mister's tightening balls felt her flirtatiousness. Her flirty attitude kept him tuned into her channel. Even his fantasies recorded her every word and gesture for later.

"I would stay and chat with you, but I definitely cannot today. I am on my way home to pick up the kids." D giggled like a giddy schoolgirl in trouble, but still she kept on dishing out her version of erotica. "I hope you weren't just about to start bearing your sole to me."

"As a matter of fact, I was going to tell you about my dream and get your take on it. But since you're busy, maybe we could talk some other time?"

She looked at him, smiled, then gave out the yes nod in agreement. D's smile was anything but a smile. It was a sultry smirk that almost leveled him into a pile of melting goo.

Their short word exchange made Mister's unmolested cock instantly grow inside of his boxers. He hoped D would not notice it. Although Mister did not know if she had seen his pant bulge yet or not, he turned his hips to the side to avoid any kind of embarrassment.

"Yes! We will have to talk later. Let me know when you are available." She paused to get up the moxie to say more. "But, Mister, I really think you came down here to my office just to get another look at my nice juicy ass. You did, didn't you, you bad boy?"

At first, Mister played dumb, then a minute later coped to it.

"You caught me, D. I could not resist seeing your butt one more time before you went home. But I am not the only one guilty here. You wanted me to see it. I know you did. Do not even try and deny it either."

His first day back from a thirteen-day sabbatical was too god-damn perfect to even be believable. The office vibe felt better, and their previous animosity was almost vaporized. Even though everything felt right, something still felt wrong. Sometimes Mister questioned himself why he kept holding out hope to be with D, and other times he vigorously wanted to pursue after her just to force a decision out of her, though there was a part of him that still needed to keep the possibility of making D his alive.

In her office that afternoon, Mister came as close as he had ever come to grabbing her and pushing her down on her office desk. He decided not to do it out of respect for her marriage. He did not want to be the sole cause for their marital breakup. So he always made sure to keep enough physical distance between them to prevent an accidental slip. Ultimately, Mister knew that D would not give him what he wanted, which is why he went through with his personals ad.

What D liked about Mister was his attention and personality. Most of all, she liked his unrelenting attempts to bed her. He gave her the kind of attention she needed to have to live through her sexless marriage. His attention was flattering, and it made her feel sexy. D knew she could get away with making him hard anytime she wanted. She also knew he would always be a gentleman in respect to her boundaries. She took Mister's tease like any frustrated married woman would, with comforting grace and naughty guilt. She felt comfortable flirting with him because she knew he would not cross her well-established line. D talked with Mister many times about leaving her bad marriage behind, but so far, it had just been an empty promise. But still, she liked Mister's naughty attention, and he liked her tease. Their friendship was as simple as that.

"Sorry, I cannot stay longer and talk, but my kids will be mad if I am not on time to pick them up."

D strutted her hips toward the exit, but for brief seconds, D thought about "accidentally" rubbing her hips against his boxer-wrapped cock, but a traffic-stopping smile and low-pitched vibrato goodbye would have to do.

D secretly wished that Mister would have made a move on her that very second because she would have unequivocally let him have her in her office. Instead, she looked back into her office and said something equally hot.

"Hey, Mister, whatever you do, don't cum on my desk. You can think about it, but do not do it. And be sure to lock the door when you leave because I think the janitors have been stealing my candy. And you know how much I like to suck on hard things."

She wanted to say and do so much more than walk away, but still she kept on walking down the long hallway alone, horny, but gloating that she made his cock flutter. She walked out of the building with a smile and ever-increasing wetness flowing out of her tight Amazon River.

The temptation of watching D's voluptuous figure strolling away was too great to not admire. He peeked his head out of her office doorway to watch her sashay out of view.

D confidently knew that Mister would watch, and he did. And she purposely swayed her hips from side to side like the fierce tigress that she was.

D's hallway prance-around show gave him hot jerkoff material for the month. Mister stayed in her office to get back his lost composure before he really did shoot his steamy semen all over her desk. He turned the lights off and stood there in the dark for a few minutes, hoping that his erection would disappear all on its own, but it was too strong to go away without help.

CHAPTER 6

• • • • • • • • • ● • • • • • •

Restroom Break

The darkness of the office and the sweet lingering scent of her per-fume-stained leather chair drove him fucking nuts. D's titillating departure left Mister's thoughts in a place they should not have been while at work. As he stood in her dark office, he trembled with horny confusion. He did not know if he wanted to remain a working pro-fessional or cross the line and be that naughty-desk-cum-slinger that D instructed him not to be. Serious considerations of breaking D's only rule would have been imminent if it were not for the footsteps coming down the hallway. They forced him to put his weak thoughts on temporary hold while waiting for the sounds to be gone. But while standing behind her partially open door, he formulated a plan to do something about his protruding cock before it spontaneously combusted in his pants.

Mister poked his head out her doorway to make sure the coast was clear, then beelined it into the closest men's restroom to carry out his plan without interruption. He walked in through the bathroom door, then paused at the sink for more than a minute to inconspicu-ously look around for other occupants. Fortunately for Mister, it was empty, but still he chose to make one last attempt to silence his raging erection by splashing cold water onto his face. He was torn between selfishness and professionalism. Unfortunately, the cold water only fueled his bad-boy desires to take it out and get it off.

With all three stalls empty, he picked the far-right one for its privacy factor; the adjoining corner walls lent him the best conceal-ment while being the farthest from the entrance door. He boldly walked into the stall, closed and locked the metal privacy door, then steadied himself against the two back corner walls. At first, Mister struggled with his zipper, but with a little patience and a lot of deter-mination, he got it undone. The anticipation of his pending orgas-mic release made him shake all over. His trousers and boxer briefs were the only things standing in the way of his cock being in his hand. He unclasped his pants and peeled back his fly, exposing his satin black boxers while being nervously horny. Despite the "being caught" potential, he unsnapped the remaining silver-tabbed boxer button and freed his hard dick from solitary confinement. It stuck straight out in the air with commanding arrogance. Before gripping it in his hand and stroking it off, he looked downward and proudly admired its hardness. His dick felt like it could not get any harder. And he was right; it really could not grow any bigger. It was fully pumped up with rushing blood and flowing testosterone. As Mister stood in the bathroom stall with little Mister in his hand, he tem-porarily became the most powerful man in the universe, although a man with his own cock in his hands without a cued-up fantasy was dangerous.

He closed his eyes and pushed Play on his hottest memories of D. He started up the high-definition projector in his twisted mind of naughty perversion. As the bright light shot out of the projector, it played back D's first day on the job with amazing clarity. Even their dialogue did not escape his etched-in impression. He knew what he saw, how he saw it, and what it did to him. Mister even remembered her facial expressions when she caught him looking up her skirt that fateful first day. That was Mister's favorite memory of D. He had several other alternate endings of the same events, but the real events from that day were what made his erection go away faster than any other.

It was D's first official day on the job. She wanted to leave an impression on her new coworkers that she deserved to be there, and she did with her dress-to-impress ensemble. Yet this companywide dress-down day made her severely overgussied up for the occasion. Her white-and-black-pinstriped power skirt suit stole the show. D's worn attire had purpose, a strong statement to let everyone around her know she was important. Thin black pinstripes ran vertical over the top of a stark white background giving D empress-like power. Maybe it was the pinstripes or its visual acuity, but whichever it was, she felt like a goddess in control of everything around her. The banker's stylized vest was made to be dramatic with its plunging V-shaped neckline, while its simplistic material-covered buttons fastening it closed helped to downplay its sexiness. She wore the boss-like outfit to comfort herself more than show anyone up. The skirt stopped mid-thigh, while the dyed white silk stockings went higher up. The rest of D's unmatched undergarments depended on the satin white garter-belt to keep her stockings in place. She was garterless; who needed the garter when she had the thong to make a much more dramatic statement? Although it was D's sense of professionalism that made her wear the satin slip, she took extra comfort in knowing that it also kept her hidden assets top-secret. Despite her professionalized appearance, she stuck out like a naked movie star on center stage, due to everyone else being dressed down in jeans and polos. Even Mrs. Tsar could not take her bewildered eyes off D. From her press-pleated skirt to her unblemished lipstick to her white three-inch heels, not one flaw was seen. Everyone positively paid attention to D that morning, especially Mister. Instead of being bothered by the competition, he looked forward to getting to know her via their week-long training sessions.

During that period in Mister's career, he did not know anything about Mr. Tsar's future plans to hire another salesperson. So when Mr. Tsar showed up in his office with D before the quarterly meeting, he was starkly confused. Yet it all made sense when Mr. Tsar introduced D as the new sales rep. At first, Mister was shocked, then curious. But after Mister got a whiff of D's lingering perfume during Mr. Tsar's brief introduction, he wholeheartedly embraced his new competition. The one thing Mister was certain about was that D smelled better than sin on a Sunday morning.

D's first day coincided with their company's quarterly growth progress meeting. That was the day they announced promotions and other noteworthy company news. Mister's ritual was to go down to the conference room ten minutes prior to its beginning and order up a vanilla latte prepared by the standing-by baristas. Coffee was necessary to stay awake during those dry company meetings. It was usually a fifty-five-minute process that came with day-long aftereffects. Mister walked into the conference room as usual and preordered a free sugary vanilla latte when he noticed his usual seat taken, forcing him to find a new spot. He always downplayed his job's importance, yet this was one of those mornings that Mister should have arrogantly declared the conference room as his own, ousting the stranger that occupied his space. But since Mister was not a condescending prick, he let D keep his spot without provocation. He could have easily caused a spectacle, but Mister's moral character immediately gave in. Although he afforded himself a sigh aloud. Not only was D beautiful, she took his spot. The only other open spot was on the other side of the room directly across from where D sat. He took it with an agenda to secretly spy on D without being obvious.

That specific Tuesday, God sent Mister a new jerk off memory, a steamy new one at that.

Mister played off his displacement with gentlemanlike integrity. He took the latte drink back to his new seat and sat quietly as his internal upheaval dominated his OCD ritualistic feelings. Through it all, he inconspicuously spied on D out of his peripherals, immediately noticing her hidden nervousness. She was all alone, looking for someone to help her get through her first day. Immediately, Mister was drawn to her nervous insecurity as though it was his responsibility to be that welcoming friend. Before the Tsars walked in, Mister made eye contact with D, smiling and giving her an approving nod. D's smile back at him opened the door to their first conversation. Minutes before the meeting was supposed to start, Mister stood up and walked over to D. Despite the room being noisy with chitter-chatter, he gracefully broke her nervousness and calmed her fears with his flirtatiousness.

"D, is it?"

As his words found her freaking-out psyche, he stuck out his hand for a more personalized introduction.

"Good memory! Yes! I am D. You are Mister, right?"

That was how Mr. Tsar introduced him as. Everyone called him that in the office; no one ever called him by his real name, C. He preferred it that way. So when Mister paused and stared at D, his uncomfortable silence sent chills down the entire length of her body. He took the pause to help him think up something witty to say.

"Yes, I am Mister, and you are in my seat."

His comments were followed with a lighthearted chuckle that disarmed the situation.

D laughed and coyly let him have her hand in what turned out to be a very proper businesslike handshake.

"Sorry, Mister, for sitting in your seat. I did not know it was yours. In my defense, it did not have your name on it, so I just assumed I could sit wherever I wanted to. Do you want me to move?"

Mister did not exactly know what to say to her rebuttal, but he spoke the first thing that came to his mind.

"No, D. I was just joking with you. I saw you sitting all alone, and since we will be working with each other, I wanted to properly introduce myself. You need to forgive Mr. Tsar for the initial improper introductions. He can be socially awkward like that."

D smiled, laughed, and innocently flirted back with Mister.

"Well then, I appreciate your comedy, Mister. You already know me so well, because comedy always calms my fears. I bet I look like a nervous wreck. I am sure I will make friends as time goes on, but for now I feel all alone. So thank you for helping me acclimate. But I do agree with you about Mr. Tsar's social awkwardness. I saw that firsthand when he walked me around the office with short intros. But he seems to be a good guy with a good heart."

Just when D started to feel welcomed, Mrs. Tsar called the meeting to order. Mister gave her a parting smile and walked back to his seat across the room. From where Mister sat, he saw D's nervousness return with more vigor than before.

He replayed every exchanged word as if they were being spoken real-time in the men's bathroom stall.

The conference room table easily fit thirty-five people around it, which left fourteen to sit in the overflow chairs that lined up against the outer walls. Two of the four conference room walls were made with ice-block-styled glass for the privacy effect while the other two were sheetrock-covered and earth-tone-painted. The carpet was snowflake white with a powder-blue border that outlined the table. The elongated table had a fresh fruit platter on it with bagels and fancy cream cheeses next to it. All the chairs in the room were made of the same black leather that everyone had in their own offices. The magnificent conference room's splendor ended with an in-the-ceiling projector, speakers, and a drop-down screen that only came out for special video presentations. The room was a well-put-together artistic expression that projected company success.

However, this hour all eyes were on D. Even though the meeting was not really all about her, it was *all* about her. Mr. Tsar's wife started out the meeting with the usual words of encouragement and cheer before turning it over to the CEO for the serious parts.

"Welcome, everyone! We made it through another quarter. Yes, we did, and we did it because of all of you. Every one of you should be proud to be part of our growth. But do not fall complacent now. We have many more things to accomplish."

As Mr. Tsar took the stage, he included the specifics of how the company was doing, which included future plans of expansion. It was a slow work up to D's official introduction in dramatic fashion. The CEO's slowness caused D's nervousness to grow so much so that she was completely oblivious to any of her jittery mannerisms. She had been dangling her heels on and off her feet for more than ten minutes. The nervous shoe dangling made her thighs more parted than she realized. That was the second thing Mister noticed about his new trainee, the first being her wedding ring.

He was excited to see what he saw but quickly turned away as if he never saw anything at all. A few minutes passed before Mister looked over at her again. He knew it wasn't the right thing to do, but D's outer beauty had pulled him into her magnetic force field. He found her shyness positively exciting to watch. Whenever she moved around in the seat, he looked away, hoping not to get caught, but his view was perfect from the limited angle he had. Excited confusion overtook his businesslike professionalism. With an unobstructed nine-foot separation, he was given a direct view right up her white pinstriped skirt. He tried to remain a gentleman, but still he wanted to see more red. D's nervousness distracted her from noticing the obvious; her parted thighs gapped more than a professional business-woman's legs should ever be. And then D glanced over at Mister for moral support; she saw his eyes glued to something else, her open skirt. Right then D picked up her strong-calved thighs of creamy steamy delight and recrossed them with sassy attitude as if to say, "No, no." At that very moment, when she crossed her legs, Mister knew he had been caught. He refocused his eyes back on her face to see her reaction.

His being caught played out in slow motion. Every passing second felt like an embarrassing eternity. His face was flushed, and he sweated. The only thing he thought of doing was playing it off like the slick salesman he was. However, it was too late. D already knew that Mister saw something he should not have. D ended the awkwardness with a dirty but sultry hot scowl of disbelief. Her panties were bright cherry red with shimmery gleam to them. Mister knew it was not intentional that he saw what he saw. Nonetheless, he saw something that made him erect.

Were they cheeky or thong-styled? Were they wet? Wedged between her cheeks? Perfume-scented? That was all he could think about. He could not tell, but he wished he knew what they exactly looked like. It was lucky for Mister that he had a notebook sitting in his lap to hide his erection from public view.

D lightheartedly scowled at him for the remainder of the meeting to discourage any more of his perverted attention.

It would have been a hot memory if their intertwined beginnings stopped there. But they did not. And neither did his ongoing DVR recording. That day, Mister won the perfect trifecta. His perfect memory of D's first day on the job only grew from there.

Mister started her training after they both filled up on coffee and cream-cheese-covered bagels. And since there beginning started awkward, so was training. He liked his job and did not want to lose it because of any sexual harassment scandal. It made him a lot bit worried, so he kept his distance. It showed when he began her training regimen. As it neared the middle of a hot June afternoon day, the air conditioner was set on high. Not even the silly old air conditioner could cool them down; they were too excited with each other's morning antics to be cooled off by anything. Even though nothing sexual had happened, their imaginations kept them both on the edge of ecstasy. Their all-day-long tension escalated to uncomfortable levels that had to be extinguished. That was when Mister came up with an exercise for D to do just so they could be apart for a while. For an hour and a restroom break later, D endured unexpected excitement all by herself. Their break from each other almost worked.

D armed herself with a newly refilled ballpoint pen positioned in one hand and a sassy smile in the other before walking into his office to interrupt his training plans. Mister was looking downward when D shyly walked back into his office. Her doorway presence was prebroadcast from the sounds of her heels seductively echoing down the hallway right into his open office. The sexually alluring sounds of her three-inch heels talking acted as an aphrodisiac to Mister's sexual depravity. Those kinds of sounds were a rare commodity around the office anymore, so when Mister heard those unique sounds stop at his doorway, he blushed. After seeing D standing there with one hand on her hips and the other one holding paperwork, Mister was speechless for the third time in all his life. His earlier "getting caught" embarrassment vanished after seeing D's sassy arrogance standing in his doorway. She boldly touted her five-foot-nine-inch frame full of sass and splendor while asking silly questions about her new job. D confidently stood there at the head of his dark-stained Brazilian cherrywood desk while waiting for answers. Piles of paperwork and a laptop were the only physical things keeping them separated. Mister answered all her questions except for the last unasked one.

"Will we be doing sales together or going out on our own?"

While waiting for the answer, D's frivolous pen play purposely landed her expensive ballpoint onto his office floor. The loud sound of the pen hitting the hard granite floor sent an echo through his office which broke Mister's attention fast away from answering.

"Oops! I am so sorry, Mister. Sometimes I get carried away with my nervousness. But I am sure you already know that from my earlier mishap."

D's pen came to rest slightly off to the right, in between his desk and the book credenza.

She walked over to where it landed, turning her back to him, then bent over and picked it up off the floor. She did her morning leg stretches right in front of Mister's bulging eyes. She let her body stiffen while bending over to retrieve her dropped pen. Her pinstripes rode up over her curvy hips confirming what Mister had imagined; it was a thong. She got his attention on her terms. D felt it was necessary to answer all his unasked questions from earlier, and in a small moment of sexual brevity, every one of his perverted questions was answered.

D proudly stood upright and returned to her earlier spot at the head of his desk flaunting a smile that stretched from coast to coast. In that chaotic quiet office moment, nothing but whispers of the usual workplace background could be heard. Mister's heartbeat stopped just as all space and time did. For an agonizing twenty-nine seconds, D allowed herself to be sexually compromised. Every bit of her earlier payback plan worked.

"I am not usually that clumsy." Naughty giggles streamed from her throat. "Are you okay? Mister, are you okay? Say something if you are okay. Please!"

She knew that he was okay, but she felt that it was her duty to all womankind to keep pressuring his cock to stay nice and hard. Just a little payback was what she sought out for his peeking up her skirt without permission.

"Yes, I'm all right! Ahh. At least I think I am okay. Uh-huh! Yes! Wow! All righty then!" All Mister could do was mumble incoherent things. Then he thought up something worthwhile to say. "Wow is all I have to say about that. I am sorry you dropped your pen too. Not!"

"Do you approve?"

"Approve of what exactly, D?"

"You are awful at this game, Mister! You know, the panties that I am wearing? That was one of the questions you wanted to ask me. Was it not?"

"Ahh . . . How did you know I wanted to ask that, D?"

"Call it woman's intuition. I really did not mean for you to see them earlier, but I am glad you noticed them, and me too. Yes, they really are sticky wet too, no thanks to your honest attention. You see, I am attention-starved at home. I cannot remember what it felt like to be ogled at with pleasure in mind. You strongly reminded me of its glowing aftereffects. So thank you. Thank you for noticing me. It felt wonderful to be ogled again. Do it some more. Please?"

While Mister stood in the men's room, he recalled blushing because of what D said. The warmth on his face from his intense blushing over their private office meeting transcended to his bathroom memory romp with himself. There was no doubt that their friendship was just "meant" to be. Mister knew it, and so did D. No matter how professional he tried to be about seeing her scandalous red thong, he could not get it out of his head. It was stuck in between her butt cheeks just as if he had wedged it there himself. Her naughty sex show in his office made him keep recording her every gesture on his internal DVR.

In his office that day, Mister almost unloaded his creamy orgasm in his slacks at the exact moment when D touched her toes, but he refrained from giving into his strong desires out of fear of ruining her marriage. Mister knew she was married from seeing the wedding ring on the left hand, so he hid his real emotions for her out of marital respect, but he was glad that D could not see under his desk. What she would have seen would have been one of the most delicious erections of her life. Sure, D could have been more of a lady in picking up her dropped pen, but she chose to let him see her most prized possessions as his reward for paying attention.

"I definitely approve of your panties. How could I not? I thought I was lucky this morning when I saw a glimpse of that bright, shiny red satin. However, this sweet supplement was much more than I could have prayed for. It was that sizzling hot to me.

I know we should not be having this conversation right here, right now, but I need to tell you something. You almost made me orgasm in my pants. I think you should know that. But somehow, I think you already knew, didn't you?"

He remembered everything they both said, verbatim. Sometimes it was the word exchange he remembered more, and other times it was seeing her wet red thong that did it.

"Mister, to begin with, I was not exactly flaunting myself to you this morning. It was an innocent mistake on my part. Obviously, I was more concentrated on the meeting than you were, and you took advantage of my nervousness. But I liked it. I admit that when I saw you looking up my skirt without my permission, I got embarrassed, then frazzled, then wet, excited, and turned on."

D confidently stood tall and cocky in his office. She felt it more than appropriate to shift her hips into that flirty pose every woman knows about while using her sass to dial it up a few notches. She made Mister drool, confirmed by his audible sighs and unintelligible talk.

"Obviously, you were more interested in seeing my panties more than attending the company meeting. So I thought I would show you what you did not get to see earlier. I know a man like you would appreciate seeing the finer details. But now that you know, let's not make this awkward. Okay?"

With his memories of D continuing to play in high definition, he spat into the palm of his hand a few more times to make his right-handed love tunnel sloppy wet. This day, this time, he only thought about seeing D bent over in that perfect symmetrical A-shaped stance getting an extra butt lift from the heels she had worn. The way her hair dangled downward with blood rushing to her head was priceless to Mister. That was the first time that he ever saw a woman look at him upside down and backwards through her parted legs. She gave him a little extra thank-you by the way of a few well-performed butt twerks simply because she could get away with it. D confidently held all of Mister's attention in the palm of her hand, and she was not about to release it anytime soon.

In Mister's private bathroom reality, he was very close to having his own spewing orgasm, but he could not let himself come just yet. He had more sexual energy that he needed to get out of his body before he could let it all go. The only thing that he could do now was let his fantasies take over.

Mister stood up from his chair and walked over to where D stood in his office. The closer he got to her, the more palpable her sex smelled. He positioned himself behind her with one sole purpose in mind, lifting her straight-edged, strict-pressed, pinstripe-colored skirt up while feeling up her assets. First was a playful slap on the butt to see if he could get away with it. The subtle sting got half of her attention, but it was the second spanking on her ass that got all of her attention. It was a little stronger than the first, but still, she did not complain. However, the third and final spank was more than just a slight sting. It made her whimper in painful ecstasy. All his caring punishments made her aware of his naughty intentions. Lasting memories and fantasies of D's first day on the job constantly stuck with him.

The mere thought of Mister getting to taste her sex ended his fantasy in one big bang. He stood in the men's bathroom stall, dependent on the tiled walls to support his wobbly knees. It took him a few minutes to ride out the orgasm and catch his breath. He pinned up little Mister and cleaned up his sticky spilt mess on the floor before anyone figured him out. Wiping up the semen with toilet paper, he flushed it down the drain, then creaked open the stall door and walked over to the sink as if nothing had happened.

While washing the liquid orgasm off his hands, another coworker walked in. His perfectly timed exit was met with a brief hello from one of the interns. Mister said his hellos and made his exit. Walking back to his office just as if he never left it in the first place. He leaned into his computer, turned it off, and walked out the office door. On his jaunt out to the Humvee, he realized his workday was completely wasted. At least it was Friday, and he was off to a great weekend start.

CHAPTER 7

• • • • • • • • ● • • • • • •

Surrounding Mister

Mister drove his fancy Humvee onto the cobblestone-paved and horseshoe-shaped driveway to park it in its usual spot. His successful back-to-work debut could not have been planned any better. He climbed out of the Humvee and walked right into his twenty-six-hundred-square-foot home with a specific agenda, to relax and get it off again. Although Mister's everyday getting home ritual could easily be predicted without a mind reader present, the day after his lucid wet dream was not so predictable.

No matter how good or bad Mister's day went, he always left work stress outside the front door where it belonged, always slipping into the cloak of positive mystique before the front door closed. Priority one was letting Rocket in from the outside dog run. Then if Alex was around, he would go back into the family room and make small talk with him about sports and current news events. However, some of their conversations went deeper than just the usual "I know what you are saying" kind of agreements. Alex was a psychology major, and that gave him the kind of character and depth that Mister enjoyed being around. While Alex secretly looked up to Mister, admiring his personality and moral character, Mister silently wanted some of Alex's carefree guiltlessness. Neither of them knew what the other thought due to the unspoken universal man code of "keep feelings to thyself." Nonetheless, they bachelor-domed it under the same roof for over two years without any issues.

Mister's house was bequeathed to him six years earlier when his parents tragically passed-on. Even years after they were departed, he strongly felt their appearance around the house, so he kept it in the condition they would have wanted it. Although Mister added his own subtle touches here and there, it was still his parents' home. He took care in not detracting from their vision. They had the house custom built sixteen years earlier using simplistic sensibility and classy elegance as their guiding light. They designed it with three bedrooms and four baths. Then Mister and siblings had just entered their teenage years, and it showed in the way the house was designed. Each bedroom had its own bathroom so that there could not be any squabbling arguments over bathroom rights. His parents mixed common sense with creativity to make their dream home come true. Mister applied those same principles whenever he changed something major around the house.

By far, Mister's added water fountain feature was the best. In one of Mister's most depressed weeks alive, he added the fountain and the backyard barbecue bar area at the same time to make himself feel better while changing things up around the house. His parents occasionally talked about buying a water fountain for the front of the house but never had the extra funds to do it. So when Mister spotted the life-sized dolphin statue on one of his sales calls, he impulsively bought it and had it delivered to the house. It did not sit around for very long before Mister had it spouting water out of its blowhole. He paid a contractor to build an in-ground koi pond to catch the dolphins' water spew. At night, different colored lights lit up the entire dolphin water feature, which quickly set the estate's mood. Though the backyard had been halfway designed by his parents years ago, getting it finished became Mister's responsibility. And in fine Mister style, he added a gazebo-covered hot tub right next to the BBQ pit. The outside yard was sexier than sexy, while the inside house was not so sexy more than it was simplistically functional. The inside decor was not exactly Mister's forte, but he knew the exact look he wanted—simplistically sophisticated, just as his parents would have wanted it.

The house worked for Mister, not being overglamorized nor undersimplified. His bedroom was a modern-day bachelor-pad marvel. Beside the medium-stained cherry oak bed, there were two matching nightstands to complement its original design. The bed was comfortable but felt lonely without a cuddling partner. So Mister made the sitting area his favorite place to be. It had a suede-covered lounger that sat directly in front of the fireplace. And since it was still a bachelor pad, the required sixty-inch flat-screen TV proudly hung on the wall above the mantel. Sometime before the TV was mounted on the wall, Mister had a table made to seamlessly conceal his new wine refrigerator into the room's decor without notice. Despite its lack of wine, the usual root beer, water, and dark-chocolate-covered raisins were always freshly stocked. Despite the changes made, the room remained simplistic with a touch of chic. From the thick plush cream-colored carpet to the earth-toned paint job, the room was sexy as well as highly functional. It worked for Mister, and that was all that mattered. Although if his bedroom walls could talk, they would need a psychologist and extra Zoloft to treat their sad loneliness.

By far, Mister made the house's most functional change himself. It was the finest side-yard dog run in the state. He built it himself, paying specific attention to his best friend's amenities. He put blood, sweat, and tears into building it for Rocket. His private dog run door was specifically cut into the house to allow Rocket in-and-out privileges. Mister handmade Rocket's doghouse with insulated walls, AstroTurf floor for easy cleanup, and a running water spigot that was activated by Rocket's licks. A hand-carved sign with Rocket's name on it hung above the doghouse's front door. Rocket had the best made doghouse in the entire state; Mister made sure of it.

Mister's single-story house sat on the corner of the third-busiest street on the edge of middle-class suburbia. The neighborhoods per-fectly manicured trees and shrubs that lined up and down the curbed streets are well-maintained by the city. Each house in the neighbor-hood had at least one-half acre of land, except for Mister's property. His parents purposely bought two parcels of land. On the square-acre estate, there were lots of exotic plants, flowers, and jacaranda trees spaciously spread out. The entire yard was planted years ago by his mom, and out of love for her, he kept the yard looking spectacular all year round just as his mom would have wanted it. Lots of grass and big boulder rocks were strategically placed all around the yard with creativity. Paving stones lined the grounds in sweeping half-curves to make a pathway around the yard. The expected seasonal changes dramatically made the barren drab browns go away, replacing them with a vibrant color assortment of blooming buds. Everyone in the neighborhood marked that time of year on their calendars. For those two weeks of the year, every morning showed off dramatic new changes during Mother Nature's awe-inspiring fashion show. Despite the large amount of dead leaves falling all over the property, Mister, with Alex's help, maintained the yard with determination. Besides sharing mowing and raking responsibilities, Mister and Alex also shared the cooking responsibility.

Their menus were always simple, including things that they both could make and eat. Their cooking responsibilities changed every other day just so that neither bared the full responsibility. Everything ran smoothly for the most part. Mister and Rocket had their own side of the house, and his roommates had the other side. Originally, his parents designed the house to keep the kids on one side and the adults on the other. That same layout plan helped Mister's roommate idea work perfectly. It was not the exact plan he had envisioned for himself, but when his last relationship ended with his ex-fiancée, he did not want to be alone in the roomy house. It was much too big to let the space go to waste, and besides that, Mister welcomed the extra company and distractions that roommates brought to the equation.

A few roommates drifted in and out of the house over the last two years, but he specifically sought out the twenty-something male crowd. He liked living with males because there was less drama to deal with, though Mister got along with everyone. The mid-twenties crowd offered him a variety of personalities he could vicariously live through while being wildly entertained. Of course, there were drawbacks to the twenty-something crowd, but it was what Mister needed to have around him for now. The house did not have many parties, but that was just the way Mister wanted it to be. But the obvious parties, such as the Super Bowl and World Series, celebrations were mandatory. But months back, Mister had to kick out one of the renters for throwing a Friday-afternoon party when Mister was not around. The party upset the neighbors, then upsetting Mister when the police were called. For now, Alex was the only roommate living there.

Mister gave up some of his privacy just because he did not want to be alone. He has not had a steady girlfriend since his breakup with his ex-fiancée, so privacy was not a big priority then. He would rather have a live-in girlfriend to stay with him, but for now, his roommate Alex would have to do. Besides being roommates, Mister and Alex were good friends despite their twelve-year age difference. They were bros; that was all there was to it. They spent a lot of time together; however, that chilly spring night, Mister needed to be alone. His overwhelmed jubilance and sexual frisk from D's earlier office tease forced Mister into alone time. Mister's mind was in the middle of a big orgy that put himself on an unexpected fuck ride that he did not want to get off. Mister's earlier work restroom orgasm should have been enough to calm his anxious energy, but it was not.

Firstly, he was getting a drink of whiskey, then showering. Before settling in for the night, he walked down the hallway into the kitchen and grabbed the bottle of Gentleman Jack out of the liquor cabinet. On the way back to his room, he spotted Alex in the hot tub with a bubbly brunette sitting on the top step. Without disturbing them, he walked back to his room with a plan to keep his somber buzz going all night long. Gentleman Jack was one of those drinks that great men sipped on. However, that night, there was not any sipping of any kind, just straight shots of guilty pleasure to soothe his thirst and quench his remaining virility. Next came the steamy hot shower. He molested his cock with slick soap and two hands, once again fantasizing about D. But this fantasy was more about him fucking D hard from behind, pulling it out and squirting hot semen all over her desk and keyboard. His orgasm was not as stronger as his earlier bathroom one at work. The post-orgasmic bliss mixed with soapy hot water greatly calmed his randiness right on the spot.

Mister had another double shot of caramel-colored heaven to keep his chillax vibe intact. With his lucid wet dream, finally in the rear-view mirror, Mister focused on finding the delicious things it foretold. Although having a woman in his life was on his to-do list, he had kept himself single due to his previous self-inflicted torment. His being single was a necessity needed to heal himself from the inside out. And now that his past torment was done and over with, Mister concentrated on the things yet to come.

While waiting for his laptop to warm up, he threw back the second double shot of the smooth-tasting whiskey to speed up its after-effects. The alcohol quickly replaced his horny edge with an alcoholic buzz that he needed to have. Filling up his shot glass for the third time, he settled into the loveseat like a lost romantic, hoping that his new Miss had already read his personals ad and wrote him back. But that was not the case at all. As soon as he saw that no one had written, disappointment settled in. No real responses to his ad made him second-guess what he already wrote. After all, Mister was a perfectionist with everything he did. Another reread of his ad revealed a few weak spots that he wanted to improve on. He made several small changes to it so that he could be completely confident that his ad would find, locate, and lure in his future Miss. The changes were subtle, but they made his confidence soar high above previous expectations. Everything after Mister's lucid wet dream led him down a different pathway than the one he was previously on, pulling him apart from his once-strong religious morals. Even if he wanted to, Mister could not restain the monotone shades of gray, only accept them now for what they once were. Up until now, Mister's simplified life was just that. He ate, slept, worked, and did it all over again. He only dreamed of going on wild spontaneous adventures, but those were just late-night erotic thoughts that never went anywhere. On many occasions, he tried to break out of his self-made prison, not ever succeeding.

With no food and three double shots of whiskey in his bloodstream, the room spun around with dizzying consequences. The little sobriety that he had helped him make it into the kitchen to get something to eat to counteract the alcohol effects. He picked out tortilla chips and made nachos. Just when the microwave dinged, Alex walked in to the kitchen to get a few more beers for him and his date.

"It looks like you have a hot half-naked sweetheart out in the tub. Good job, Alex!"

While Mister poured the nacho cheese dip over the chips, he and Alex conversed.

"Yes, I do. She is a friend I met in class. I have been flirting with her off and on for a few weeks. But then in class today I got the chutzpah to ask her over for a movie and a dip in the hot tub. I won't get lucky, but you know I will try."

They chuckled together, then Alex made a bowl of nachos for his hot tub date.

"Have any special plans for tonight, Mister?"

"No special plans, just taking it easy. I am already buzzing hard. I had an indifferent day with a weird ending. So I am keeping to myself. Good luck with the bikini!"

Mister smiled, winked, and walked back down the hallway. But before disappearing out of sight, Alex gave Mister a courteous thank-you and good-night.

"Thanks, I need all the good luck I can get. Good night, Mister."

Shakily, Mister made it back to his room with his lonely alcohol-induced buzz worsening. It was a given that whenever Mister drank whiskey, he sought after a brief timeout from life. Although this night, he drank for several other reasons than just a break. The ending of his two-week sabbatical mixed with dreaming up his lucid wet dream, culminating with D's hot little office tease made for one unbelievable week. The dream was still too new for Mister to completely trust in the fact that it was his new future path, but he felt positive beginnings of everything good finally coming together. The night flew by in a jet-like flyover. He was a lot more buzzed than he normally ever got. Even though it was just after midnight on a Friday night, he was wiped out beyond repair but felt the need to check e-mails one last time before bedtime.

The one good thing about Mister's ad was that it had a hit counter that tracked how many people saw his ad. So when he saw that eighteen people viewed it so far, it gave him encouragement and a peace that he could fall asleep to.

That night, Mister went to bed buzzed on alcohol, yet he had vivid clarity of things to come. He now has what he had only seen others have. Mister never thought that was possible, but it was finally his turn.

CHAPTER 8

• • • • • • • • ● ● ● • • • • • •

Choices

Mister got up Saturday morning as if he were an eight-year-old on Christmas morning. The built-up excitement convinced him to roll over, sit up, and grab for his computer. He needed to find out if anyone had yet responded to his personals ad. While waiting for the computer to turn on and connect to the internet, he stood up and stretched. He spent the first five minutes of every day stretching. Morning stretches were never calisthenics, only a little something to slowly tease his senses awake without sacrificing a lot of effort. That day, Mister intended on sleeping in, but emotional mind excitement made him be up at sunrise. Feelings of possibility and potential cut Mister's stretching regimen short.

Mister stopped stretching and took his laptop over to the love-seat and checked for new e-mails before getting on with his day. High hope existed before he signed into his e-mail account, but then zero hope remained after no new e-mails were found. For the second time in ten hours, there were zero responses to his ad. Despite the negativity, he shrugged it off as if he knew what to expect. Along with emotional sadness, the alcohol from the night before had severely dehydrated him to the point of being parched. An unexpected apple juice craving took him by surprise. Rarely did Mister have strong urges like drinking apple juice, but his dry throat gave him the motivation to go get some. He weakly wobbled into the kitchen and poured himself a short glass of cold thirst-quenching sweetness. After drinking down the first round, hunger pangs erupted aloud. Mister decided on having another glass of apple juice along with a mixture of unsalted almonds and dark-chocolate-covered raisins for breakfast.

It was not like him to smell the roses, but that morning, Mister took a brief timeout from life to whiff their distracting essence. He stood in the kitchen and peered out the window. The morning's beauty was breathtakingly divine as the rays of sunlight illuminated the backyard patio table. There was an iridescent glow all around the table that clearly spoke to Mister, "Come and sit." He obediently walked outside and sat at the glass table under the center-poled umbrella. As Mister jumped in and walked out of a real-life daydream, the morning unfolded before his very eyes. He watched the rest of the sunrise while sipping on sweet apple juice and chewing on raisins and nuts. The nippy morning air congealed well with the beautiful baby-blue sky. As the sun arose, its illustrious beams of light highlighted all his mom's hard yard work, which brought Mister back in time. Forgotten memories of seeing his parents having breakfast at the very same table he sat at gave him a much different view of how good they were for each other. He remembered them holding hands and laughing, kissing, and hugging while sharing morning coffee at that very same table he now sat at. His parents were in love; that much Mister knew. They had the ideal marriage, something Mister had been jaded on for a long time. It was Mister's jadedness that forced him to seek out the alternative via a personals ad. The motto Mister firmly embraced was "Hurt me once, shame on you. Hurt me twice, shame on me." He was once emotionally scorned, but that morning, he finally got it. He had to be vulnerable and open to find her. Just then, he decided to not second-guess himself anymore and accept his new path of unbound freedom. It was that morning at that breakfast that Mister positively knew that his personals ad was what he had to do. So with strict obedience, he kept pursuing after his sexual soul mate with determination. It was "Find Miss or bust." The sunrise ended, and so did Mister's childhood flashbacks. With urgency, Mister walked back to his room, grabbed the laptop, and brought it back to the patio table to begin his own search for Miss.

Still dressed in satin blue pajama bottoms and a plain black cotton T-shirt, Mister searched through the entire personals website database using an eighty-mile radius and a select keyword search. He typed in *soul mate, passion, adventure,* and *tease,* then waited. Pending possibilities gave him many new ideas that turned him on to plausible hope. When the search results appeared, goose bumps shivered him all over. Mister's post lucid wet dream persona broke off the usual stigma associated with internet dating, making it okay in his own mind to browse through the personal section without shame. He figured out that he could order himself something that was not on his normal narrow-minded menu.

Mister sifted through the three ads that matched his multiple keyword and eighty-mile criteria. He checked each one of those ads with much expectation, but all he found was disappointment. With not much luck, he discarded that search and started another. The second attempt yielded more success. He went through every ad with a fine-toothed comb. As the minutes passed, the warmth of the hot rising sun and a dying laptop battery made him continue his search indoor. He sat down on the loveseat and refocused his attention on finding his hot sexual soul mate temptress through the expansive green and rose-petal-filled Garden of Eden. He read many ads, never finding the right one. Mister needed the ad to cause butterflied chaos. He did not know that finding the right one would be so daunting, but she was. So many ads, too little time, but he sought her out from his shade-drawn bedroom.

With continued desire in his aching soul, Mister spent three hours meandering through the localized possibilities that existed within his eighty-mile range. Through his search, he discovered a lot of sad stories about loneliness and hurt. Some were shy about their quest, and others were bold and desperate. Some were unrealistic, while others were depressing. But one ad caught Mister's fancy. He reread it four times over before knowing she was the one. Her ad got his attention with her naturally flirtatious personality and clinched victory by displaying her intimate sincerity with sensualistic parables that described her life in a way that Mister got.

Hello there,

I am Mister, and you have my attention. What you say makes total sense to me, which is why I am writing. The way you used parables spell-bounded me. To be honest, this is my first go-around with the online personals dating scene. Just the other day, I posted my own ad out of curiosity. Then today, I decided to read other people's ads in an attempt to find the right one for me. I read many ads but stopped reading right after I found yours. To be honest, it was the only one I wanted to respond to. Really! You made me smile big as well as keeping my hopes of faith alive. Now that you know I am interested in you, maybe you should read my ad and see if you feel the same way about me. I have this internal feeling that you will like all that I say, but do be careful. It might stir up wanted and unwanted emotions somewhere deep inside of you. All I can hope for is that you will be half as intrigued in me as I am in you. Until we talk again, I will try and be patient while waiting for your reply. Have a great day and know that you have a secret admirer.

Intrigued!
Mister

The approach was a long shot, but he kept his hopes up. If it were not for the lucid dream a few days previous, he would have never written her. With anxious hope, Mister sent off the e-mail, then looked at his inbox one last time before taking a much-needed break from virtual reality. Although his intuition was wrong last time, this time it was right. A new e-mailed message emerged. He did not think it could be from the woman he just wrote minutes ago, and it was not from her at all. An unknown e-mail from an unknown woman made Mister egotistically smirk. He acted as if he had the eighty-million-dollar lottery ticket in his hand. Mister gave into his excited nervousness and read it with a macho confidence boost.

Mister,

If that is what you want me to call you, then I will. But I am certain that a true name like Mister does not exist, although I guess it could, given the billions of people that live here on planet Earth with us. Anyway, we can talk about that later. But for now, I want to talk to you about your personals ad. That is why I am here, right? Two words that I would describe what I read: *wow* and *impressive*. It intrigued me in more ways than you will ever know. It stood out far above any other ad, and I like that. That, my sexy man, thoroughly made my heart skip a beat. It made me want to find out more about the mystery man calling himself Mister. You have exhilarating passion, and I like that. It is refreshing to see. To me, "Mister" suggests you want anonymity. So for now, I will let you have that, but only for now. Nevertheless, your name hints at you being a gentleman full of mystery yet someone that could brandish a whole lot of naughty mischief whenever he wants to. I like it. When I read it for the second time, I felt like it had my name on it. Did you write it for me? Because it spoke to me more than you might ever know. Tell me more, Mister, because I want to know.

As for me, I am new to this site too. Coincidence or fate? We can be each other's firsts if you want. Do not expect to be inside of me on the first date, Mister, for I am much shier in person than online, although I will be highly disappointed if you do not try and get into my thong on the first date. I feel as though you do not like disappointment, so I will exactly know what to expect. LOL! Somehow, I just know what you are about, and that thrills me a lot. Your intellectual stimulation seductively intrigues my fancy. I like how you know what you want and subtly went for it in the alluring manner that you did. This world needs more men like you in it. I feel as though we already know each other intimately. You know what? You make me feel like the prom queen without a date. We see each other from across the room, both walking to each other at the same fucking time. We meet in the middle of the dance floor and start dancing. The music beats are erotically rhythmic, and so is the dance between us. Our dirty dancing ends with a show-stopping dip as you firmly grab my ass and support my bent over stature with your strength.

I swear, no one "gets" the dance anymore, yet somehow, we both understand it well. I can only admit my instant crush on you. Maybe you will go look at my profile and see some things you might like to see. Sorry in advance about my no-picture policy, but a woman must keep some things secret. Right? I like keeping the man in my life on his tippy-toes. So, Mister, be prepared for the unexpected. Besides secrets, I want my man to be more attracted to my personality than my looks, and vice versa. It was hard for me to not compete and put up my picture, but I need and want substance. Can you give me substance, Mister?

Impatiently waiting,
S

Now befuddled, Mister had to take his overdue break to figure out what to write back to S. He closed the laptop and walked out to the kitchen to get Alex and go grocery shopping, although for the last week, Alex had been wondering what Mister was preoccupied with. Yet still, they went out and shopped and guy-talked about bachelor things.

"You seem to be preoccupied these days. What gives?"

"Ahh. You know me, Alex. Been busy with life and the pursuit of happiness. But the pursuit is much different than before." Mister chuckled aloud, then spilled the beans. "I put up a personals ad on a dating website a few days ago. And then today, I looked through the other people's ads to see if I liked any. I have been thinking about finding someone to spend time with. I guess I am deciding to move on and stop feeling sorry for myself."

"Oh wow! Good for you, Mister. It is about time. I was beginning to wonder if you had become asexual or something." They both laughed hard with Alex's joke cracking. "Watching baseball and soccer, working hard, and being a bachelor can only last for so long before you go ape-shit crazy."

"I totally agree with you, Alex. And that is why I put up the personals ad. If I can't have D, then I need to move on. Right?"

"Yup. That is true. I have been saying that for months. I say, go for it."

They grocery-shopped, and Mister thought about things to write back to S. He did not want to repel her away with some stupid response, but he also did not want to turn her off with mediocrity. He knew he had to be smooth and clever with however he responded. After Mister helped put the food away, he sat down and wrote S. At first, he struggled with what to write, but then the perfect words just flowed out of him.

Good afternoon, S.

How are you? I am great now that you wrote. Before, I was a struggling romantic clamoring to find his groove, and now I am a starving artist seeking out a muse. I am glad you like my name. I like being called Mister for the exact reasons you suggested. I hope to live up to your expectations because I do not think either of us can take any more disappointment. The main reason behind my ad was that I had a life-altering dream a few days ago that changed me from the inside out. After I dreamed it, I knew exactly what I had to do. The ad is part of the change. I put it up for the world to see. If you stay interested, I might share the dream with you. However, you should know that I am interested in knowing more about what you said about Mister being a man of mystery cloaked in naughty mischief. I like your open-minded flirtatiousness. But I must tell you that I am a lot bit sad to not see your picture on your profile. Leaving it blank is extremely risky on your part; however, I do like solving a good mystery. I don't want to admit it, but not including your picture was an ingenious idea. I know the world mostly gets caught up in looks rather than substance. You just like being a tease. Don't you? I am sure you did that on purpose, probably because you wanted an intellectual man as your sole captive audience. I admire your intelligence; it goes way beyond the ditsy stigma associated with a certain colored hair. I love a smart, sassy woman. Don't change a thing. Even if we never meet, don't change. I feel just as you do about character. I think I have great character, but only you can be the judge of that. I do hope we get to talk more because I am interested.

Mister

He sent it off with internal expectations that she could be the one. It was not like him to pursue two women at once, but hearing intern stories made him stay open to anything conceivable. As Saturday night fast slipped away, Sunday morning set in. With Mister's hazy mindless three-day sex binge over, his entire weekend vanished. Something that naively started Friday morning tiringly ended at 4:30 AM, Sunday. For one entire weekend, Mister intoxicated himself on sex. Sex on the brain, sex in the pants, sex on the computer, sex in the bathroom stall, and sex behind the shower glass.

A binge that began with a wet dream ended with Mister's insides bursting with possibility galore. His binge ended out of complete exhaustion from being up all night dicking around with his past, present, and future.

CHAPTER 9

Male Bonding

The mixed scent of raw meat and sweet mesquite brought Mister out of his long Sunday afternoon sleep coma. He napped the afternoon away, and still needed more sleep. And now, the unmistakable smell of barbecued steak made his hunger pangs go ping. Yet still, he swooped in and fell out of sleep consciousness while halfway paying attention to the exquisite scent of meat cooking on the barbie. In the quiet background, Mister heard a faint unrecognizable sound chiming on and off every so often. His grogginess kept him from auto-recognizing that faint sound. But when a crashing-down barbecue lid starkly startled Mister awake, he confusingly sat up and scooted over to the edge of the bed, not knowing what to think.

"What the hell was that?"

Mister added the smell of steak to the sound of the crashing down BBQ lid and got the "suppertime is ready" answer. While thinking about biting into that juicy rib eye, he heard that faint sound chime again. That time, Mister was more awake to recognize the sound. The reoccurring chime came from his laptop signaling new messages.

"Yes! New e-mails. I hope at least one is from the ad."

Mister's dilemma—steak or e-mail. He decided on e-mails, then dinner. Four new messages existed. One offered him mail order brides, another was for a house refinance loan, and the last two messages were crappy infomercial sales pitches. His excitement quickly turned to frustration when all that he saw were junk advertisements. He quickly deleted the four messages only to find out there was a brand-new message delivered. Mister traded in his downtrodden demeanor for excited hope but then decided to savor it for a bit.

Mister and Alex made Sunday-night steak dinners habitual, but that evening, Mister needed to do dinner alone. It was not that he did not want to read the unopened message, more than it was his body needing fuel for reenergization, for he had only eaten two meals in three days due to his concentrated efforts to search for his sexual soul mate. He was famished and ready to eat.

Mister jumped up off the loveseat with Rocket hot on his trail. They walked down the hallway into the kitchen, looking for food. It just so happened that it was Alex's turn to be the chef. Mister and Alex sequentially took turns making dinner. By far, Sunday dinner was the most important of the week. Whoever that night's chef was, they always made a fresh green salad mixture with a side of fresh vegetables and beer to supplement the main course. The third-course selection was limited by their confectionary-cooking abilities narrowed down to frozen-apple turnovers and boxed brownie mixes, though sometimes Mister turned semipro and made a Black Russian cake full of liquor, chocolate, and sin. They quickly bonded over baseball at first that soon kaleidoscoped into much deeper intelligent conversations. Mister and Alex made sure to get together at least once a week to console themselves about being lonely masters of the universe. Weekend nightly normalcy included sitting around the living room, watching TV or listening to music while shooting the proverbial shit. Even if they had movie dates, Sunday night steak and baseball was served. They rooted for the same sports teams, making them more friends than roommates. Sometimes entire weekends were spent jabbering about baseball and unexplainable phenomena about big bang theories, life after death, and the unknown. Without the estrogen factor being present, their laidback personalities made the house a melodic retreat from chaotic tussles that everyday life presented. Only sports and other climatic events of life were the only house drama that existed. They cherished the no-estrogen-drama zone with tenacious verve.

Though that night when Alex stoked up a conversation with Mister, Mister only tolerated it.

"Man, the Yankees look great this year. Let's hope that they can get back into the playoffs again. It should be easier with their off-season trades and acquisitions."

"I know, right! I hope that too. I have complete faith in them that they will make it back to the playoffs." Mister felt urgency to get back to the waiting e-mail, trying to oversteer the conversation that way.

"As sad as this might sound, I have not exactly been paying attention to their preseason antics due to other distractions going on around me."

Alex knew something bothered Mister as soon as he stumbled into the kitchen off-balanced, but held his tongue until the time was right.

"Mister, are you okay? You do not look so good."

Alex stated the truth, and Mister knew it.

"Lately I have not been sleeping very well. Not to mention my allergies combined with planning my future has distracted my usual baseball fanaticism. Then last night, I mixed Benadryl and whiskey. I now realize that was not a good mixture."

Mister chuckled, then began thinking clearer, though in the foreground of his mind he severely wanted to find out what the e-mail said.

What does it say? What does she think about me? How interested is she? Will she keep liking me for who I am? How do I keep her intrigued?

Even while Mister walked around the kitchen, pretending to listen to Alex, those were the secret thoughts he waffled back and forth on. All Mister heard Alex say was "Blah, blah, blah" while conjuring up speculation on unread e-mail.

Alex knew there was more to Mister's "distractions" excuse than met the eye.

"I can understa—"

Mister cut Alex off before he could finish his retort. "Nothing personal, A, but I am not in the mood for conversation nor company tonight. Thanks for making dinner. It smells delicious as always. But tonight, I am going to eat in my room if that's cool? Night!"

Alex was not buying what Mister sold, yet he respected his excuse with a nod of agreement. Mister grabbed dinner and took it back to his room with Rocket following. The eleven minutes that Mister spent in the kitchen getting dinner made him feel like a six-year-old boy trapped inside a candy store. He strode across the heated granite hallway floor on his way back to the loveseat, where he made himself comfortable in front of the TV. He used one hand to cut into the juicy rib eye while the other helped balance the laptop steady so he could read what she had to say.

CHAPTER 10

· · · · · · · · · ● ● · · · · · ·

In Pursuit

Dearest Mister,

Oh, how I like calling you that. It rolls off the tip of my tongue with such bling-bling panache. I know my dating profile is not as exquisitely written as yours was, but God did not bless us all with the gift of writing, now did he? It took me forever and a day to get my ad just right, but then I slowly forgot about it, not ever expecting something to come from it. I put it up over six months ago with not one good substantial response. Ugh! To be honest, I have been stupefied as to why I have not attracted my kind of man. All the responses were undignified in their own way, so I just figured all the men out there were that way. I mean, is my ad really that bad? I could have flirted too much, swaying the readers to believe one thing when I was nothing like what they thought. Yes, I deliberately planted sneaky sexual innuendoes all over the place, but now, think I should have planted my genuine sincerity. But I wanted to be different than every other ad out there, using my flirtatiousness and comedy to get the man of my dreams interested in me. To be honest, I am confused as to why you did not treat me the same way the others did. All the other responders were completely unworthy of my time despite my giving them some of it. I am not going to lie; the dating scene sucks! However, knowing that a man like you could exist makes me quiver all over with intrigue. However, I am more than a little skeptical about what you want out of this. What are your intentions, Mister? Honesty counts!

Speaking of honesty, Mister, I reread your profile several times to convince myself to write at all. I was not going to write you back, but after every reread, I liked it that much more. I like the way you write; you have an interesting lyricism about you that I cannot get over. Even though you did not write one dirty word, every word you wrote came across just like it was hot pillow talk that we could be having some day. You have a knack for getting people's attention, especially mine. Whatever you do, keep it up. LOL! Okay, fine, I want to tell you another truth. Your mysterious eroticism and wit got my attention, while your clean words turned dirty kept it. It has been a long time since anyone has captivated me with generalities, let alone complimenting me with "beautiful" and meaning it. At least that was how you made me feel. So thank you for that. And now, I must reciprocate.

Your looks match up with your personality perfectly. The exact words that you write to describe yourself painted me a vivid portrait of an intriguing man cloaked in mystery. If you had not used a picture in your ad, I would still know how you look; that was how vivid you described yourself to me. The way you did that was extremely hot. I can only admit one last truth; you have the sexiest eyes that I have seen in a long time. I do not know if I should print your picture out and put it in a silver-bordered glass frame or stick it in my purse and carry it everywhere I go. Humph!

I get this weird vibe from you that I need to figure out. Most men are full of dirty words, but they cannot make them dance and sing like you did. Yet you take the most boring word and make it sound so damn delicious. You have a very smooth way about you, Mister. It is downright sexy. Somehow, I just know that you are one charming man that all women and some men need to fear. If I were not so gun shy and jaded, I would be over at your place right now, but my broken heart of feelings past have taught me to watch out for my future. One-half of my brain tells me to throw caution to the wind, while the other half says hold back, M, hold back. So while I figure myself out, you should try and come up with a strategy to win me over.

Interested and intrigued,
M

After Mister read that, he was an excited mess. He went from a zero to a stud in an eye blink. What she wrote made him get that same silly feeling in the bottom of his stomach that he felt when he picked up that faded-blue notebook to take notes on his lucid wet dream. Internally, Mister felt like he had to strike again while M's iron burned hot. Luckily for Mister, he had a few free hours to construct a well-thought-out response to rock her emotional boat one last time before bed.

M,

I am glad you thought me worthy enough to write back. Are you challenging me already? I like it. But you should know that I am the kind of man that will always rise to the occasion, accepting every challenge presented. So when I say that I am going to the boardroom to prepare a foolproof strategy to penetrate your defenses, know that I am doing exactly that. For now, I will respect your "feel it out first before proceeding with caution" theory, but only because I am that way too. I am a "proof is in the pudding" kind of man, although I must admit that I am also skeptical, but in a different way than you are. We are two skeptics going on a skeptic-less trip together. My honest prediction: interesting times ahead, especially after I dreamed another déjà-vu-like dream the other day. So I am going for it, just as the dream foretold me to do. I used to not be like that, but now I am. No more smoke and mirrors or bullshit, just straight honest talk that will earn me a place into somewhere hot and wet. Oops, did I just say that? Bad Mister, bad!

Seriously though, my dream changed me overnight. Know that you are now talking to the new Mister, not the old one. The old Mister deliberately put obstacles of all kinds in his way, whereas the new Mister has a clean slate without obstacles. The old Mister would not have ever placed a personals ad, nor would he have ever checked out the personals website where he found you. It is the new Mister that is choosing to slide across the fine green felt table all his remaining black and purple chips. Right into the middle of the pot they go, all-in. As I ambitiously wait for an answer, I get the moxie to ask the dealer to start a countdown timer on your hand. Now you have three minutes remaining to decide our fate. You know you have a great hand. Your heart is racing, and you are trying hard not to give any tells away. You know you cannot fold your hand, but you also are scared to see mine. Whatever are you going to do? Call? Fold? Or re-raise?

Wanting to know,
Mister

It was barely 11:00 PM, and both he and Rocket were in bed. Mister did not know if or when she would write back, but he hoped it would be sooner than later. Mister was trying to be calm, strong, and confident with M, but only because the new Mister was in effect.

Morning time quickly made Mister awake without assistance. Despite every Monday being his least favorite workday, he was up earlier than he should have been. He groggily lay in bed, yet he was superbly awake. His first morning thoughts were of S and M in compromised and uncompromised positions. But without any caffeine in his bloodstream, he was confused as to which roles he wanted the girls to be in, submissive or dominant. Either way, they made his morning greater than great. He did not know if M had read his last night's e-mail yet or not, but he was eager to find out. He rose out of bed with positive buoyancy only to be sunk back down after discovering zero new e-mailed messages.

• • • • • • • • ● • • • • • •

Reconnecting with Forward Movement

D's sexless weekend and rekindled friendship with Mister made her reconsider his past offers. But D, being the loyal wife that she was, made her husband his favorite oatmeal-raisin cookies to show him she cared about their future. The more her husband failed to pay attention to her efforts, the more she thought about giving herself to Mister. Her Sunday-night shower emotionally cleansed her more than it washed her clean, sobbing to mourn her dead marriage. As D towel-dried off, she reminisced PG-13 moments that she and Mister shared over the last few years. Clear memories of working late and taking early lunches with Mister made D want more of Mister's attention. With every intimate memory remembered, her pussy got moistier over their fully clothed bonding. She slipped in between the sheets, laid her head down on the pillow, and quietly masturbated to thoughts of Mister spooning her from the backside. Pleasure filled her heart with guilty freedom, yet her shed tears melancholized her soul. D awoke Sunday with renewed hope of having a good family structure as she preplanned shoe shopping for the kids' shoes, lunch, and an afternoon matinee for the entire family. That was not D's idea of a great weekend, but it happened just like that.

M discovered Mister's Sunday-night e-mail during her Monday morning "get ready for work" rituals. She did not expect another one from him so soon, but there it was, and with sleep-tossed hair, she read what he wrote.

M,

I am glad you thought me worthy enough to write back. Are you challenging me already? I like it . . .

As Mister's words danced across her computer screen with convincing charm, his words spoke to M's wide-open soul. His e-mail left Miss with an overwhelming need to reciprocate, but Mister would be forced to wait due to M's prior work and school commitments.

Mister went about his day as normal. First stop, coffee with D, then two scheduled sales appointments after that. They met at the sandwich place and sat at the only open umbrella-covered table. Over the next thirty-eight minutes, they drank lattes, ate egg-covered bagel sandwiches, and talked about work and outside-of-work things. The bright sun and crisp spring air lent them a memorable picturesque backdrop right out of a fairy-tale fantasy. The air could be smelt, and the slightest breeze could be heard as it whispered bye. This was the big opportunity that D had been waiting for. She jumped at the chance to try and mend their fractured friendship.

"You know, Mister, I still feel horrible for winning the sales comp the way I did. It was completely unfair, I realize that now. As you know, I am a competitor, and I saw a way to get my husband to pay attention to me. I know it was not the best way to win, but I knew that if I did not flirt and subtly flaunt my assets the way I did, I would have lost by a landslide. All that I could think about getting into my husband's good graces. I tried hard, and now I know that there is nothing I do can to get my marriage back. And that makes me want to give up. But . . ."

Tears streamed down D's cheeks as she opened up to Mister. He patiently listened while D shared her sadness. She let her real feelings go, knowing that Mister would not tell a soul.

"Well, D, I will always be your friend no matter if your marriage survives or fails. However, don't feel bad for winning. But remember, paybacks are a bitch." Mister sarcastically chuckled, then continued. "I really do appreciate all your gestures, especially the provocative massage with the extra happy ending you had her do. Let's just say it was an explosive ending. I was stupefied when she changed her massage techniques. The way she changed from strict massage techniques to much gentler touches that targeted my nipples, balls, and shaft." Mister's sinister cackle turned into a naughty grin letting D know he liked it. "I am glad you still consider me a friend, D. You made me wonder if we were friends anymore when you played that contest dirty-D-style. I will try and forgive you, but give me a little time. Okay, D?"

"Mister, we are friends, I promise. I will back off until you are ready. Now I feel bad that I told you what I did this morning."

"Do not feel Bad, D. I am glad you told me. We needed to clear the air. In all honesty, I was more hurt by my own feelings. You squashed my ego hard with your dirty tactics win. But losing to you internally wrecked me more than your flirting did. The loss made me feel sad and depressed, like I was expendable. It gave me impressions that I was not the company hotshot anymore. In retrospect, I needed that bruising. So thank you."

"Well, okay then, Mister, you are welcome. But just in case you forgot, we are *way* closer to each other than me and my husband ever were. Take that to the bank."

"I never knew that, D. Thank you for sharing."

"No problem, Mister. I was not being fair to you or myself. So thank you for making me see that. Does that mean that we can put the contest debacle behind us and never bring it up again?"

"Maybe . . ."

A small pause followed up with a big smile from Mister to D concluded their breakup and started their makeup.

"I do know one thing, D. I wished it was you giving me the two-handed happy ending. Though I would expect the same outcome, with a few changes. You dressed down in a satin purple and black bra, black leather-and-lace thong with thigh-high fitted, zipper-closed boots. Only then would I allow you to take her place as my private masseuse."

They both looked at each other in the eye and simultaneously smiled, signifying a rekindled friendship. As the sun passed over the top of their table and the last of their lattes were finished, Mister wanted to tell D about his personals ad. Instead, Mister hugged D compassionately, then drove off to his afternoon appointments.

He arrived ten minutes early to his eleven-o'clock, which allowed him to take deep breaths so that he could put on his game face. He exhaled out thoughts of D, S, and M and inhaled thoughts of iron-clad contracts and signed agreements. Two minutes before eleven, Mister confidently walked into his sales appointment, carrying with him a blank contract and product literature. He walked out forty-two minutes later with a signed contract as well as a signed three-year extended-service protection plan. The sale was one more notch toward his monthly sales quota, and the extended warranty contract built up his end-of-the-month bonus.

As Mister drove down the roadway to take a well-earned break, he thought about the girls. He efficiently put work first, but now, S's, M's, and D's personalities loudly resonated in his private think tank. Just when he pulled into his usual lunchtime parking spot, text messages rang his phone. He did not have to look at the display to know it was D. She texted him friendly messages of salesmanship camaraderie.

"Go, Mister, Go! Sell it, and *no* is not an option."

Mister rather liked D's encouraging text message, but right then, he needed to hear sexy words from S or M to counteract D's earlier love potion effects. D's earlier attention retriggered him to redesire her in many positions, many ways. Instead, what Mister felt was past thoughts of torment and inadequacy. He thought up all kinds of crazy things that were unfounded.

"Did S and M know each other? Are they in cahoots with each other just to fuck with me? Is this some sort of fraudulent scam? Maybe payback? I wonder, did D put them up to playing a trick on me?"

While Mister's seat was tilted back, background rhythms played as he struggled to be confident. Despite teeter-tottering confidence, he put the girls out of his mind and began preparing for his last appointment of the day. With the sun shining in through his closed sunroof, he spent the next ten minutes getting into top salesmanship character, then drove off. He met with and made another sale at his two-thirty appointment. Just as he shook hands to seal the deal, Mister's phone quietly vibrated against his hipbone. Even though he wanted to look and see who it was, he downplayed the interruption and played up welcoming a new client. But the moment right after the welcome-aboard handshake, he walked out the door at the same time he reached for his phone. It turned out to be an e-mail from someone that he wanted to hear from.

M had ants in her pants over writing Mister back. She never broke any company rules, but one rule begged to be broken—the "do not use the company computers for personal reasons" one. It begged to be broken, especially since M did not yet own a smartphone.

Mister,

I finally got a break, and I decided to write you back. I bet you have been in suspense all day? Haa! Today was crazy busy, so please forgive my lack of attention. It really was not my fault. I swear. Everyone picks me to gossip to and ask favors of. I sometimes hate it, but other times I love it. I really like helping everybody. That's me! Your message . . . I did not get the chance to write you earlier, but only because I just read it this morning. I hope that I did not give you the wrong impression. So here I am.

And yes, you have been in and out of my consciousness all day long. How could you not be after writing me that sexy note? I am interested, what can I say. But don't go getting a swollen head just yet, Mister. A little part of me is unintentionally scared of your intense personality. I am not used to talking with such a confident man. This is new to me. I am just the average girl next door, not causing or seeking out any kind of drama. I guess you could say that I am a prude, never a temptress. Believe it or not, you are challenging a lot of my beliefs right now. It is hard for me to get a pulse as to who you are, but I am trying. Really, I am! Give me a little more time to figure you out is all I ask.

Still intrigued,
M

After he read M's ego-boosting message of encouragement, Mister was determined to keep her intrigued. He was not about to back down from the challenge. While maneuvering his way through traffic, Mister's mind ventured somewhere it should not have been while driving. He thought up many different ideas to keep M intrigued despite shitty static bleed over from his self-tormented past. His unsurety of freedom and happiness kept hindering his ability to decide on what to do with the girls. Serious doubts kept infiltrating his new plans.

"Can I really do this? Which one should I choose? How will I know she is the right one? Will she like new Mister? What if she doesn't? Will I have enough confidence to keep her fascinatedly intrigued? What if I can't, then what?"

That was what he thought about while being stuck in stop-and-go traffic. Despite the distractions, he tried to sort out which one of the three girls was Miss.

"Was it S, M, D, or someone else?"

Just when Mister became completely frustrated about making decisions, he drove up the driveway. Confusingly, Mister parked under the shaded tree and turned the idling engine off. Profoundness kept him inside the Humvee for longer than he wanted to be. He succumbed to the moment and surrendered his will. He closed his eyes and went on a road trip deep into his subconscious, a place that he had never really explored before. He once studied about the subconscious in college but never could get all the way in. Mister visually saw, felt, smelt, and tasted his Miss from within his concealed subconscious psyche.

"Who is my Miss? Really, man! Who do you want her to be, Mister? Come on, think . . . Hmm, flirtatious with a girl-next-door appearance. Taller than shorter. Dominantly tart yet submissively sassy, knowing exactly when to be each. Prominently alluring, yet casually coy. Eyes powerful enough to hold a conversation when she can't speak a word, yet dirty smirks that can instantly make me hard . . . Yeah, I would like that a lot. Hmm, confidently smart, yet hypnotically sultry. Seductively smooth, yet charmingly hot. Boldness to take what she wants, yet shy enough to beg for more of it. Hearts of gold, skin of silk. Ladylike acts, yet slutty-enough transgressions. A come-hither call that makes me weep, yet sincerity that can soothingly calm. A woman that can sigh breaths for me when I cannot breathe. Her left to my right. A thickness to her dangerous curves, enough so that I can roll my collector's edition Matchbox cars up her perky peaks and down her gentle valleys. Compassionately giving, yet selfishly needy . . ."

"Woof . . . woofffff . . . woof, woof."

When Rocket's barking expeditiously squashed Mister's subconscious enlightenment, he walked into the house with an agenda to grab onto M's soul and not let it go. Specifically, one idea stood out far more than any other. With a heightened sense of lust, up sprouted a risky idea from his wicked arsenal of dangerous liaisons. He decided on using a nonfictional fantasy about an unknown man named Mister and his would-be Miss to test M's boundaries from afar. Mister passed through the kitchen, giving Alex a welcome-home high-five while celebrating the Yankees' earlier win.

"That's number 2. Only 160 more wins to go."

They exchanged joyously high-fives, laughed, then parted company. Mister's plan to think up a steamy romance novel to tell M could not have been a better night to write. Alex was preoccupied with entertaining his date with a dramatic movie flick playing loudly through the THX surround sound system. Firstly, he checked out his e-mails, paying close attention to the subject headers. Instead of the e-mail being from M, it was from another. At first, he was curiously puzzled but then remembered he was talking to two women at once. Before he wrote M back, Mister read S's message with expectant enthusiasm.

Hola,

What is up with my lover boy Mister? It is Monday already, isn't it? I rather like working, probably because I am a workaholic. Shhh! Don't tell anyone that though, okay, Mister? You better promise? LOL. But of course, the weekends are by far my favorite days, but they always do a fast touch-and-go routine that I just do not like. My workaholic mentality is a curse, especially where I work, primarily because some of my coworkers are constantly getting on my nerves. If I did not have a few close friends there, I would have already left. Ha . . .

Okay, sorry, I got off topic. I am back now. Sorry again for not including a picture of myself in my personals profile, but sometimes a woman wants to be mysteriously anonymous. Beyond that, I need and want to connect to someone else on a much deeper level than just dating. I sometimes feel that my looks attract the wrong kind of man. I want him more interested in my intellect than my body. Can you blame me? It is okay if you do. I won't hold it against you. Ha! At least for now I won't. Seriously though, I am looking for someone that I can sit across from and smile at or lay next to and spoon against before I coax him into repeatedly making hot love to me as if my tight vaginal walls only accepted his pleasure instrument. I say that here and now, for I am sensing that you can handle my provocative innuendoes with ease. Am I right, or am I right? Anyway, sit back and get hard for me because I am wet for you.

Sweet dreams, Mister,
S

Mister's amazement of S's boldly written reply instantly caused his blood to rapidly rush into his flaccid cock without warning. Mister just discovered that S was an excellent tease just like he was. He never expected to find two different women, with differing personalities on the net at the same time, but now recognized the real probability. The thought of talking to S and M at the same time made his ego want them both, together if possible. His thoughts were overzealous but not completely out of the equation. For now, Mister conjured up perverted fantasies involving S, M, and him. He had not ever felt that strongly about wanting two women at once, but he felt a hot connection to them both.

With S's words fresh in his syllogism, he hesitated writing M back out of a guilty fear that he might accidentally mix up their personalities. He rather liked the way M played along with his story writing, but on the other hand, he liked the way S boldly flirted with her "read between the lines" kinds of innuendoes. M held nothing back, yet S held most everything back except her sexual prowess. Nonetheless, S's peculiar mysteriousness made Mister want to know more about them both. He logged into the personals website and reexamined S's and M's online profiles with a magnifying glass, paying closer attention this time around. What he first noticed about M's profile was that it was more impressionable with a lot of sincerity mixed with some creativity. After he felt good about M's persona checking out, he moved on to S. The first thing he noticed about S was when her sign-up date was. She made her profile last week on the same day that he made his. But when S's seductive dominance teased him in all sorts of ways, he let his suspicions go. He printed out both of their profiles and put them side by side. Where M was not afraid to reveal her physical appearance with a picture, S appeared cautiously mysterious without showing hers, though S's written-in description more than painted a visual likeness of her outer looks to circumvent the need for an actual portrait. Where the two girls' profiled personalities were completely opposite, Mister's ideas about them both was the same. Despite M being the innocent girl next door and S being the sexually aggressive one, Mister put them both on his to-do list. What Mister really wanted to do was put them both in a blender and get his ideal woman out of the mixture, Miss. But since he could not exactly do that, he had to choose one, but for now, he indulged in having them both. What Mister knew was that he could not write M back in his erectified condition. He had to do something quick, explosive, and naughty to make his erection disappear lickety-split.

Mister's selfish needs drove him to stand up, push down his boxers, and plop back in the loveseat so that he could hypersonically make love to himself. With Rocket being his only audience, Mister went for it. He spat into his right hand a few times to make his self-made pleasure cavern moistier to fuck. It took Mister under four minutes to get there. His powerful orgasm started with spasmodically quivering legs and ended with a steamy hot avalanche of creamy semen exploding all over his belly and hands. He quietly sat on the loveseat, sprawled out, as his orgasm dried. Unbeknownst to Mister, he had an audience of one; Rocket stared at him the entire time. Out of fear that Rocket would sniff out his drying orgasm, he stood up and pulled up his shorts to discourage Rocket's curiosity. He almost fell over from shaking legs and a dizzying head but used the loveseat's overstuffed arm to hold him steady while he got his compass back.

With extra help from Gentleman Jack, Mister snuck past his mental protection guards, landing in the deep end of his unfiltered subconscious psyche. He downed the remaining glass of whiskey and refocused on writing M something back to turn her on, tease her wet, and get her off.

CHAPTER 12

Mister's Miss

M,

I understand exactly how you feel because I feel that way too. But right now, I want to take you on an emotionally provocative road trip with me because I don't want to be one of those "other" guys that you said came and went. I am not looking to come and go, rather just come. As I sit on the loveseat in my bedroom, I feel compelled to transcribe you my exact thoughts and ideas that I am thinking up. Let my unadulterated hieroglyphics be something playful and fun yet naughty enough to make my intentions clearer than crystal.

My story is a secret guide to navigate through me. I recommend grabbing your seatbelt, fastening it snug, and staying buckled for the entire ride. It might hurt my feelings if you do not like what I think, but it will not stop me from chasing after you. Why? Because deep in my aching soul, I feel like this is what we both need. That is just a feeling that I get, and my protruding feelings are never wrong. Her name is Miss, and she will be my nucleus. Though I have yet to meet her. For all I know, you are her. Every Mister needs a Miss, just as every Miss deserves a Mister.

Only if you want, close your eyes and take up a deep breath. Breathe me in and let my words make love to your bare-naked soul so that you can be wet while tasting Mister's sweetness in the back of your throat.

Miss awoke from a short but heavy night's sleep. She felt the slightest chill in the room as the subtle air moved about in her smaller-sized fortress. She felt an internal warmth that made her content with where she was at in life despite the reasons behind her strategy to make and keep herself busy to drown out the loneliness. Like many, Miss longed to find a deep soulful connection with someone other than herself. She kept a watchful eye out for him, but he has yet to show himself. Her holding pattern for the last year was officially over, and now she welcomed change. She was not purposely seeking out any kind of change, yet it tracked her down all on its own.

For the first time in a long time, Miss wanted to go somewhere, anywhere, but where she was at. Previously, she made her life a constant rush-hour traffic jam, but now, she was tired of being stuck in traffic and wanted to go off-grid. Then when a midnight dream was dreamed, she knew change was coming. She could not remember many of the intricate details, yet she yearned to know them all. She felt exactly like someone had broken into her head and pushed Play on all her life's highlight reels. While comfortably lying in bed, her mind drifted off to a place where only she and Mister existed. Decades past, months present, and years future showed up in her dream. He snuck into her head and latched himself onto her intellect. Though she thirsted after a friend, lover, and soul mate, all she found was lukewarm possibility. So when this peculiar man named Mister showed up, she let her subconscious take her on a wild dream of exploration.

Miss stood on a busy train station platform, waiting for her train to arrive. Many trains came and went, but still hers had not come in. Then when she least expected it, the train station's intercom echoed and repeated her name, "Miss, to platform X, please. Miss, to platform X." Out of the corner of her eye, she saw the sign pointing her to platform X. She pushed herself through the crowded terminal and boarded the high-speed phenomena. Her walk over to the train seemed to be time-shifted, for what was a five-minute walk turned into nanoseconds. Miss walked onto the train, noticing that the train car seemed to be void of all human life. As the train ramped up speed, she grabbed onto the back of seats while shuffling to the middle of the car, where she sat in the seat next to the window. Puzzled by the empty train, she looked around while trying to figure out where she was headed. When nothing gave away the destination, she stared out the window to calm her anxiety. Miss watched the landscape change as the train charged down the tracks at medium-fast speed. At first, the ride was smooth and scenic, then everything around went pitch black.

The dream transported her to her bedroom in front of the TV. The TV was off, and the house was silent. The next thing she knew, her TV turned on, and the picture displayed a reflection of her standing there. She was confused, but when she waved at the TV, a soulful flute music mix began playing. Then highlight reels of her life forward advanced. Warm midrange and deep bass were felt as her dream played video clips and pictures of her life. Some she recognized; others she did not. She figured that all the memories meant something, yet the specifics were completely obscured. When the last recognized video clip of her life stopped, new pictures and videos played of her future. Even though she saw many fragmented memories of her future life, her subconscious did not let any future impressions cross over to reality. Miss felt as though she was in her room and in the dark train tunnel at the same time.

Suddenly, the TV turned off, and she was back sitting on the train, watching extraordinary scenery rush by. For a moment, Miss felt like she was being watched. And when she looked around the train to see if she was right, she noticed a silhouetted image of a man sitting alone. The bright outside scenery washed out the man's face, keeping him in a silhouetted shadow. He sat two rows in front of her adjacent, yet his face was blacked out. She knew that his silhouettedness must mean something more than just a person in her dream. She could see that he was strong and healthy, taller than smaller, but no other details on what he might look like were obvious. He had on a long black trench coat and a top hat, which terribly confused her. The silhouetted man continued watching her for the rest of the train ride, though he would periodically stand up and change seats. No matter what seat he sat in, he maintained eye contact with her. That special kind of attention made Miss feel like she was on center stage at a strip club. Every time he changed seats, she hoped that he would come sit next to her, but he never did. Miss remembered feeling something hot and sensually erotic about his little game of mystery that they were playing. It was his eye contact and mysterious appearance that kept her intrigued. He did not have to physically touch her to make her as excited as she was. This hot little game of "duck, duck, goose" made her want to be his goose. Although she wanted him to touch her, he never got close enough to "goose" her. The last seat that he "ducked" into was directly across from her. Three feet of walkway space separated them. Despite his being close in proximity, she still could not make out any of his facial features. As he sat there for a good amount of time, he eventually reached out and touched her bare-naked thigh. She heard him sinisterly cackle, then heard the train's powerful whistle blowing. Its power and purpose were felt all the way through her, but right when the trains whistle stopped blowing, Miss abruptly woke up, wanting to know more about this man that just played the sexiest game of "duck, duck, goose" with her.

She kept hearing the same question echoing over in her head. Am I his Miss?

Mister's hot little written-down fantasy ended as fast as it started. He created something short but sweet enough to keep M intrigued. If it were not for the limited number of words and attitude that M already showed Mister in her writings, he could not have painted a vivid fantasy so real, it made M think she really was his Miss. Even while being drowsy and intoxicated, he never lost sight of what he wanted to express to her. In the remnants of a late Monday night, Mister eloquently created something erotic for his new pen friend. He wanted to write her more, but then he thought that what he wrote was a good start to test her limits.

Moments after he sent off the e-mailed message, he ejaculated his hot semen all over the inside of his boxers. The entire time that he was typing out the fantasy, he was as hard as a man would ever want to be. He was too amped-up on perverted thoughts to not finish himself off. With the subtlest of several rubs along the head of his penis, Mister came for the second time that spellbound Monday. It was pathetic the way he took care of himself, but it was M's unexpected control that he submitted to. Mister knew that he was a man like no other, and he wanted M to see that from the very beginning. He laid it all on the line to share his hot thoughts with her. He created, he conquered, he came, and he crashed hard on the floor right next to Rocket.

While Tuesday was M's quiet before the storm, Wednesday would be the eye.

CHAPTER 13

Reactions

M was half-awake yet half-asleep in the comfy confines of her well-deserved condominium. She begrudgingly looked over to the white glass-and-wooden-made nightstand to see what time it was. This morning, M was a lucky lady to be waking up a few minutes earlier then her alarm clock went off. She was not a morning person and always late to everything. How could she be early to anything when work, school, promotions, money, and damaged friendships constantly distracted her every thought? Somehow though, M's last night's sleep was exactly what she needed—solidly solid yet shortly short.

As M awoke, she reluctantly rose out of bed. Lucky for her, the room's coldness gave her extra incentive to get moving. M needed more than a paycheck for motivation, so she always counted on self-ish shower pleasure for the right amount of incentive. She meticulously carried out the morning climax ritual for the last fifteen years without fail. That naughty kind of circadian love that M made to herself never really depleted a lot of time or energy, and it always gave her the necessary carefree attitude she had to have to face the trage-dies and comedy of the world. Ever since she discovered just how fast Mr. Massaging Showerhead could get her off, she has been religiously addicted to his pulsating pleasure. Missing it made her one sensi-tive bitch that was mad at the world. At first, morning masturbation started out as curiosity, then exploration, and now it was an addictive necessity. She could not ever purposely deny herself the pulsating streams of warm water jets rhythmically massaging her clitoris; however, on rare occasions, it had to be skipped. Even when her menstrual cycle came, she still orgasmed hard without excuse or regret. Having that once-a-morning orgasm kept her grounded which allowed her to be focused on work and school. Money and orgasms gave her the perfect balance to push through a day that she would rather have slept through. Up until the last two weeks of inventory hell, she had not missed a morning orgasm in more than four years. She could count the times on one hand of the missed morning climax, yet last week alone, she missed two. Certainly, M was not about to let a third one get missed even if that meant being late.

The morning's good news was that M stood on her own two sock-covered feet, but the bad news was that she inched ever closer to being late for her own promotion party. She yawned and stretched her arms out to the side to help properly mix her endorphins and estrogen in a cataclysmic newsworthy event. M always fought for more sleep, but her sleep-ins have been limited to weekends, always sleeping in until she could not sleep any longer. For the last two years, she never got more than five hours of sleep every weekday night. Compounding her maladjusted sleep patterns were nightly bouts of tossing and turning. She worried about things she had no control over. So when morning came, M usually slept through her sounding alarm clock, never hearing it go off. But this morning, it was different; she naturally woke up all on her own.

M finished her morning stretch and walked off to the kitchen to get the first round of coffee going. While impatiently waiting for her one-cup-at-a-time coffeemaker to dish out hot coffee, she shoved a single slice of wheat bread into the toaster. The brewed coffee and the last bite of toast usually finished at the same time. On a typical morning, her finishing breakfast was always impeccably timed, but sometimes not exact. For this morning though, breakfast would be eaten at work brunch after her promotion. She filled her porcelain coffee mug halfway full due to her klutzy-klutz factor as she recognized her shortcomings. She took the coffee back with her to the room to sip on it while going through her unopened e-mails; after all, the aftereffects of caffeine were just as important as having morning orgasms. Together, caffeine and pleasure made M a force to be reckoned with. She was proud of herself for making it to the bedroom without spilling a single drop, though her victorious snicker would not last long.

Excitedly, M sat down in her annoying squeaky bedroom desk chair and dove right into her unopened e-mails one at a time. M never really had that many messages, so her checking it was almost an obsolete event, yet she held out hope that one day a noteworthy suitor would unexpectedly write her, kind of like what Mister had recently done. Now that Mister had vied for her attention, she excitedly started to check out her e-mail account more than ever before.

Six new messages. She quickly scanned them, hoping one would be from that new guy Mister.

"If he writes me again, maybe I am back in luck."

M's groggy-froggy vision barely adjusted to the beams of sunlight shining through her window, causing her to squint to see who the messages were from. Out of the six new messages, she only wanted to read one. Seeing Mister's e-mail in her inbox was all it took to make her smile bigger than she had smiled in months. Just the other night, M had thrown herself a pity party suited for royalty, and now, she was the royalty. Before opening it, she had to wipe away the sleep that clung to her eyelashes so that she could clearly see what he said. Mid-wipe, M's phone rang. It was a text message from Kodi.

"Hi, VIP. Congrats on the promotion. Growllll, go, M, go! See ya soon, VIP."

Kodi was M's best friend and coworker that got M the job that she had. Kodi wanted to be the first to congratulate M on her promotion, and that, she was. Kodi's text message made M gloat all the way up to and through the company meeting. M fought hard for that promotion, and she would not let anything get in the way. Not even tardiness brought on by Mister's seductive charm could ruin her day. She would not even know what to say for that kind of tardy excuse anyway. Other than having her morning orgasm, she was excited by the idea of being paid a yearly salary in lieu of an hourly wage. She gladly traded in hourly pay for more benefits and a helping hand up to the bottom rung on the corporate ladder of success.

"Yaaaaay, *me!*"

Literally, it was the second time in all of M's life that she was truly proud of herself for accomplishing something good out of nothing great. Sure, there were mediocre accomplishments along the way, but none as more deserving than this one. The promotion humbly meant something to her. She kept those feelings to herself, only sharing them with Kodi.

Before M read his e-mail, she silently paused to enjoy the bittersweet triumph of life upgrades. It just so happened that Mister's e-mail was the chart topper. It had been more than six months since her friends pushed her into putting up her own personals ad. It was during a night of wine drinking, shot chasing, memory reminiscing and life celebrating that Kodi and friends dared her to do it. At first, M said, "No way," but then buckled under her drunk friends' peer pressure. The morning after she made it up, she forgot all about it until two weeks later when she was surprisingly reminded about it from her first response. Then as she received several more messages over the next several months, she became more disappointed in men when they all turned out scandalously disastrous for one reason or another. She kept reading the new responses but blew them all off. M secretly held out hope that she would find at least one intelligent man, but instead, the ad only brought her cheap, cheesy assholes wanting one thing. They were not even charming, just the usual bar lines followed with a second message asking them to go on a date. There was no "get to know me" chitchat, just "meet me and let's get it on." Quickly M's frustrations about the ad turned into anger when the intelligent knight in shining armor coming to her rescue was MIA. She kept her feelings to herself about how the ad made her feel, hoping that her friends would forget about it. They did, and so did she.

That was until Mister happened. An excited pause followed by nervous anticipation kept rocking and rolling through her stomach. At first, M did not want to read it, then she wanted to, then she didn't. It was too early in the morning for her to be overly excited, but in the back of her mind, she buzzed with bubbly positivity. M decided a few months back that she was not going to settle for any more stupid boys. She wanted and needed a real man that could accept her for who she was and who she wanted to be. So far, Mister's personality has pleasantly surprised M, but then again, she really did not know him well enough to be confident in her judgments. The one thing she positively knew about Mister was that he was not a stupid boy at all. She could tell from his confidence alone. He knew exactly what he wanted, and that made M intrigued. Mister was much different from any other guy she dated. He was sophisticated, genuine, compassionate, daring, sexy, charming, and downright naughty. Mister's opulent splash turned her on more than she had anticipated. M liked everything about him except his smooth erotic seductiveness. That bothered her. M was the sweet innocent girl next door that always pursued after the bad boys. She saw a little bad in Mister but saw a lot of good in him too. Even though M was in her late twenties, she never had sex on the first date, yet Mister's erotic subtleness made her want to.

With his third e-mail sitting in front of her, she acted like a giggly teenage schoolgirl. M wanted his e-mail to do something to her soul. Anything, but nothing she could not accept. She could not take any more direct "I want to get into your pants" bullshit. Mister's reply caught M with her panties down. She was expecting him to write back, but when he did, she fully paid attention. At first, his words were normal, and then they were not. Her jaw dropped to the floor, and her body tingled all over from his G-rated words that turned into R-rated thoughts of lyrical intrigue. When she saw that his message was much longer than the first two e-mails put together, she stopped reading it out of doubt that she could finish it before leaving for work. But curiosity inspired her to do a quick skim over the rest of it to see how it ended. The more she skimmed over it, the more she wanted to read it unskimmed. Before M knew it, she reread it from beginning to end. She could not help but fidget around in her squeaky-assed chair while digesting his e-mailed thoughts. The more sentences she read, the hotter she became. Midway through, she took a closed-eye pause and sigh break.

"Oh my god! Who is this guy? Like really, who is he? Mister sexy is what he is."

She reopened her eyes and kept reading. His frank words unexpectedly got to her. More squeaks and squirms came from her office chair as she consumed more of his electrified eroticism. The only thing that kept M from making selfish love to herself was finding out how it ended. Her eyes bulged and heart raced with what-ifs.

"What if I meet him and like him too much? What if I want him to make love to me in the exact ways he describes? What if I want to cuddle with him afterward? What if he makes me want to be held and kissed ten times a day every day? What if he truly gets me? What if I like him more than he likes me? What if he is not like the man that I think he is?"

Nothing could take her mind off Mister's vivid sensuality, not even if her beating heart leapt out of her body and landed on the floor in front of her. She was as moist as she could be for an early weekday morning. All she could do was shiver and quiver and be confused. Confused because she was always attracted to controlling assholes, and Mister was anything but one of those. He was caring, gentle, nice, and sweet, which sneakily kept M drunk on his smooth talk. At the snap of his fingers, she let her convertible top down and let his fresh air in while levitating her right off this fucking planet. M wondered how he could turn her on like that without any kind of physical stimulation. She had never been turned on that much before for a man she had never seen, heard, or smelt, yet she was completely seduced by his swagger.

Then everything shuddered to an abrupt stop. M's blissful utopia was interrupted by the freestanding household grandfather clock dinging out the 7:00 AM chimes. The interruption made M a conflicted mess of confusion. She was torn between work and pleasure.

M's estrogen was about to erupt all over her insides. She felt as though she was floating on an inflatable raft heading downstream, racing downhill, headed for a fifty-fucking-foot cliff that ended in a dramatic splash of opulence. M spewed out fire from her erect nipples only to have it reenter her directly through her tight little twat. She stopped her morning Kegels mid-squeeze. M knew all about Mr.

Kegel and his unobtrusive exercises. She constantly exercised her pelvic floor muscles everywhere she could, driving to and from work, in the shower, watching TV, even while sitting at her desk at work. She always kept up on her Kegels. M liked knowing she was tight. Sometimes doing Kegels made her orgasm, but sometimes not. The outcome depended on what her thoughts were focused on while exercising her pink vaginal walls. Though this morning, M's clitoris had a mind of its own.

One pulsating twitch after another overtook her mound of fleshy goodness. That morning, she did not need to play with her clitoris; the rhythm-like sequences kept replicating themselves all on their own. M's naturally induced contractions kept her body stuck in sexual chaos more than she needed to be on a workday. She never thought her promotion day would turn out that way, but then again, she could not have predicted that a man named Mister would have been able to describe sensuality to her as vividly as he did either.

His words jumped off her computer screen right into the depths of her innocent soul. They came at her with a three-dimensional latitude that only made sense to her. M tried her best to squash the tidal wave of gushing excitement without climaxing, for she knew she was too oversexed to have her morning orgasm end her insatiable need to come. The more she tried to ignore her aching pelvic pleasure, the more she had to tightly close her thighs to stymie the pleasure ripple effect.

As the clock chimed out 7:30 AM, M positively knew she crossed her on-time threshold without even taking a shower. She made a new plan to take a quick shower and do her makeup and hair primping on the drive over to work.

"Damn that man!"

Mister's words of descriptive pleasure were written with enough class and eloquence that M believed any woman would submit to his irresistible charm. Instead of Mister's words being a vulgar turn-off, they were a sizzling red-hot turn-on. M's once-fragile self-esteem was instantly mended while feeling Mister's charm tease her wet. An instant magnetism existed that M chose to keep a secret from everyone, especially herself. The one thing that she did not want to do was give him more power than he already had. Mister seemed to have his own version of hypnotizing power over M that she has yet to understand. The man that she has yet to formally meet has already broken into her head and stolen the key to her private thought chambers. What impressed her most was what he said and how he said it. It was like Mister already knew her from the inside out.

It made M seriously think about using her own special exponential power of estrogen. M knew about its effects, whereas Mister had not one clue. It was not a state secret to know about the exponential power, but much of the world wished it had a top-secret classification. She never really wanted to have the power, but she was glad that she knew of its existence. Innocently enough, M's mom passed it down to her. She wanted M to know about it before she became a woman so that she could handle all the immature boys wanting into her pants with confidence. Her mom once told M, "It takes a special woman to confidently walk in that kind of power and get away with it." She knew M would be in trouble without knowing of it. Sure, it was dangerous for a young woman to know about it, but her mom knew that it was the more secure way to keep M on a different path than the one she traveled down.

Because of her mom, M knew exactly when to wield it and when to yield it, which made M a more efficient provocatrix. The deceptive part of the exponential power of estrogen was that it could not ever be seen, only felt, and by that time, it was too late to easily run away from it without feeling its strong effects. The exponential power of estrogen always started out innocent enough, but its addictiveness was far greater than anyone could ever dismiss. At its core was "For every emotional action, there is always a physical reaction." Fortunately, for all men and some women of the world, M was too shy to flaunt her knowledge of the power. But if she turned it on, with a word she could get what she came for. She was a famous stairway song of the seventies past. Right at the apex between every woman's thighs sits a mound of pleasure that is so great and powerful that it hides the entire purpose of all creation inside. It is soft and moist, intoxicatingly wet, and mesmerizingly alluring. It is the most sought-after asset in the world. It looks like a beautiful flower on the outside while the inside is a flesh-colored moist cavern meant to seduce all the world. Even though the vagina is not a rare earth magnet, it should be considered one. Its strong power attracts everything near and far. Despite what scientists say, that mound of delight is arguably the most powerful magnet in the whole fucking universe. When you mix shimmering glances with well-pronounced girly mannerisms, smiley smiles, smelly perfume, and teasing laughs with estrogen, you get the most potent cocktail in the universe. No matter who knows about the exponential power of estrogen, there is no stopping its effects. Ever since Mister's omnipotence showed up on scene, M thought about dusting off her "exponential power of estrogen" halo and test it out on him.

M's dusty halo sat on the top shelf in a box for more years than she could count. Nevertheless, she wished he was standing in front of her that morning. She knew exactly what she would do to Mister's intoxicating persona if he knocked on her bedroom door. She would have opened it with her shiny halo freshly polished up. Greeting him with a sexy smile and puppy-dog eyes would secretly earn her a ton of favor over in Mister's world of confidence. As soon as he felt and saw her well-pronounced mannerisms, he would cavalierly puff out his chest to defeat her attempts at seduction, not knowing anything about the exponential power of estrogen. M would clearly anticipate Mister's body chemistry, confirming he fell for it. Seeing the conviction in Mister's eyes would make M turn up the secret exponential power cloak of invincibility to further bring him in under her control. Other than hearing his buttery smooth voice uttering risqué questions, M did not want to hear anything else.

"Baby, can I please have a taste of you?"

M had a sincere answer for him if he asked, but since he was not there, neither of them would get to know the answer. Her natural instincts were to introduce Mister to the exponential power of estrogen right away, but she knew its effectiveness would be better felt when they met each other in the flesh. One of M's power-wielding specialties was knowing the exact time and perfect place to use it. So for now, M remained boggled about how the fuck Mister got into her head so damn fast.

"How is it so that this evil man can paint me such a magnificent Picasso? So real. So alive. Man, I need him to come over here and use his soft-bristled brush on my pliable canvas."

Mister purposely let M see inside of his twisted world of erotica. That was no accident. He designed his attentive writings to tug on her innocence.

Freshly out of her "what if he were here" fantasy, M needed more caffeine to stymie off his sexual hold. As she picked up the coffee cup to take a sip, she accidentally spilled some of it on her chest. The hot splashes of coffee landed directly on her left nipple.

"Ouch! Shit that fucking burns! Holy shit, man. Dammit!"

The burn from the splashed coffee made M's swollen nipple intensely ache. The sting added more frustrations to her fast-paced morning, yet there was nothing that could prevent her from reading the last paragraph. While reading his last written words, M's coffee-stained shirt kept aggravating the pain. M did not want to admit it to herself, but the stinging pain was unique. It was not like the usual burn someone would get on their arm or hand. Instead, feelings of pain and pleasure came to her breasts. M had no desire to properly care for the burn, but more than that, she was not about to dip her nipple in anything cold that early in the morning, although she briefly thought about it. Instead, she hastily walked over to the full-length mirror to look at the damage. When she went to pull away the shirt from her chest, she accidentally pinched her tender nipple along with the shirt, causing more conductive feelings of something amazing. Absolute confusion struck her psyche.

"Shit! Dammit. How could I be that stupid!"

While belittling herself, she tamped her toes into the carpet to stifle her wild needs to orgasm. M never had her nipple burned before, but when the sting from the hot coffee merged with her dumb titty-twister, it gave her maximum pleasure and pain simultaneously. M did not expect the sexually hot erotic sensations that the pain caused. When they gave her irrefutable reactions of pleasure chills and burning pain, it excelled her need to come more than any morning before. She was wet, and she was turned on. No matter what she did or did not do, she could not extinguish the sexual fire that was freshly lit under her ass. Instead of fighting against not cumming, she feverishly fought for it with all she had.

M's mind went blank, and her eyes rolled into the back of her head at the same time she cupped her bare breasts in the palms of her warm hands. She massaged them in the exact way that she would expect Mister to. Her touch was gentle and seductive, yet it felt more naughty than nice. As she prominently stood in front of the full-length mirror, fantasizing about a man she had never met before, the stinging pain was replaced with searing hot pleasure. Her reflected impression was not what she ever remembered about herself. What she saw was a beautiful woman with richly shaped curves, wavy dark shoulder-length hair, voluptuous lips, and sweltering hot hips. M excitedly admired her outer beauty while getting off on her newfound beauty. The truth had always been exactly what she saw standing there in that full-length mirror, but previous reflections had been distorted by sadness, depression, and loneliness. Right at that moment, M rekindle the love she once felt for herself. As she played with and pinched her erect nipples with feather-like gentleness, Mister's sexually potent words echoed up and down her spine. She wiggled her other hand into her panties and massaged her clitoris. And in minutes, M collapsed to her knees in front of the mirror while laughing, smiling, and crying with hedonistic joy.

Now M had no time to waste. She flew through the shower like an angel flapping wings on the way up to heaven. With no time to finish her makeup and hair, she ran out the front door, hopped into the car, and drove ninety-miles-an-hour down the roadway just to make it through the office's glass front doors eight minutes late. Despite her rushing around, M's burning nipple served as a strong reminder of her super-fantastic solo show.

CHAPTER 14

• • • • • • • ● • • • • • •

In Her Head

Despite leaving the house later than she wanted, M made it to work before her boss did. That was all that mattered. M owed her tardiness to Mister's scandalous writings, but she was okay with that. She was more interested to have read all about Mister's naughty little story starring his dream girl Miss. She was amazed at the numerous similarities she had in common with Miss. That specific reason vividly resonated with M on many levels.

He knows me already. But how could he understand me when we have never met? Did he jump into my head somewhere along the way? This is scary! Does he "really" get me? Maybe he really is too good to be true? Is he?

She did not know if he was really in her head or not, but it felt like he was gathering all her most intimate thoughts that she did not share with anyone. Even when she tried not to think about Mister, she thought about him more. M got her panties charmed off, and she could not understand how. Though hours after digesting his third e-mailed note, she began to wonder much more about his sweltering unsolved mystery.

As she sat in her cubicle, M anxiously counted down the minutes for the company promotion meeting to start. It was hard for her to concentrate on work, but somehow, she got her shit together by taking a quick timeout. She did not have much time to close her eyes and slow down her breaths, but she made the most of the stolen four minutes. From that moment on, she was all business. It was game time, and M was dressed to kill. She knew it, and so did everyone else. That morning, M earned every last polka dot that decorated her fancy new outfit, including the ones all over her white and pea-green-dotted tanga.

Right after M found out that she was being promoted, Kodi instructed M to shop for a new outfit to wear just for the promotion. On a slow Tuesday, the two girls took an extended lunch break to do just that. Kodi steered M in one direction, straight toward a spring polka-dotted surprise that included nude silk stockings with matching garter belt, cream-colored heels, and a prissy hair scrunchie. Of course, Kodi had her own hidden agenda for coaxing M to get that outfit. Fortunately for Kodi, she enjoyed M's eight-minute modeling exposé before directing her to charge it. Kodi enjoyed M's mini fashion show a little too much for her own good. She saw M sway and stand, turn and twist, and primp herself in many ways. M had no idea that she had secretly made Kodi's panties moistier with every twisty turn. M bought the entire ensemble for less than three hundred dollars over two weeks ago. It neatly dangled in her closet until the promotion day ceremony, as to which she sassily debuted her new sophisticated look.

The company-wide midmorning brunch was preplanned right down to the fresh fruit platters and bell-folded napkins. It was the company's twice-a-year scheduled performance and promotions extravaganza. It had been decided weeks ago that M would be promoted. Ever since Kodi got her the job, M worked exasperatingly hard to move up in the company. She gave more than 100 percent to get noticed. Over the years, she got plenty of kudos from her immediate boss but just thought her work ethic went unnoticed by anyone else. However, her harshest critic always put in good words for M because she had no plans to stay in that position forever. The company purposely timed it with new growth attempts, but the timing was never right. That was until this time around. The company aggressively put their expansion plans to the front burner. All management wanted M to be a boss, and so it was.

M walked into the meeting, cocky as hell. Her confidence out-shone everyone in that room, exactly showing off the pretty penny that she was. Her copper brilliance could be seen miles away. As soon as M sat down in the media room, it was her room to have. The sassy dress amplified her arrogance, yet it was her sweet girl-next-door persona that sold her best. If it were not for her snug-fitting tanga wedging itself up her ass, she would have continued to own the room. Instead, she was forced to downplay her cockiness because of her wedgie. What she really wanted to do was pluck that mother-fucker out of there.

That morning, M's concentration was barely there, but still she patiently sat at the end of the sixth-row seat, waiting for her name to be called up on stage. On the outside, she looked all business, but inside she was high on Mister. His words were the sole reason that M had all that extra energy flowing out of her. Kodi noticed it from across the room and thought she could calm her down with a distracting text message.

"Are you okay? You seem nervous."

The unexpected text jolted M right out of her seat. M forgot to put the phone on vibrate, so when its obnoxious sound inter-rupted the entire meeting, her face turned cherry red. In a panic, she covertly slid her hand into her tiny purse and silenced it as fast as she could. Luckily for M, there were many people in the auditorium, so pinpointing where the sound came from was near too impossible. The CFO disappointingly proceeded to tell everyone to silence their phones at once.

Kodi was the only one that ever texted M, so M already knew who the message was from. M chuckled aloud because it was Kodi's drunken dare that brought her Mister. While nervously gloating, M waited a minute before texting Kodi back out of fear that she would be outed as the company disrupter.

"Yeah, I am okay, I'm just nervous about the promotion, is all."

She sent off the text and smiled over at Kodi to let her know she replied. Kodi and M were good friends inside and outside of work. They shared everything work-related, and some personal-related things too. Although the personal-sharing side still needed major work, through the years they kept working out the kinks.

M kept waiting for her named to be called, but the CFO kept dragging it on and on with company progress updates and plans. Seconds before her anxious patience snapped, she was called up on stage. M popped up out of her seat, arrogantly strutting up on stage. The polka dots gave her way more attention than she needed to have, but she fully enjoyed all of it. M smiled the entire time she was on stage.

"Without M, we could never have maneuvered ourselves past the competition, so congratulations M on your long-awaited promotion to department manager."

Mr. CFO handed her a red envelope and let her briefly have the microphone. M was always a woman of few words, but her unexpected managerial promotion truly left her speechless.

"Thank you. I am a lucky woman to go from where I was at to where I am now. And thank you to everyone for giving me the opportunity to thrive."

After her thirty-second emotional thank-you speech, the CFO announced her as the new department manager instead of assistant manager. At the last minute, the chief decided to give her the full title. That surprise announcement put M on the bottom rung of the corporate ladder. It was exactly what M had been secretly waiting for, and now it was hers to have. She barely contained her outward excitement, limiting it to a fist pump and a few high-fives. Manager M walked off stage with everyone clapping. Inwardly, M was an emotional wreck.

Kodi could tell M was about to lose it, so she made sure to be at the bottom of the steps to greet her with a congratulatory hug to break her emotional inflictions. She wrapped her arms around M's shoulders and whispered something in her ear that only M could hear.

"Who is he?"

M was caught off guard with Kodi's directness, but her haughty retort put Kodi back in her place.

"How do you know it's a man?"

M voiced her words louder than a whisper and sarcastically broke their embrace.

"So a woman then?"

Kodi deviously smiled back at M, knowing she hit one of M's biggest hidden nerves.

"Wouldn't you like to know?"

M's haughty sarcasm fed Kodi's curious wonderment. Then as M turned around and walked off, her cute polka-dotted dress quickly faded away. When M walked back to her cubicle to grab her purse, she was greeted with flowers and balloons adorning her chair and desk. Despite the company being small, they kept growing threefold every year, which allowed them to keep up good company morale. When M saw the flowers and balloons, she felt wanted, alive, and appreciated. M planned to go to the catered brunch, but with her new manager position title, she needed a few minutes to herself to regain emotional composure. A five-minute timeout was all she needed.

M strutted out through the glass doors in an attempt to leave the building without being seen by anyone, especially little Miss Bitchy Bitch receptionist. Little Miss Bitchy Bitch, also known as Miss BB, was the office gossip queen that always kept the gossip circle thriving. M made it down the hallway and out of the building without Miss BB seeing her.

"Phew! I made it."

M tried to make the most of her alone time while everyone else was preoccupied with the catered brunch. With new work expectations and Mister on her mind, M tried to detox from both as she sat on the stone-made bench. The warm spring sunlight shone down on her while the chirping birds lulled her into springtime sanctity. Finally, she closed her eyes and shut out the world. No bosses, no Kodi, and no Mister, just amazing peace penetrating her deep inside. Five minutes of splendor is what she got. Then the sexiest breeze blew in through the smoker's pit openings. The soft breeze slightly lifted M's skirt as it delivered Mister's presence right into her magnificent V-shaped playland. Erotic whirlwind kisses of air allowed Mister to creep into her every thought. Spring was M's favorite season, only second to summer. It was the "pure, with all things new" atmospheric phenomena that made her like it most. Despite the pit's chilliness, warm sunrays kept its internal barometer warmer than it felt. The former company's outside smoker's pit was turned into her company's new gossip corral. Only one employee used the smokers' pit to smoke. So when Mrs. Tsar named the old smokers' pit "the pit," it caught on. When the Tsars first started the company, Mr. Tsar worked long, late hours, and sometimes Mrs. Tsar would go out to the pit to ponder a future life of success and wonder if that might happen. The Tsars held up and sacrificed many things to make the company succeed. No one knew if the company would grow, but they had many coworkers relying on its continuing flourishment.

Intentionally, the walls were made of sandstone bricks built up to the six-foot-high mark. No doors, just openings on two of the four sides, allowing people to come and go as they needed to. It once was a smoker's paradise, and now it was the informal conference room. Even little Miss BB could not see over the wall, so it was the perfect hideout for anyone wanting to chillax. On the two walls that did not have any openings now had half flower beds with brilliant colors of blooming petals and amazing smells. Where once there was sand, there is now green grass. The pit was an amazing get away to calm down from the business-day chaos. Early afternoon blowing breezes were always present. And now the air caused M's oversexed body to shiver in exquisite delight. Briefly she opened her eyes to see if anyone was around, then closed them shut to get back to Mister. Mister's vivid words secretly made love to her once-broken spirit. It was right then that M knew she wanted Mister in every way conceivable. And in a midmorning instant, M's heartbroken spirit was mended. Overwhelming feelings of joy made her want to be alone and cry. Of all places to cry, work.

M stood up and contemplated going out to the parking garage. Every workday, she parked in the same spot on the bottom floor of the underground parking garage. When she first started working there, that spot was the only one available. She began parking there on her first day with mixed feelings. The back-corner parking spot was not well lit or protected with video surveillance. It took her a few months to get used to walking out to the dimly lit spot, but then got used to it when one day she needed to take a lunchtime nap. Quickly finding out the benefits of the dark bottom corner spot, M lost her fear of the dark parking garage rather fast. Privacy, the only place she could go without interruption. Anytime of the day, no office stress, just quiet and peace. As she stood up, salty tears welled-up in her eyes before heading out of the pit. Despite tears, she experienced every emotional state in compacted minutes. How could she not conjure up new fantasies involving chivalrous danger?

Hmm, I know, I know. He would be secretly waiting for me in the dimly lit underground parking garage behind the elevator shaft half-wall. Then as I pass by the half-wall and turn right, he would quietly sneak in behind me. His sneaky sneakering would allow him to get right behind me without being noticed. I put my key in the door and turn it open. I would lift the door handle and swing it open, still hearing nothing. Then with the blink of an eye, he would forcefully place one hand over my mouth and the other hand on the center of my left pelvic bone and spin me around. His leather-gloved hand stays over my mouth, while the other one reaches up my skirt and swiftly pulls down my panties to the floor. I would be trembling scared, but so fucking turned on that a man wants me this much that he cannot wait.

As M stepped through the invisible pit door, she heard her name being called.

"Wait up, M! Wait up!"

M recognized the voice even before turning around; Kodi's shrilly voice was unmistakable. She knew Kodi would be looking for her, especially how their last conversation ended. She just did not know it would be that soon. M reluctantly turned around, hoping Kodi might disappear, but she did not. M was too emotionally caught up in her own eroticism that she wished Kodi would go away, whereas Kodi wanted answers. Nonetheless, M waited for Kodi to speed-walk across the driveway to find out what Kodi wanted.

"You have to tell me who he is."

Kodi stood in the bright sunlight demanding answers.

M thought about what she could say to Kodi to get away, but she was too mind-fucked to spin anything to anyone, let alone her girl crush Kodi. M wanted to cry on Kodi's shoulders, telling her everything, but she did not want to break down in a sobbing mess at work.

"You know that ad you made me put up?" M's giggle let Kodi know she was seriously interested in someone.

"Yeah, and?"

"I have been talking to someone. He responded to my ad a few days ago."

"Are you going tell me the details, or do I need to pry them out of you?"

Kodi pressed hard.

"Have lunch with me tomorrow, and I will tell you all about him."

M's invitation made Kodi ease up on her only a little. Their friendship was unique. She first met Kodi while taking her first college course four years ago, and their friendship has been growing ever since then. M had not trusted Kodi at first, but now she confided in Kodi with everything. Kodi understood M and vice versa. It was uncanny how Kodi could read what M thought and felt. Whenever M needed space, she could tell Kodi to back off, and Kodi would do it. That was one thing M liked about their friendship, no prejudgments or drama, just a true friendship that they found in each other.

"Okay, fine! But at least tell me something about him over brunch? You are going to get something to eat, aren't you? I want some of that fresh fruit. Did you see the jalapeno cheddar bagels? Come eat with me."

They walked back into work, heading for the cafeteria. While they were in the food line, everyone kept walking over to M to congratulate her on the promotion. M disliked being the center of attention and suggested to Kodi that they take their brunch out to the pit. Kodi agreed, and they got their food and walked out to the pit. Luckily, they made it past Miss BB as she was too busy chatting it up with the IT technician to notice them walk by.

"You know I can see right through you, don't you? You like him. I can tell."

M was not about to divulge too many of the sordid details to Kodi. She did not exactly have many to share. She chose to tell Kodi about the generalities and possibilities of Mister, intentionally leaving out her desires to ride him fast and furious in the back seat of her car.

"He is sweet, nice, and good-looking too. He knows what to say. And he likes to tease and flirt with me. I feel like he pays attention. His subtleness turns me on."

M smiled, then both girls giggled at the same time.

Kodi was no fool. She saw that M was completely hot for him no matter if she admitted it or not. Kodi just knew. Everything was confirmed when M's face turned red.

"You do know me, don't you, Kodi? It's like he makes me feel special and excited whenever I read or write to him, and it's driving me crazy that I can't give him the attention that he deserves to have. I don't want him to lose interest."

Kodi blurted out the obvious.

"Are you fucking kidding me, M? You are a great catch! If I were a guy, I would hit on you every second of every damn day. In fact, I am making a move on you now, girlfriend."

Kodi's left hand grabbed M's exposed thigh in a playful embrace. When Kodi moved her hand further up M's exposed thighs, she embarrassingly giggled. When Kodi saw M shiver, she knew what she had done.

M took Kodi's risqué gestures for playing around, but when M glanced over at her friend, she saw a sincere gleam in Kodi's eyes that spoke something specifically different. M felt Kodi's eyes brazenly ask her for a taste. Kodi's unexpected lunchtime flirtations kinetically sent chills all the way up and down M's central nervous system. At that moment, their eyes made an organic connection that stimulated them both beyond their preceding limitations. And at work no less.

"Kodi, stop that!" M's shy voice spoke up. "My god, you have no freakin' idea how sensitive I am right now. I could not even concentrate on the meeting this morning. Please don't touch me like that."

With M's hand on top of Kodi's, she helped Kodi remove her hand from her upper thigh. Kodi took the slow movement gesture as having future potential.

M admitted all the feelings she had for Mister to Kodi. Kodi's excitement for M got worse thinking about M's sweet love spot. Kodi's panties should not have been soaking wet, but they were definitely damp. The creamy wetness enveloped her stainless-steel piercing. Kodi had her clitoral hood pierced. She never told M about it, always hoping that M would find it out all on her own.

An uncomfortable silence settled upon them both. The sexual tension was high. The crisp spring breeze was real.

"M, I just want you to be happy again. No matter if it is by him or me." Kodi snickered.

M was too paralyzed to say anything. Just when the intensity needed to be broken, little Miss Bitchy Bitch came strolling into the pit with her fake tits, fake attitude, and fake friendship to smoke her brains out. Kodi quickly stood up and pretended nothing was happening, but Miss BB saw something that should not have. M and Kodi were practically in each other's laps with M's skirt pushed up higher than it should have been. Miss BB deciphered their closeness as scandalous. Miss BB smiled with glee as she tried to start up her own conversation.

"Congratulations on the promotion, M. You deserve it. I hear good things about you through the company grape vine."

"Thank you. I worked my ass off to get that promotion. You have no idea how many extra things I did out of the scope of my job description to earn it. But thank you!"

"I know I saw how you stepped up and did things. Don't think I don't hear about things like that. I do."

"Thank you, Miss BB. I appreciate that. Since we don't smoke, we will let you enjoy your vapor pipe alone."

M and Kodi gathered up their plates and departed for friendlier territory. There was no hiding what Miss BB saw, but the two girls could not downplay what just happened either. Kodi kept all the company's accounting straight, and she would not have any problem doing the same with Miss BB, except she just gave Miss BB superior ammunition. Kodi was known around the company as a bad girl with an attitude to match. Even the outfits Kodi wore were borderline inappropriate, but she liked to push all the boundaries, even the ones with Miss BB. Everyone in the company overlooked Kodi's inappropriateness since she was a whiz with numbers, but Kodi was the subject of numerous gossips. Her smarts kept her employed and her bold flirtatious personality kept everyone wanting a piece of her. From the outfits she wore to the suggestive comments she made, Kodi collected a group of followers that hinged on her devotion. Her brunette hair was a telltale sign of her standalone personality. As soon as Kodi got blonde streaks through her hair, a few of the other office girls did the same thing, except the color was different than platinum blond. Kodi kept her hair cut in a short style, showing off her sensual neckline and cleavage. M never admitted to Kodi the crush she had on her. Even moments ago, she could have told Kodi about the crush, but she did not. M was more of a shy woman that liked her secrets. They were the best of friends, but it was never more than that. Their kisses on the lips were meant to convey playful friendship more than anything else. The most intimate thing that they did was masturbate in the same room together. M knew that, but Kodi did not.

It was late one night, three years ago, when Kodi and M went out for a girls' night on the town. They went to a few bars, had many drinks, played a few games of darts, played a short game of truth or dare with two younger guys at the bar, and ended up taking a yellow taxi ride home together. Both were well over the legal limit to operate a motor vehicle, so M slept at Kodi's place. M never really had a girl crush before, but that night, she liked watching Kodi manipulate the men, so much that she started to have a secret girl crush on her. If that evening's new girl crush was not enough, M got to listen in on Kodi having phone sex with her boyfriend. Kodi's dirty talk and moans made M want to find out what Kodi tasted like. She crushed on Kodi's demanding control over her boyfriend. Hearing Kodi manipulate her boyfriend to talk dirty to her made M absolutely get off too. She stored their shared masturbation memory shallowly for the last three years without telling a soul. From that moment on, M kept that very private moment in the forefront of every solo orgasm she experienced.

That night's solo-shared, estrogen-made cataclysm left a confusing impression on M that has yet to be resolved. Kodi did not want what she started with M in the pit to end, whereas M needed it to stop fast. She stomped her heels into the dirt pit floor, immediately halting escalating tensions.

"Ladies, I need to go inside and be the boss. Talk to you girls later."

M stood up, walked out of the pit, and got back to work. She knowingly left Kodi in compromising situations with Miss BB. M did not want to, but it had to be done due to her moistening pussy. She was torn between Mister's morning-time penmanship and Kodi's noontime lipstick twist.

CHAPTER 15

• • • • • • • • ● • • • • • •

Reacquisition

S and M had begun to lodge themselves deep inside his psyche, especially after last weekend's three-day binge. It was as if both girls walked in through the front door, right into his bedroom, and stood at the foot of his bed demanding attention. So far, M spoke to Mister's soul more than S did. He was defenseless against her innocence. To him, it felt like M bound his ankles and wrists to his king-size playland so she could palm his super sensitive balls, preparing to never let them go.

Mister's worst days of the week sprouted wings and flew off, leaving the best ones to come. Mister's 10:00 AM appointment was across town, but he needed to go into the office beforehand to pick up product brochures and blank contracts. He woke up on time, but after he stubbed his little toe on the bed post and spilt droplets of coffee on his freshly laundered pants, all time was lost. Right away, Mister knew it would be one frustrating day, so frustrating that he did not remember driving to work, but there he was, parked in his usual spot. Even then, he was barely present. Hump day was one of his better-performing days, yet his constant thoughts about S, M, and D discombobulated his every move. While Mister sat in his Humvee behind the limo's tinted windows, he sighed, fully exhaling out every emotion he had in a final attempt to get his mind right.

Within minutes, Mister calmed down and started purging impure thoughts of sexual liaisons with all three ladies. Just when he began to focus on monthly quotas, D pulled up and parked next to his driver's side door. D did not pay any attention to the what-ifs as she got out of her car. She wore a new outfit specifically for Mister to enjoy. So when she used his window for a mirror, she was oblivious to his presence. D gave him a front-row seat to a show that she unknowingly starred in. He watched her shimmy out of the car, close the door, walk around to the passenger side, fiddle with her outfit, reach in and grab her purse, and fiddle some more. Her use of his driver-side dark-tinted window as her own personal makeup mirror was creative. As she boosted up her cleavage and reapplied her Ferrari-red lipstick while making kissy expressions, Mister got to watch from the other side of the tinted glass.

The four-minute show left Mister speechlessly erect. The entire time, Mister wanted to roll down the window and kiss her back, but refrained. As the seconds passed, he saw into her unguarded soul right through her eyes. He learned something that he wished he never found out. Her sad eyes revealed just how trapped she was. He knew she felt trapped but had no idea the extent of her dark loneliness. It was much deeper than he imagined. D's eyes spoke of a much sinister sadness that he did not want to believe, and since Mister was D's best friend, he was not about to cause her any more trepidation.

Right in front of him, he watched her chameleon-like transformation from extreme sadness into elated bubbliness before walking off. As D disappeared into work, Mister's mind turned to S; he owed her an e-mail. There were things about D that made him think about S. Maybe it was S's sass and flare for innuendoes, or maybe it was how she frankly spoke. Whatever it was, he knew he had to write. Mister could not tell S that he forgot about her, so instead, he told her vague truths.

Hello, my secret admirer,

It's Wednesday already. Ugh! Can you believe it?
I know I can't! Last I remembered, it was Friday,

and the weekend was just beginning. Nothing major to do except the usual "get ready for next week" shopping spree. The weekend flew by, and now it was freaking Wednesday. I should be happy that I made it through last weekend in one piece, but instead, I am sad I had to live through it alone. However, I completely agree with you about the "Mondays suck" theory. I dislike them all. LOL! Hmmm! It sounds like we are a lot alike in that respect. Interesting! So then, about not writing you back right away. I am sorry about that. I hope that you do not hold that against me. Although if you do, I will have to find a way to make it up to you.

I am sorry you feel that way about your work environment; it must be a challenge to work around a bunch of people you do not like to be around. I can only imagine working with people like that. As for the rest of what you said, I am speechless. You intrigue me with your for-wardness. Whatever you are doing, keep it up. But only do it if that's really what you want to do. I don't ever want you to be someone that you are not. Speaking of personal character, I am a tease. A very big tease. So watch out, S. Oh, and a friendly batman tip: be careful with your sexually laden innuendoes because I have a lot of my own that could instantly make you wet your panties. Hmm, speaking of all things sexy, when do I get to see a picture of you? You do realize that it's not fair that you know what I look like and I don't know one thing about your physical appearance. You did not even give me some sort of written description so that I can properly dream about you. That is just not fair, S. You know that, right? Are you really going to make me guess what you

might look like? Because if you make me guess, I
will be forced to punish you accordingly.

Mister

Mister sent those exact words off to S just before he started up
the Humvee and drove down the city streets to his first appointment.
Even though he just sent the letter off to S, he eagerly wanted an
immediate response. Something spectacular with pictures, descriptions, and steamy innuendoes was preferred. That was his hope, but
reality always dictated much harsher outcomes.

D usually saw Mister every Wednesday, which was why she purposely dressed up. She liked his hump day swooning. It gave her
enormous confidence to see Mister mentally drool all over her. Her
deprived attention starvation at home made her seek it out from
Mister at work. Their fateful beginning was the first time D felt okay
to let someone other than her spouse give her that kind of attention.
It was an unspoken expectation on both of their parts for Mister to
give her validation, and for D to accept it. Mister's appetite for skirts
and dresses, silk stockings and lace thongs, buttons and zippers, heels
and sparkly lip gloss was everything D had. She was a girlie girl all the
way down to her manicured and pedicured cat claws. She kept herself
looking beautiful from every angle, always hoping for her husband
to notice, but his interests were misplaced on his career. All it took
was Mister's looking-up-the-skirt incident to make D aware of her
sex appeal. From day one, she gathered information on Mister's likes
and dislikes and played to them accordingly. Through many conversations they had, she discovered Mister's weaknesses one at a time,
including thong panty lines and protruding nipple erections. When
D recently learned of his liking for exposed lace-topped stockings,
she made it her business to give him what he wanted. Just like that
morning, she wore a new skirt purposely short enough to reveal her
silky lace tops when sitting. She constantly exploited his weaknesses
using them to her advantages whenever she could. But since Mister
was not around, she could not flaunt her goodies to him like she
needed to do. D purposely planned her Wednesday schedules around

Mister's just so she could spend time with him. She saw his Humvee in the parking lot, so she knew he had to be somewhere close by. Her giddiness was evident in every motion she made. She casually strolled past his office to say good morning to him before going to hers. But when she noticed his lights and computer were off, she kept on walking down the hallway. D turned on her office lights and computer, then walked down to the break room to get a hot herbal tea. She steeped the teabag in her company ceramic logoed mug while pondering Mister's whereabouts.

Where is that man hiding at? I know he will want to see my new outfit. I cannot wait to see his reaction. I am wearing everything that he likes, although he won't be able to see my panties. Bummer! God, I want him bad. Why can't I let myself take him to bed with me?

She took her piping-hot tea with her on a casual tour around the entire building specifically seeking him out. He was not in the conference or copy rooms, he wasn't in the break-room either, and he certainly was not in his office. She even walked over to the storage room to see if he was there loading up on sales literature. But after scouring the entire building, she gave up and walked back to her office in disappointment mode. Before sitting, she took a quick look-see under her desk to see if he was under there. Mister constantly teased D with surprising her like that one day. His deliberate teases were simple attempts to flirt with D in an unrealistic, comedic-like manner. Though his flirts were just words, deep down, D loved the attention. So when Mister was not under her desk, she rechecked the parking lot to see if his Humvee was still there.

Did I miss him somewhere? Is he playing with me? Humph!

D sighed while standing up. She walked out to the parking to discover that his car was gone. It was gone, and so were D's hopes of showing off her newly procured outfit to him. She knew that he would have liked her new skirt, especially if she was sitting, for it rode up high enough on her thighs to reveal her lace-topped stockings. It was not just about showing off the outfit more than it was feeling his desires to have her. She had to have his approval. Mister was the only one that she wanted to validate her sex appeal. He did it impeccably well, considering D did not belong to him. When she could not locate him anywhere, she was tempted to phone call him. But then she let it go. Their friendship had been slowly mending itself from catastrophe. Even though his friendship was one thing she did not want to lose, she wanted him more than she admitted.

Did he go out the back door? I wonder . . .

While D pondered his whereabouts, her phone rang. She hoped it was Mister, but it was not him at all. It was D's 2:00 PM sales appointment wanting to push their meeting time back to 2:30 PM. When she went to update her calendar app, she noticed Mister only had two appointments for the day—one at 10:00 AM and another at 3:00 PM. And there it was turning 9:10, and he was gone.

Where did he go? Maybe he went down to the coffee shop or was parked over at the park. Why did he not want to see me?

All D knew, was that she wanted to find him bad, but Mister was AWOL. It drove her nuts not knowing where he went, so she decided to do a quick drive-by at the café and park. When she spotted his Humvee parked under the tall oak tree, she was relieved then disappointed that she could not show off her new skirt to him. What D really needed to do was connect with Mister to get rid of her held-in past weekend's lonely neglect and trade up for Mister's sex-crazed devotion.

Mister made it to his morning appointment on time, walking into his 10:00 AM on time with a confident swagger in his step. However, just when he got out of his big rig of visual delight, his ringing phone alerted him to new messages. When he looked to see who the messages were from, he noticed it was an e-mail from S. An urgency to get back into his Humvee and read all the way through her message was dominant, but in the end, work prevailed. He was charged up and ready to make his third sale in two days. Yet it was his 10:00 AM's CEO that slowed his supercharged salesmanship down with her rare need to talk with some references before signing on the dotted line. While Mister waited for his 10:00 AM to contact references, his mind went stir crazy trying to guess what S's messaged note said. He imagined all sorts of things from dull to titillating. With the passing of every minute, Mister plucked his arm hairs one at a time. As the third hair fell to the floor, his 10:00 AM handed him a signed contract with a handshake and a smile. He gracefully thanked her and took the signed paperwork with him out the door. He was happy for the sale but happier still to be free to read S's unread e-mail.

Mister,

You do know how to make a woman's morning, don't you? I did not think I would hear back from you. You took forever and a day to write back. I thought you forgot about me. I am happy that you remembered I exist. And since you made me feel special, I cannot hold it against you. You are forgiven. Just don't disappear like that ever again. Okay, Mister? Mister? That is one sinister sounding name you have, but it makes me curiously intrigued. From the first time that I saw your profile on my computer screen, it gave me chills up and down my entire body. Mister? What kind of name is that? It sounds seductively powerful. Are you seductive? Powerful? I cannot lie, I already like your mystery. Serious, I do! So, Mister, why do you need to know what I look like? Are you going to try and find me through the vast size of the town I live in? Do you even know if we are in the same state or country for that matter? Hmm . . .

Even if you mysteriously showed up at my work unannounced, I would still have to be your boss. You know that, right? That would be the proper way since you would be on my territory. I would get to tell you what to do, or not do, and you would have to do it. I am liking that idea, Mister. Me, S, the boss. On second thought, maybe you should try and find me, Mister. I feel a weak spot for a man named Mister. One rule though, you cannot be a dick.

Okay, Mister? I am tired of always finding jerks. I deserve better than that. Really! I have a lot to offer. But my college graduated education does not stop my self-doubt. No man has ever really validated me before, at least not in the way I need to be. As for my picture, you will have to be patient, Mister, for I am loving this mystery far too much to end it. I want to be able to tease you and make you erect without touching you. I want to make you beg for things that you do not yet have. I am going to enjoy our mystery for all that it is worth. I hope that you do not mind. You know, you and I could be a hot item. But only if you have the missing ace up your sleeve. Well, do you?

It is funny how I earlier suggested to you to come and find me. It's funny because I keep fantasizing about a man coming into my office during the middle of a busy workday just to have his way with me. It goes something like this . . .

I am typing away in my office when this confident man struts himself into my office and demands my immediate attention. His grand entrance into my workspace instantly makes my hidden entrance immediately ready for his hard shaft. He would wear a mask of mystique over his eyes and nose, just like Zorro. He would let his actions say everything that needed to be said. He would walk right over to my chair with one purpose in mind: fucking me hard in my own office. He would not be afraid of getting caught, only concerned with his desires to come deep inside of me. He would smoothly walk around my desk and position himself behind my swiveling chair. Then swiftly he would force my chair around 180 degrees to look me in the eye. He would grab my hair at the base of my head and pull my head upward while inserting his tongue into my salivating mouth.

All I would know is that his lips would taste so incredible that I would make him kiss me again before I let him do anything else. He would indulge my need for more intimate kissing before selfishly spreading my legs apart with his leather-booted foot. His deliberate moves would instantly make my uterus weep for his penetration. He would use his arm to instruct me to rise, our eyes locked onto each other's. Both of his strong hands would grab me around the waist and spin me around. As I face away from him, his right hand pushes my face down into the desk while his left hand tears off my panties. This guy would firmly spank my ass twice before thrusting his thick stick into my weeping twat. My slick labia lips of silk pleasure would coax him to squirt his liquid orgasm deep in me. Then as fast as he showed up, he was gone.

Oh, wow! Now I did it. I am so turned on right now. I cannot handle your mesmerizing heat anymore. OMG! Look what you're doing to me, Mister. You are corrupting me, you dick. You make me want to close my door and silently get off to thoughts of you fucking me hard in my office. I need to go and take a break before I explode. As I said, I like our mysterious game of tease, but I cannot reveal any more details about me just yet. But, Mister, please tell me more about you. I must know more. Please tell me.

Goodbye, my sexy Mister. Bye.

S

After Mister read her intersecting words of chaos, his mind turned to liquid mush. He sat inside of his blacked-out Humvee in the city's busiest parking lot and imagined S lying on her tummy with her legs bent upward and her thong tightly lodged between her cheeks while she hunt-and-pecked out her naughty office fantasy on her tablet. Mister would have given anything to secretly watch her body bend and fold with every thought she included.

What made her send me such scintillating words of pleasure? She writes good. I wonder where she was at when she wrote this. That was one hot fantasy. But I wonder if she really was that sexually excited or if she was just flattering me. Dammit, I want to know.

With visions of grandeur, he wanted to see D. With hours between appointments, Mister drove back to the office for a second round of D.

While D stared at her computer screen, she heard Mister walk by her office door and pleasantly wish her a good afternoon. D was in between bites of her lunchtime salad when she looked up, smiled, and said hello right back. D wanted to follow him down to his office but held back to finish off her salad. She gave him time to get settled into his office before revealing her new attire.

Mister sat at his desk, searching for information about his next appointment while waiting for D to make an appearance in his office. Then light knocks on his partially closed door let him know she was there. Mister looked up and saw D staring him down with a smile that ruled all smiles. Her outfit and smiles made him want to thrust his hips into something soft, wet, and pink. But it was not the time to let her know how he felt. Instead, Mister steered the conversation back to business. They casually talked about sales quotas and customer experiences to break unspoken tensions. Mister knew better than to gloat about his sales due to D's hidden assets, but he let her know he was close to meeting his goals. D told him that she surpassed her quota already, but she was curious to know his numbers. When Mister kept those numbers to himself, D put her hands on her hips and gave him one sassy stare. Mister snickered, then smoothly changed topics.

"You know, D, I was inside of the Humvee when you parked next to me this morning. I watched you get out of the car, and I immediately saw your new skirt outfit. I wanted to get out of the Humvee and throw you in the back seat and take advantage of you. I would have if I did not fear any sexual harassment charges being levied against me."

His chuckle was sinister, but so was D's grin.

"I hope that you saw I didn't leave you any come on your desk. I thought about it hard, but I didn't do it."

His naughty cackle caused D's nipples to harden up and all her other glands to salivate.

Neither of them gave up any clues or answers to the unanswered questions that they both had on their minds. Yet in game play, Mister had the upper hand this round. He knew it too. She obviously wanted to get some sort of reaction out of him, but he did not give it to her. He was a smooth playboy how he handled it.

Though his desk comment added high-octane gasoline to her smoldering fire, she did not let him know that. Instead, she wanted to enjoy his compliments later in private.

Just before Mister was about to leave for his 3:00 PM appointment, D reappeared at his office door with flirting on her mind. But instead of allowing D to speak, he boldly jumped in and shut her down.

"I am off to my afternoon appointment, but we will catch up later. You can count on it."

D smiled and gave him the usual "knock 'em dead" colleague cheer before taking his sexually provocative ideas with her back to her office.

He ran his last sales appointment of the day with 100 percent accuracy. It was not until the last five minutes of the appointment that he made the sale. He had to work hard for it, but he ended the day on a sales high.

"Finally, two sales on the same day without much opposition. I like it. I need more of that."

He strutted back to the Humvee, climbed up into it, and drove home to relax. After all, it took a lot of energy to make multiple sales and tease multiple women at the same time. That kind of tired was okay to feel; he would not trade it for anything.

D made it home to be that faithful wife that she was. Even though there were not any accolades waiting her arrival, her kids liked having her home, and that was all that mattered to D. She took well care of them, always making them colorful dishes to fill up their bellies. She also took the time to always read them a good-night story. Even while working a full-time job, D religiously kept the house looking good and the laundry caught up. Those were a small sample of the many marital vows she regularly kept. D made the kids first priority no matter what. D knew what the kids needed, and that was what kept her stuck in the shitty marriage. As for her husband, he was another story. The two marital vows that he kept were family security and being faithful to D, although D had her suspicions about his faithfulness. She stuck it out for the kids' sake and no other reason. But now that the kids were getting older and their marriage was splintering more, D reacquainted herself to being a single parent.

Through her marital downfall, D was still a woman that needed attention. She could not handle any more neglect. When it came to intimacy, D's husband wanted it on his terms, not hers. The affection that he gave her in between his once-a-month bout of making love to her was pathetic to say the least. No cuddling, no touching, and the kisses were pathetic. Pecks on the lips with no tongue action cause a lot of self-doubt and hurt. She made most of the family's frivolous spending cash, always selfishly sharing her small fortune and decent bonuses. Her sharing still did not stir up any extra emotions that it should have commanded. Her sad situation was hard to see from the outside, but somehow, Mister's friendship and listening skills were exactly what she needed. She knew that he did not have to pay attention to her like that, but she loved every moment he gave her. D knew that Mister wanted to make her his, and that one concept kept D going back for more. She would always lead him on just so he would keep making her smile and feel good about herself. Mister's attention was addictive. Mister was her surrogate donor of emotional affection that she could not find at home. That was D's boring married life outside of work. Nothing special. No hot lover boy to go home to. No romance or porn either, just a lot of sexual frustration and emotional neglect met her at the front door. Getting and keeping Mister's attention was D's one guilty pleasure she let herself have. For the rest of the day, D tightly held onto his flirtations, replaying their hot word exchange at bedtime.

M's Wednesday was as busy as it could have been. She got a little management training, then went to night school. On the even days of the week, M had no energy to do anything other than just be present. Even though she got to have her usual morning shower time orgasm, she was forced to be sexually frustrated over Mister's whimsical word play penetrations. On the twenty-two-minute car ride over to school, M transformed herself from a strict business manager, to an A+ student debutante. She made it into the school parking lot, looking all preppy and astute in her polka-dotted skirt ensemble, having had no time to change after work. She was about to make all the boys hard with envy without even trying.

As soon as she stepped out of the car, her body cried out for sleep more than it danced for sex. She got neither.

CHAPTER 16

Notes and Dreams

M arrived home just as the clock struck twenty-one minutes past 10:00 PM. That was her usual get-home time for the nights she went to school. The work then school schedule was grueling, but that was how she needed it to be. Week after week of nonstop busyness kept M focused on her future. She made that commitment three semesters ago to avoid residual effects of a bad breakup. Even though M missed the standard amount of daily sleep, she kept trudging through. By now, she was used to the long hours, but lately, they had been sucking the life right out of her. Up until now, she accepted the self-inflicted torture, but now, she wanted it to be done. The new catalyst driving her thoughts was Mister. He was the X factor in her unpredictable equation of chaos theory. Even though it had only been a week since they started talking, she constantly had thoughts about a man she has yet to meet. Even while she was being a straight-A student, M silently daydreamed about him. To make matters worse, she went home to two catty ladies and an empty bed.

M walked through the front door, making it into the kitchen before finding her roommates watching reality drama. M never "got" reality drama, so she kept away. Even if she had liked those sorts of shows, she would not have had the time to "get into them." Before M said hello to the girls, she noticed a wine bottle on the counter. She picked it up, poured the remaining wine into a blue solo cup, and gave out a group hi.

"Heya, ladies. Wine and reality TV? Really?"

Her two roommates echoed the same answer in unison, "Yes, really!"

M retorted with a straightforward sentiment that made sense at the time.

"Maybe if I had more free time, I would watch the shows with you. Unfortunately, I don't have much time at all. I know, sad, right?"

A lighthearted cackle came from M's mouth before she finished her thoughts.

"But you know how it goes. Never a dull moment. Oh, and I took the rest of the wine and now going to bed. Good-night, ladies."

M took the plastic cup of wine back with her to the bedroom and got ready for bed. She wiggled out of her polka-dotted skirt outfit and slipped into what M liked to call the Velvety Ones. The two-piece pajama set always kept her warm at night. Even the skimpy fitting style-matched cheeky-styled bottoms were made of soft crushed velvet. The Velvety Ones accentuated her every curve perfectly. They made her feel like one of those hot models that she was not. Somewhere coveted inside M's subconscious were self-esteem issues that were brought on by childhood razing. The Velvety Ones were one of her simplest pleasures that always boosted her self-esteem. M did not know if it was their color, fit, or feel of the velvet touching her clitoris that made her feel like a seductive temptress. Whichever it was, she appreciated the Velvety Ones for all their unexpected attitude adjustments. The funny thing about the Velvety Ones was that she bought them on a three-for-one sale over one year ago. She did not even try them on, just laid down the credit card without giving it much thought. Her impulsive buy got her the best pajamas ever. The first time that she wore the Velvety Ones, they made her come alive with sexiness. They boosted her confidence right out of the solar system, always making her feel like a sweet piece of eye candy that needed to be licked. The first night wearing the Velvety Ones since Mister wrote her was nothing less than risqué.

The heat between her and Mister quickly turned into an out-of-control inferno. M has not had the time to think about what she would do now that Mister was boring a hole into her impenetrable defenses, but she had to figure it out before he got all the way in. There was no undoing M's erotic cherry; it was already busted all over Mister. No matter what time of day it was or where she was or what she wore, M quickly got used to his constant attention.

M went through half of the day without any food at all, so the bedtime wine swirled into her bloodstream with much stronger effects. She felt tipsy the moment she stood up to walk across the room to get her laptop off the desk. M brought it back with her to bed and flipped it open to get right onto the World Wide Web. M settled in and grabbed the nearby pillows and propped herself upright. She deepened the mood of sexy by cueing up some funky rhythm-filled songs by the artist known as a symbol while swallowing the rest of the tart-red wine in remembrance of Mister's naughty ideas. He intrigued M in many ways that she did not understand. What made her most impressed was Mister's ability to take the simplest of words and make them sensually come alive and dirty dance with each other. She did not know if she wanted to encourage his naughty talk or downplay his pornographic portrait altogether, but she knew she had to react somehow.

Mister,

> I spent all day trying to figure out where you got your smooth gentlemanlike persona, and I still cannot pinpoint anything specific. I rarely tell people what I am thinking, so you should feel lucky, Mr. Mister. I just got home from school, and the first thing I am doing is writing you. Okay . . . fine, it's the third thing, but I had to say hi to my roommates then get into my pajamas. Yes, I did say I just got home from school, and no, you are not robbing the cradle. I promise. I am trying to further my education and advance my career so that I can make my own financial

security. LOL! Well that, and I also needed the school distraction. I went through a bad relationship breakup over a year ago. He broke my heart, and I went back to school to forget about him. But now, I am growing weary of constantly being busy and want change. It felt good to be single, but I don't want to be single anymore. I did not know it then, but I needed personal time to myself to grow and learn who I am. Before that, I went from one relationship to another, never really evaluating what went wrong and why it happened. I thought that I was the problem, but what I learned was that it was not all my fault. Ever since I grew into womanhood, I never truly allowed myself to know who I was and what I wanted out of life. Being alone helped me learn a lot about me. It helped me fall back in love with myself. I finally understand me, and it feels great. I am glad I took the break. You could say that if I had not taken that break, we would not be talking right now. But enough about that.

I have no idea how this kind of relationship is supposed to go, Mister, so please be patient with me. To be honest, Mister, I do not know if I want what you want. It has nothing to do with you, and all to do with me and school. This semester is almost over, but next semester is right around the corner. But for now, I am choosing to stay and find out more about you, if that is okay. You have my undivided attention. I do not mean to cut this note short, but I am tired, and I need sleep. But while I sleep, you need to answer me something. Can you keep me intrigued? Good night, Mister.

M

M sent her reply to Mister, then closed her pink-accented laptop, put it on the floor, and passed out from exhaustion.

As Mister was falling asleep, the vibrations from a noisy phone e-mail alert startled him up. At first, he did not want to read it, but then he reached over to the nightstand and grabbed the illuminated phone. With the room dark and Rocket stretched out on the left side of the bed, Mister lay still while reading her late-night thoughts. His grip on the phone was tight while his mind was loosely focused into everything she had to say. His tiredness was soon replaced with some ego-boosting giddy up and go. Even though M's words were not sexual, it was the potential that made Mister's sheets rise to the occasion. Even with Rocket asleep on the bed, Mister rolled over onto his belly and thrust his hard cock into the soft satin sheen until hot sticky semen burst out of his hard cock. It was not his fault that he woke up Rocket; rather, it was a girl on the internet that deserved the blame. His orgasmic release was powerful and perfect. It made him not want to move anywhere at all. He closed his eyes and fell asleep in his own wet spot.

She had been lying in bed half-awake yet half-asleep for the last thirty minutes thinking about his smooth words of soft-core porn. Her thoughts and ideas ever changed while the minutes passed by. Strangely enough, M woke up Thursday before her alarm clock had the chance to go off. That was not like her at all. So with exigency, she peeked her head out from under the sheets to do a time check. Relief was restored when she saw that she had woken up earlier than late. Since going back to school, she never really slept solidly during the weekdays, only weekends. That morning, M woke up one grateful girl that the universe still loved her.

The dark-blue room made M feel warm and wanted. That was all that mattered, yet it was the idea of Mister being inside of her that made M linger in bed longer than she should have. She had not expected those kinds of emotional reactions to him just yet, but it was the serious mixture of passion, desire, want, and need that inspired his existence in her soul. Throughout yesterday, M thought up several things she wanted to ask Mister, yet she was too tired to even ask him one. She wanted to write them down so that she would not forget to ask but was too tired to get out a pen and paper. Although she liked the new path she was going down, she was more than a little scared to travel it without a GPS. The feeling of not knowing made her pulse race. She was used to knowing where she was going, but obviously, that time of knowing was done and over. M now lived on a borrowed path. Mister was the last thing she thought about at night and the first thing she thought about in the morning, even more so than work and school combined. Morning reflections relaxed her enough to lull her right into dreamland, where she was dropped off in the middle of a dream about a man named Mister.

Visions of Mister standing upright at the foot of her bed, calling out her name in his low-pitched vibrato, willingly seduced M under his control. His stocky physique made her feel safe, like no one could harm her or take away her newly discovered happiness. Sitting up in bed, she stripped off the covers as fast as she could. M's undercover warmth was immediately interrupted with a cold air blast that gave her goose bumps a big dose of morning reality. Even her nipples instantly hardened as the change of temperature bit at them hard. It had been far too long since anyone had touched them with wanting desire, so long, that she had forgotten what it felt like to have them fondled, kissed, and sucked. But in her new dreams, she dreamed Mister sucked on them with exotic precision. She imagined his soft, wet tongue making love to her erect nipples as if they were his. Their hardness was almost too painful to experience, but when she thought of them being in Mister's mouth, the stinging pain became quivering pleasure. As M touched herself, all her unspoken fantasies came alive. She hallucinated that Mister was standing in front of her. She had many questions she wanted answers to.

"Would you wrap your arms around me? Could you pull me into your warm chest, pet my hair, and tell me I look pretty? Would you kiss me with unending passion? Could you look at me with vivid intensity? Would you compliment me on my sexy morning attire, or would you strip it off just so you can make love to me before we part ways for the day?"

Not one of her fantasized questions were answered, yet she yearned for them to all be answered in time. M drifted in and out of morning fantasyland consciousness while fantasizing that Mister knelt to his knees and massaged her erogenous zones with delicate gentleness. Like a never-ending kaleidoscope twisting in and turning out rested, her neatly trimmed volcano erupted all over the palm of her hand. Gushing sugar cane lava flowed everywhere. M collapsed backward onto the bed at the exact time her alarm clock sounded. She wanted to hit the snooze button in a selfish attempt to keep the dream going, but after she came, all fantasies of him were wiped clean.

The Velvety Ones and lust-filled thoughts were her only protection against becoming a frozen popsicle, yet she was overheated from the strong orgasm. She wished to dream more about Mister being in her plush bed of serenity, but work won out this round. M arose with deep sexual spry. She wanted him there to stroke her hair and pet her soft skin and tell her everything will be okay. Instead, Mister was too busy soundly sleeping across town to know he was needed. She took her dream and his words with her into the shower with naughty intentions of making love to herself again. And that was exactly what she did.

CHAPTER 17

• • • • • • • • • • • • • •

In the Office

Mister woke up refreshed more than any man could ever be on a workday morning. His sales mojo was through the roof after his last flawless sales performances. That Thursday, he rose out of bed with a cocky edge and an erection that begged him to take it out and get it off. The funny thing about it was he fell asleep getting rid of one. Instead of making it go away, he fondled it while writing S an over-the-top fantasy that included mystery and dominance.

S,

You will be happy to know this morning I exchanged my sales job for a temporary private-eye gig, no thanks to your concealed mystery. You make me want to take a guess at whom you really are, so now I must fantasize up a woman named S. My thoughts are to create you in my head just like this.

Mister walked into his hallway coat closet, opened it, and took the long black trench coat off the hanger and slung it around his shoulders while slipping his arms into the sleeves. Right away, he walked into his home office and stepped into character, rereading their past correspondence, specifically looking for any details as to her identity. What Mr. Private Eye found was her uniquely assigned internet protocol address while cleverly sifting through every possible clue. He used special GPS triangulation and algorithm software ahead of its time to find her embedded digital footprint with pinpoint accuracy. He grabbed the car keys and headed out to the suspected coordinates. Mister spied around the industrialized area, eliminating insignificant locales. He narrowed it down to two possibilities, then to one.

Mister PI pulled into the business complex's parking lot, parked, and grabbed the binoculars and scoped out the place for more clues. He noticed surveillance cameras and a female receptionist as the only deterrence of getting in. Mister Private Dick watched the front desk girl's comings and goings through the transparent front glass doors while hiding behind his tinted window fortress on wheels. When he saw the receptionist walk out of the front door and to the side of the building with the phone headset on a few times to smoke, he planned his way in.

Mister Private Dick waited for the receptionist to walk to the side of the building to smoke, then he snuck in through the front door. He had a specific task to carry out. It was to find out more about the elusive woman named S. The building had two floors filled with offices that were connected to a larger-sized warehouse on the back part of the building. He roamed the halls, looking for a woman he had never met before. The only clues Mister Private Dick had of her looks was her sensualistic personality she told him about. He also knew of her office surround-ings from previous e-mailed writings that she told him about. He roamed down the hallways, trying to be as inconspicuous as possible. Then he located her shortly after he began his search. She was talking on the phone and working on the computer inside of her enclosed office that was sandwiched between a row of connecting offices. She had no idea he was watching her; he was just that good. After all, Mister Private Dick was the MVP of the private-eye world. He quickly retreated to the closest bathroom to formulate a plan to begin his cunning fuckery.

It was midday, and everyone around the office seemed to be too enveloped in their own working world environment to take notice of a stranger's suave swagger down their familiar hall-ways. Mister Private Dick made up his cunning fuckery plan in the little boy's room while incon-spicuously washing his hands. He then reentered the hallway and snuck down the winding hallway right into her office undetected by anyone, not even S. The click of the lock being pushed in is what first got S to look up. When she looked up and saw a man dressed in black standing behind her locked office door, she instantly had wetness flow out of her. Black silk pants with a silk black button-down shirt and glossy black dress shoes covered his underlying physique. S had no idea what was next, but when she saw his naughty smirk, she quivered from anticipation. Using his deep soothing voice, he calmed her down by tell-ing her exactly what he was there for.

"I am Mister, and I found a girl that could not be found. I am here to take my prize."

He walked closer to her, and she could not move anywhere. She was frozen from the shocking excitement ensuing. He walked around her desk and got behind her rolling leather chair with dominance. S struggled to keep her eyes on him as he stood completely hidden behind her chair. In not so many gestures, he forced her to keep looking straight at her door. Then when Mister Private Dick felt her sexual curiosity hit an all-time high, he traced around her sticky lip-gloss-covered lips with his index finger. His deliberate touches on her lips caused her immediate chaos. She went to grab his hand and remove it off her lips, but instead, he captured her hand in his, then laid gentlemanlike kisses on the palm of her open hand. That was when the room went silent with building sexual tension. Even though she could not see or touch him, she felt that his surrounding presence repeatedly penetrating her vaginal walls.

That is all you get for now. But, S, why do I not know what you look like yet? Please tell me. Show me. Tell me and show me. Please? I must get back to work now, and so do you.

Waiting,
Mister

Those words from Mister's naughty letter of intent came with hidden purposes. He ended his teasing fantasized e-mail to S with an attempt to get her to tell him and show him her laws of attraction. He wanted the fantasy to dangle her off a cliff without any kind of force, causing some sort of reaction.

While S dangled off the cliff of erotica, Mister doubled down with an e-mail to M. He did not want her last night's message to go ignored for very long.

M,

I can understand all of what you are saying because I have been there myself. I appreciate your vulnerability; that's a rare gift to lay your emotions out there for someone to see. I read your e-mail last night just after you sent it. It woke me up, but I was glad it did. I was feeling anxious and restless before reading it, and afterward, I slipped into a deep dreamlike utopia. Reading it produced results that you might not believe. Maybe I can tell you all about it another time when you are cuddled up next to me, but for now they must remain a secret. As far as convincing you of my sincerity, I can only throw myself on the mercy of your court. Please believe me when I say I deserve to know everything you did, do, and want to do because I am Mister. But even the times you don't want me to know what you did or are doing or how excited you are, I will know. I will just know.

Naughty ambitions,
Mister

Mister felt powerful, as he had the affections of three women—S, M, and D. None of them knew about each other, but Mister certainly knew all three of them. He knew and wanted D the most, but she would never give up her marriage, which put M to the front of the list. But one thing Mister knew that he could not ever do was give up paying D attention. He felt like it was his job as a gentleman to make her feel appreciated, desired, and wanted. That much he knew, but shallowly tucked inside Mister was a man that loved being the other man, but the going-nowhere routine numbed his thinking and flatlined his cock. And now it was down to two ladies—S and M. He wanted them both, that much was true.

Mister had enough time to make a trip into the office to get some much-needed sales brochures. As soon as he pulled the Humvee into the parking lot, he noticed that D was parked in his usual spot. Instinctively, Mister parked in her usual spot and hastily walked in heading right for D's office. Instead of going right for the sales literature, he stormed into D's office and demanded answers.

"Who gave you permission to park in my parking space, because I know I didn't?"

Complete silence silenced her twice-occupied office. D did not know what to think, but when Mister broke his serious stare, she knew he was not being an asshole, just a jokester.

"Gotcha! I'm just messing with you."

D's defunct backward smile turned right side up.

"You are a fucking jerk! But that's okay, I still like you. I think."

Mister proceeded to say, "Good morning," and "How are you?" with a touch of arrogance to his ramblings. He was already soaked in sexual depravity from writing the girls back, so his morning tease hit D in all the right spots. Mister's prowess gleamed off him, and D caught its full force.

D did not know what to make of Mister's luster. He turned her entire morning around with his speculative conjecture. D felt an aura about him that was different, but she did not know what changed. Even though she wanted him, she kept telling herself no. His light-scented cologne and pheromone mixed concoction penetrated her imaginative mind with commanding authority. She giddied up and down on his lingering smell for the rest of the day.

Mister walked out of D's office with a swollen head of built-up ego that he had not had in forever. He whistled and smiled all the way down to the storage room, quickly grabbing up the sales literature then walking out of the office high on sexual adrenaline and freshly released testosterone from teasing S, M, and D all at the same time. But only weeks ago, he could not have been doing the kinds of things he was doing now, if it were not for the lucid wet dream. It was mostly the freedom from self-inflicted oppression that gave him new hope to infiltrate S's, M's, and D's lives at different varying degrees of penetration.

M felt out of touch and blind in many ways. Unfortunately, horrible company policy dictated no personal use of the internet for personal reasons. She knew it was a spoken guideline, but the unspoken portion of that was "Proceed with caution." M feared checking personal e-mails, especially the kind of e-mails Mister wrote. That new smartphone option began looking damn good right then, but for now, there was no time to run out and get one lickety-split. Instead, M assigned herself a homework project due by next morning. In the meantime, there was an unexpected distraction by her boss.

"How are you doing with your new management position, M?"

"I am doing great with it so far. The title of manager made me realize that the company appreciates me more than ever. How do you think I am doing so far?"

Her boss handed her the newly created manager's job description and smirked at M while she read it.

"I must tell you, all that I have heard and seen does not exactly reflect your potential. Your new position comes with new responsibilities. If you can stay focused on your job, the better everyone will be."

As her boss walked off, M understood the subtle point she made, then got back to being in charge. Priority one, understanding her new responsibilities by rereading the job description and making a new goal list. She typed out goals for herself and her subordinates, all while trying to not think about him. Something so simple turned out to be a harder feat than anticipated, especially when all she wanted to do was go home and write Mister back. M passed out the new job descriptions to her subordinates and talked with them to see how they were doing and how they felt about the new department concept. M did her job well that day after she put him out of her mind. Now that Thursday was almost over with, M looked forward to another no-school night. M had plans of having dinner with her roommates and writing Mister back.

Mister,

I just got home from work. I should be visiting with my roommates and eating dinner with them as I type this out, but I wanted to write you first on the high chance of probability of my falling asleep somewhere between eating dinner and brushing my teeth. This night, right now where I sit, I feel friskier than any woman has the right to feel. Yes! Really, you did that to me again. I will write you more later, but I needed to share with you my feelings and thoughts that now race through my mind in every conceivable way.

Unanimously yours,
M

M made Mister her first priority, then joined her roommates in the kitchen and ate a Cobb salad with blue-cheese dressing. M mostly listened to her other two roommates talk about the drama TV shows that they watched. They were into watching reality TV, whereas M cared a less; she had her own sexually driven drama starting up. They sipped on wine and talked. The girls wanted to know more about M's new love interest.

"So when are you going to tell us about him? There still is a new *him*, isn't there? We wanna know about this man that makes you smile."

"Can't a girl get any privacy anymore?" She giggled. "He has an interesting personality. I like it. He is very flirtatious, and he shows a lot of passion. He is confidently sexy, and that makes me want to know more."

"When are you going to go on a date with him?"

"Umm . . ."

"You can tell us, M. We will keep it our little house secret."

"I have no idea yet. We are still feeling each other out. And besides that, he has not asked me out yet. I am waiting though. I am thinking I will say yes. What do you girls think?"

"You better say yes. But when he asks you, don't answer right away. Men like a good old-fashioned playing-hard-to-get tease. Even though you will want to say yes, play hard to get. It will make him want you more."

They all laughed and agreed as the aftereffects of the wine took hold. M felt more tired than willing to divulge any more details about Mister, so she made a fast exit. M smiled then walked off, heading down the hallway and up the stairs to bed. As M stripped down to her panties, she prepared to write Mister. But before she could type anything out, M passed out on her bed.

Mister,

Good morning, sexy man. I was going to write you something more last night, but I fell asleep. Bad me, I know. LOL. Actually, it was better that I did not write you back last night; otherwise, I would not have had this fantasy come to me. It is in my mind, and I want it to now be in yours too, for I cannot deny describing to you something you helped create. You win! Gloat as you read what I fantasize.

I lay my head against my fluffy pillow, close my eyes, and recall your charming words of dazzling wit in all their descriptive glory. My naughty thinking put us both somewhere else other than where we are at now. Despite not being in front of each other, let our desires transcend into each other's fantasies. While thoughts of a man named Mister get vividly created in my own fantasyland, let thoughts and visions of me flood yours. As my right-hand pushes my panties aside, it gets into my secret play yard. I pull on my short pubic hairs to put me in the kind of mood I need to be in.

From where you are at, you can see everything that I am doing through high-definition imagery that my eyes let you see through. I play with and tug on my soft hairs for less than three minutes, replacing soft tugs with firmer yanks to guide me in a much different direction than being relaxed. The roughness of my selfish pubic hair pulling now turns me on instead of calming me down. Petting my trimmed bush makes me feel sexy and fearless, and you can exactly understand that from seeing what you spy. To know me is to know that any kind of pubic hair play really does calm me down or excite me up, depending on how hard the pulls are. I cannot describe the feelings in words, just know it is amazing. And now that I shut out the cruel world, my fantasies rev up like an accelerating sports car launching itself from standstill to 100 mph in miniscule amounts of time. My hands go on autopilot, doing to me what I beg of you to do. When the time is right, I stop playing with my short hairs and start playing with my wet lips of silk. It feels sexy, but not as marvelous as you could do. I know you want to see me pleasure myself, almost as much as I want you to watch me. Would you? Watch me?

My searing hot thoughts of selfish lust substantially multiply and divide, equating to the vivid smell of a budding rose. My brain concentrates on you, and my hands concentrate on me. Do not be surprised when I make you watch me insert my French-manicured fingernails into my own juicy pink lips. My creamy wetness naturally helps my slick fingers slide in and slip out of my tight sugar walls all that much easier. The sounds of sloppy wetness make me want you inside of me.

Then special thoughts of firsts make me stop my selfish private plight. If I cannot have you inside of me, the least I can do is wait for you to get on my hot vibe and share this very private climax with me. It is what I want. Please, Mister, climax with me! Please! Please, baby! Please!

With M's plan almost all typed out, she wanted to see if Mister was paying attention or just pretending.

Before I go, Mister, come, and join me in the solo climatic event of the century, for I NEED you to cum with me. I do not ask; rather, I insist.

M wanted to give Mister an intimate connection with a one-of-a-kind experience to keep his interests piqued. Her invitation had to be sexually hot enough to deflect their spatial separation. Since they were not in the same room, let alone the same neighborhood, M wanted their participation experience to physically link them to each other, without really linking them together. It had to feel real, it had to feel right, and it had to mean something to make them both get off together. M wanted it to elevate his cock and sexual desires for her at an unexpected time. She wanted to play his kind of game just as he had already done to her on more than one occasion. M was not sure it would come out the way she wanted it, but she took the risk.

Mister, no matter where you are or aren't at, I need you to write me back. I am preemptively getting myself up out of bed to go over to my desk and wait for your message. Do not disappoint me, Mister. While I wait for your e-mail to arrive, I will impatiently be waiting in my squeaky-assed chair across the other side of my room. Don't make me wait too long because my room is chilly cold. At least the heat inside of my mind can make me warm while I wait. Mister, please hurry! Don't make me strictly reprimand you! Be a good Mister, not a bad one!

M

M took a seat in the squeaky cloth-covered chair, wearing her hat of impatience and the blue Velvety Ones. It had been less than five minutes since she e-mailed him, and she had ants in her pants. He was not responding to her demands fast enough, but there she sat in wait. Impatient and excited, M got a head start. She petted and pulled on her short pubic hairs while waiting for his message to show up.

Mister got her e-mail shortly after 6:30 AM. He was just getting into the shower when his phone pleasantly disturbed his quiet morning of peace. He was not used to getting any e-mails that early in the morning, let alone a message from a woman named M. Before he stepped into the tile-accented shower, he looked at the message to see whom it was from. Even before he picked up his phone, Mister felt something inside of his psyche telling him that it was from one of his three girls. Even though the water was hot and running, the e-mail stopped him dead in his tracks. He got, he saw, and he conquered her daring demands.

"Where is my silly boy Mister at?"

Eight minutes later was when she got his message. She trembled from the excitement, accidentally causing her to mistakenly delete it before it was ever opened. She internally cussed aloud in disgust.

"Oh shit, what did I do? Shit! Shit! Shit! What did I do? Ahh wait, I know, let me check my digital trash can. I bet I can restore it. Thank God for Recycle folders."

M,

What a pleasant surprise waking up to a message from you. How could I not pay attention to you? As for where I am at, I am completely naked, and the shower water is running out of the massaging showerhead. The steam is clouding up the room, and the sun is shining in through the skylight and

windows, making its brevity absolutely seductive. I wish you could be here with me. Soon I
will step into the shower and let the water wash
over my manly curves, washing away the many
semen that will soon be ejaculated all over my
soapy hands. I don't usually get off in the shower,
but how could I not with your blaring demands?
Wanna race to the finish?

Good mornings,
Mister

Seconds after Mister sent M his reply, she read it from her
podium with a squeaky desk chair. Everything she asked for, she
got. His e-mail came to her looking exactly like the sexiest pair of
heels she could ever own, steeped in sex, allure, and erotic desire. Her
eyes were mentally fixated on every word. His A+ twisted perversion swept her up into the fast-flowing river of pizzazz. She laughed,
and she cried. She touched, and she came. That morning lent her
the most intense orgasm that she ever had. She knew exactly why
too. It only took minutes for her to get all the horny out. Her idea
of sharing orgasms together was a brilliantly smart idea. It went off
flawlessly as she basked in the relaxing afterglow.

She danced down the hallway right into the kitchen and out
the front door, whizzing past her two roommates without speaking a
word. M had a purpose to live again, but for now, she had to go out
in the ginormous world of unknowns and transcend all impossibility.

After reading what M wrote, he stepped into the shower. Just
what he wrote down, he did. Her well-thought-up and written-out
words gave Mister insight into just how delicate of a woman M was.
He could take advantage of her exposed weaknesses, but then Mister
would not be a gentleman anymore. Instead, he let her vulnerabilities
levitate their friendship to new heights.

Mister liked the picture M painted for him. Her strokes might
not have been as naughty as his were, but they appeared just as intentional. As the hot water woke him up, he reflected on future agendas.

Despite work, S and M interrupted his morning's agenda. He liked the fact that S pursued him first, but then he liked the submissive sweetness of M. He still had not met either one of them, but he knew he wanted to meet them both. Mister spent several minutes thinking about them before his concentrations turned back to work.

Mister walked out of the shower and put on the finishing touches to his outward appearance and walked out the door. He climbed into the Humvee and drove down the road to his first appointment, arriving twenty minutes ahead of schedule. Instead of waiting in some scarcely occupied lobby, he stayed behind the dark-tinted glass of his military-grade ride while rereading M's morning note all over again. He smiled and felt like he was her sexual God while reading it all the way through for the second time. He wanted to write her another catchy note, but with limited time, he refrained.

Mister ran both of his meetings with an abundance of energy. Normally, it was hard to sell the extended service warranties, but he sold both systems that way. He was off to a great start on surpassing the new month's sales quota. Two repeat performances in the same day always made him want to put his pent-up energy into something soft and wet, but he knew that wasn't going to happen anytime soon. Mister had regained his lost confidence, and that gave him a cocky arrogance that lasted him the rest of the week.

Rediscovered confidence made his appointments go smooth, finishing them thirty minutes ahead of schedule. Mister knew what he wanted to do, but instead, he drove over to his favorite sandwich place and ordered up something simple. He settled with a mixed greens salad and a Fuji apple to rev down his stored-up sexuality. Mister parked under the tree in the parking lot and ate. Even when it rained, that was his spot for peace and tranquility. It was the romantic sound and visual stimulation of watching rough waters pound every fucking rock that eased Mister's tension. So he partially rolled down the windows and let in the erotic river sounds. The serenity of the overcast colors lighting up everything grey, peacefully seduced Mister to close his eyes. And then his phone rang. He wanted to pass up the interruption, but eager salesmanship made him check it out. To his surprise, it was a message from S.

Mister,

Oh boy, now you're talking my kind of language. Reading your last e-mail really made me feel like you came into my office and disturbed my office sanctity with your rock-hard shaft. As I sit here behind my desk writing you this, I must fess up to sensations of feeling wet rain drizzling out of me. It simply feels amazing to be this excited, especially at work. It's risqué and naughty, and I like it. I cannot believe I told you that, but I am glad I did because you did that to me, Mister. The first paragraph mentally made me excited, and the rest of the paragraphs made me wet. Mister Private Dick was a stroke of genius. You made me speechless. I know just how much you would like to know when I am sexually turned on, so there you go. I am excited and wet! I want you to come over to my desk right now and cum all over it. You know you want to. Don't fight it. I can always lend you a helping hand, but only if you ask nicely, because I already know that your flaccid cock is on its way up as you read this. I can literally feel its pulse while I hold it in my hand. Oh, how I wish I could help you get rid of that nice-looking erection.

Sweet daydreams,
S

CHAPTER 18

• • • • • • • • ● • • • • • • •

Selfish

M almost missed lunchtime. She was too busy pounding away at the keyboard. M could not think about breaks when she had monthly inventory and flow control reports due and a man named Mister deeply embedded in her every thought. She made solid gains, but then the internal server crashed. M's first monthly reports and forecasts were due in five days, and her anxiety was visibly displayed when she threw her pen down on the floor in disgust. Previously M typed up the reports for her boss, but now, the reports were her new primary responsibility. She was now responsible for gathering up the information from all the different department heads, formulating it into a complete slide based presentation, then presenting it to her bosses. M took her new position serious and did not want to mess up her one shot at staying on the corporate management ladder. She wanted her bosses to be impressed, yet the offline server stalled M's progress. There was not much she could do but surf the internet or break the company's most covenanted golden rule: no personal business with company computers.

I am sure that I could get away with it. I know Kodi does it all the time. Hell, if she can get away with watching YouTube videos, I am sure that I could check out my e-mails. Damn, I want to tease Mister badly. Time to go for it M.

On one hand, M wanted to tell Mister about her morning episode, and on the other hand, she did not want to tell him anything. It was an emotional breakdown that she had immediately after their remotely shared early morning pleasure trade occurred.

Up until then, it was a "give one, get one" kind of message friendship that had meshed well for them both, but M was about to change all of that. Not knowing their future certainty, she hoped that he would not run away after reading about the breakdown. But M wanted her words to hit him right where it counted.

Mister,

I had some extra time at work to think about you due to the server I use went offline. I really wanted to tell you what happened to me after our special morning bonding, but work prevailed. I would have written you on my lunchtime break, but I intend to go buy myself a smartphone at lunch. I still have an unsmart flip phone, and my laptop at home is four years old, so I am being a bad girl at work. I am breaking company policy to write you, but I feel like I should tell you about this morning. I was not going to tell anyone, let alone you, but I need to tell someone, and you are it.

What better way to occupy my downtime than writing you? So while I wait for our network technician to come and fix the server, I wanted to say thank you. Thank you for responding to my ad, and thank you for talking to me, and thank you for being the man that you are, and thank you for this morning's exemplary performance. You made our first orgasms deeply intimate. Absolutely amazing! When I got off this morning, my entire body shuttered for ten minutes afterward. That's when I knew this would be a great day. I was going to write you after I show-ered, but then something crazy happened. What happened scared the shit out of me. I am better now, but still under its influence.

I was towel-drying off when I began to feel lightheaded. I walked over to my bed, and with each step, I got dizzier. When I sat down on the edge of the bed, I felt weak all over. It must have been two minutes before it started to feel better, or so I thought. When I stood up and bent over to rub vanilla-fragranced lotion onto my upper thighs and legs, the room spun fast around me, and I started sweating. I got off balance and fell backward onto the bed. I did not pass out or any-thing, but gravity literally forced me to the bed with a heavy invisible force pushing me down. When I tried standing up again, I could only panic. I cannot lie, it freaked me out. I thought I was going through some life-ending event when I felt all the emotions that a human could feel. They hit me all at once. Happiness, sadness, pleasure, failure, anger, resentment, and guilt. The feelings were what made up the heaviness that pushed me down on the bed. My breaths got rapid, and my sobbing was uncontrollable. The only thing I could do was lie there and be still because my central nervous system was busted. For several minutes, I thought I was going to die. Then when my body stopped trembling and I stopped sobbing, I felt waves of joyful pleasure wash over me. I lay there in a fetal ball, com-pletely naked, waiting for it to end. The entire thing was done and over with in under twelve minutes, at least that was what I could guess from looking at the clock. As soon as I recovered, I sat up on the edge of the bed and tried to get going again. When my dizziness was gone and I felt normal again, there was a serendipitous joy that now existed in me.

I guess what I am trying to say is that if you never e-mailed me, I would never have felt that beautiful moment. I am glad it happened even though I was scared. I could not tell you any of that earlier because it happened right after, ah, you know. Wink, wink. But it exhausted me. I wish I could have stayed home and kept curled up under the covers, but I was not about to miss work. But one thing I know; all this has to do with you coming into my life so fast and strong. You did not give me a chance to get used to you, just, *bam*, here I am. Ever since you e-mailed me, my mind has been filled up with the scariest things that love and lust could ever make a woman feel. Yet everything feels so right that I don't want it to be wrong.

I admit that I am skeptical about you, Mister. But please don't be mad at me, Mister. Instead, show me your real intentions no matter what they are. Tell me or show me, but you cannot leave me in the dark. I beg you. Please tell me. I need to know if your words and stories are strictly meant for me or if you plagiarized them from someone else to impress me? Are you some sort of brilliant con artist trying to mind-fuck me over to get laid? Because I know I can be gullible when it comes to a good-looking, sweet-talking man whispering sweet nothings into my ear. But I don't want to be gullible anymore. I won't be gullible anymore. So please help me experience the real you.

I know we women are not the easiest to figure out, but that's just the way we are made, completely complicated. Yes, we always let our emotions control us instead of us controlling them. Sometimes that is good, and sometimes it is bad. We can be snappy, bitchy, and downright evil if we can be. But isn't that why you men love us? Admit it! You love our torture that love and lust bring. All men love the chase just as all women love the pursuit, but in the end, they both must find a way to comingle. Guess what? That is precisely why the hot and cold of our ever-changing minds of chameleon-like wants make you men keep coming back for more. Sure, we make wrong decisions based on our emotions, Mister, but don't we all? It is nothing that most us can help. After all, we are only human. It's in our female DNA to want security and be loved. It is a known fact that women are emotionally stronger than men, yet our spirits are so fragile that our glass houses can easily be shattered with the tiniest pebble striking our glass. We feel the slightest hesitation with our built-in intuition. We know when one of your strong fingers has weakened. That's exactly how I am, Mister, so you cannot hurt me. Talk is usually cheap, but so far, your talk has been anything but. It's your delicate delivery of sensuality that keeps me intrigued. I've never been around a man that treats me the way you do, so pardon my apprehensions.

Please, Mister, please don't let me down! I can accept my dominant role in your life if you can prove to me that you are capable of handling all that I might demand. I can and will put down my delicate lace, but only if you can put down your strong leather and make love to me on equal ground. No leather and no lace, just two vulnerable people sharing hot passionate love together. Can you make love to me like that?

Know that my doubts are not from anything you said more than they are from bad experiences. I am forewarning you that I will do everything I can to protect myself from heartbreak. So, Mister, I need to know something. Do you think you can win me over?

Hugs,
M

M was proud of herself for telling him what had happened despite its embarrassing connotations. Before sending it off, she kept conjuring up all kinds of bedlam to chicken out of sending it.

"I hope that he will not think of me as emotionally unstable. What happens if he does? Will he stop writing me? But he did say he wanted to find someone to have a deep connection with. Maybe telling him will show him I can be vulnerable. I bet he would like that. Maybe he will want to come and rescue me from myself. The last thing that I want him to do is stop talking to me. Humph!"

She sat at her desk weighing the good and bad possibilities of sharing it with him, hesitating to send it. But M was too excited not to tell him about everything that happened so much so that she was too zoned out to hear the company's network technician sneak up behind her. When the IT guy cleared his throat, it caused M to prematurely ejaculate the e-mail into cyberspace, forcing it down the internet pipeline at one billion miles per second. And with a bewildered nervous look, she embarrassingly turned around and smiled at the tech with a bright-red face. The tech was only there to tell her that the network server was back online; instead, he got the chance to do some R-rated over-the-shoulder reading. M went right back to work just like she never wrote Mister at all. But now M had concerns that little Miss Bitchy Bitch would find out about M's e-mail and personals ad since the network tech and little Miss Bitchy Bitch were more than friendly outside of work.

Mister was not expecting a midmorning letter of lust from anyone, but there it was. M's e-mail interrupted his in-between appointment tranquility. The funny part was that Mister was just about to write her back. Nonetheless, he enjoyed her midmorning message telling him all about her emotional morning drama. Mister liked reading about her hidden vulnerabilities and worries. Those were the kinds of details that made M's cyber personality vividly real. As much as Mister wanted to write M back, he took a pause before unleashing his realness on her.

For the rest of the day, M wondered if he got the e-mail. Since there were no real ways to tell if he had read it or not, she frustratingly waited. Minute by minute, her anxiousness grew. She was embarrassed that the network tech caught her in the middle of a tell-all e-mail. M knew she had to do something about those feelings of stupefaction. Her perplexities forced her to adapt and overcome without worrying about consequences. M knew what she had to do. And since the clock watchtower machine did not bind her to exact times anymore, M arrogantly walked past Miss BB's glaring stare fifteen minutes earlier than any other coworkers took lunch.

First stop was home then to the phone store. M wanted to see if Mister had written her back before heading off toward the closest mobile phone store to get a new smartphone. On the drive home, M decided she needed to get one of those new smartphones to keep up with him. Mister was high tech, and that meant M had to be high tech too. M flew in through the door amped up on excited energy to check her electronically mailed messages. She was so excited that she left her keys stuck in the front-door lock. Her torturous suspense grew intense while waiting for her computer to turn on and get online. Instead of waiting it out, she ran down the hallway to the kitchen and made a sandwich. It was the fastest ham-and-cheese sandwich M ever made and ate. She jogged back to the computer only to find an empty inbox. Not one e-mail at all. Nothing! Not even the usual junk mail. That shattered her fragile glass house into small bits and pieces of shard glass. She wondered where he was at and what he was doing that made her less important than she deserved to be. M knew he was fast to respond to all of her other messages, so why not this one? She wanted answers.

Where the fuck is he? What a jerk! How dare he forget about me! He comes into my life, turns it upside down, turns me on beyond belief, then does not respond! What an asshole! He is so frustrating! Ugh! I am going to give him a piece of my mind.

M turned her efforts to getting one of those twenty-first century must-haves—a new smartphone. She walked into the phone store empty-handed and walked out with a brand-new state-of-the-art smartphone in her hands. It was red in color with a big LCD screen. She purchased the new phone to keep up on all his mischievous ideas. On her way back into the office, she ripped the phone out of its new box and began to charge it up. She drove into the parking garage at ten minutes past 1:00 PM. It took her fifty-five minutes to check her e-mails and get a new phone, but at least M could proudly walk in through the glass doors with strong buzzing excitement. As she passed by Miss BB's desk, M's sassy smirk told BB to back off.

M's heart pounded just as if she ran a full mile at top sprinting speed when she had not. Mister had clever ways to work her excitement levels without doing much of anything except paying attention. His kind of intense attention was all new for M to have, and now she wanted more of it. At this point, she really did not care that he had a life outside of her; she needed to be his number-one priority. M thought that maybe telling him about her nervous breakdown wasn't such a good idea, especially since he had not written back. M went back to work with a heavy heart over Mister. It was his silence that kept her steeped in Mister's pornographic world. She had a hard time convincing herself of the obvious.

I know I only sent it to him three hours ago. Maybe he was busy with work, or something else. Relax, M. Just relax, girl. It only has been three hours. Chill out, M!

Loud sighs made everyone around her take notice. She kept rationalizing with her inner self that it had only been three hours just to make it through the rest of the day. Before M knew it, 4:00 PM screamed past in a blur. Her excited energy started back up, but then flatlined after she remembered it was a school night. Knowing that encouraged M to focus all her attention on getting her new phone working correctly. She discovered that it needed a little more setup than M was used to. She made a fast break to the restroom to find the only place in the building that lent privacy. She took her phone and instruction manual along with her to set it up. While M gave the porcelain a golden shower, she followed the phone activation procedures without deviation. The instructions said it should start receiving messages automatically in less than ten minutes. M impatiently waited it out.

Instead of Mister writing to M on his longer-than-normal lunch break, he reengaged S because he really did not know how to respond to M. M seriously left Mister speechless in more ways than one. As it was, Mister had mixed feelings between S and M, which is why he wanted to have them both. One thing Mister already knew was that he had to figure out S before doing anything else. He pulled up her last e-mail and reread it. He looked for things that might help him figure out S better. Then when he noticed one of her written statements about her desk. Baffled, he was. The "come over to my desk and cum on it" statement was exactly what D told Mister not to do days earlier.

Coincidence? Could it really be a coincidence that D told me the same thing, but with the don't*? That little bitch! Is D fucking with me? She had better not be S! I was typing up my personals ad when she walked in and interrupted me. But I was careful not to let her see. Wasn't I?*

With serious questions and doubt, Mister reread all of S's previous e-mails to see if there was any way that she could really be D. He found more than just that one similarity that made him really begin to think that S was D. He really did not know a whole lot about S, and that played strongly into his "S is D" theory. But then there was a bigger clue; S's profile was created on the same day that Mister's was made. Then there were the way-too-confident innuendoes that S wrote, as D loved the innuendoes.

Could S really be D? If anyone knew they could get away with saying some of the things that she did, it would be D. D knows me inside and out. But if she is pretending to be S, I am going to be pissed.

Even though they played lighthearted jokes on each other from time to time, this joke would be *fubar*.

Could D really have seen me making my personals ad? She did walk into my office two times while I was typing it out. I wonder.

He sighed in confusion with immense civil unrest.

He had to know for sure if D was S because he did not want to spend any more of his time talking to someone that was not ever going to give him what he wanted. If D hadn't given up her tangy berry love nectar already, she probably was not going to be doing it at all. What Mister needed was to be with a woman that would commit her entire body and sexual soul to him with every ounce of her being. He made up a plan to see if he could out her. If D really was S, his afternoon message to S had to provoke some sort of response to confirm or deny the possibility.

Sassy S,

How do you do? My morning has been nonstop work mixed with confusion. Confusion because I really thought that I saw you even though I have no idea what you look like. I was parked in this parking lot sitting in my car, minding my own business. Then someone pulled up and parked right beside me despite the parking lot being vacant. I saw this most incredible vision of a properly dressed woman get out of her car as if she was on her way to somewhere important. It was weird to feel what I felt when I saw her. I saw you in her. At least that's what I felt in the pit of my stomach. There was this incredible aura that surrounded this woman that made me think I was watching you. The entire thing was confusing. I do not know what to believe. Crazy, right?

She pulled up in a bright-red German-imported SUV, parked her car, and got out. An arrogance about her was evident in all her calculated movements. It was as if she owned the parking lot or the building or the entire city. Her arrogant attitude told me she was going into somewhere familiar. My instincts told me to pay attention, and so I did. I swear it was you that I saw. Was it? Was it really you? I could not be 100 percent sure, so I dismissed it as an impossibility, but in the back of my mind, I really think that this woman was you. What I do know is that I wanted to open the door and say hello. But since I was too caught up in watching her arrogant body movements, I could not do anything but admire her from afar. I now kick myself for not doing anything, but I cannot go back and change my zero response now.

I wish that I had said hi to her. It would have been in my sexy low-pitched suave voice that I would have spoken. I would have invited her out for an afternoon beverage or something like that. She would have said yes even if she were married just because she would have felt my passionate charm all over her body. I am that convincing when I want to be, and after minutes of hearing my persuasive charm, she would have accepted my invitation for coffee. My words of intrigue would have stoked the fires beneath her satin-and-lace panties, forever staining them with creamy wetness. This woman that I saw wore beige slacks and high heels that pushed her amazing ass higher up in the air so everyone around could admire its amazing perfection. She had a sassy bounce to her every step. I saw the most pronounced outline of a thong panty. Its sharp lines of intrigue stood out to my ogling eyes. I was glad she kept her briefcase on the passenger side front seat; otherwise, I would not have been

allowed to see the thong outline with such amazing clarity. She had no idea that I got to see the T
of it. Its ivory satin waistband was exposed when
she leaned into the car. Seeing its color and T-back
shape absolutely made my day. I even liked that
white scrunchie holding up her ponytail in such
an erotic yet professional way. Was it or was it not
you that I saw? You can tell Mister. It can be our
very own secret, but if you don't tell me, I might
have to show up at the same time tomorrow so I
can properly enjoy the view all over again.

Sweet daydreams,
Mister

He could not wait to send it off to her because if she were D,
the e-mail would force some sort of reaction. And if it was not D
pretending to be S, then S would get a glimpse into Mister's head
without even asking for it. He knew that if D were not S, he would
have a second secret admirer to keep entertained. No matter which
way Mister saw it, it kept bolstering his ego far above what it once
was two weeks ago, before the lucid wet dream.

He still could write M back, yet he needed to plan his next message very carefully; otherwise, he could very easily lose her attention
altogether. Mister gave up his attempts at seduction to put on his
cloak of sales invincibility. Excitedly frustrated, Mister drove off to
meet with his afternoon appointments. It was a three-appointment
afternoon, one after the next, with no time in between.

It had been over one hour since M supposedly activated her
phone and still nothing. That made her worry that she did something wrong setting it up. Even though she already liked her bright-
red-covered smartphone, she did not want it if it was not going to
let her get e-mails in real time. She could hardly handle the "hurry
up and wait" game. In her mind, the day went by as slow as falling
molasses.

Finally, 5:00 PM came. Time to stop work and start being a straight-A student again. Her usual plight over to school was like clockwork without any complications. M had plenty of time to make it across town so she could be in her seat by 6:00 PM. All the college boys would be highly disappointed tonight because she was not dressed to thrill. The other night was the exception. They all got lucky when she showed up in her pinstriped skirt and heels outfit. It made her feel good to see all the younger boys stare at her, giving her confidence a bigger boost than she expected. It was exactly what she needed.

Most of the time, M had a forty-five-minute window to spare before class started. She used that time to get a quick bite to eat or take a fast catnap. M liked the pizza joint just off campus, but she knew that it was a once-a-week treat due to her battle with carbohydrates. She spent her extra time trying to make her new smartphone work. M wanted to keep up on all of Mister's naughty ramblings of sin no matter what time of day they came. She double-checked the instructions to make sure she did it right. As usual, she missed reading the fine print. If she would have read the bottom of the page, under a side note, it explicitly said there would be an e-mailed confirmation sent to her e-mail address that she would have to respond to. What that meant was M was not going to see any of his e-mails until she got home and read the confirmation e-mail. She turned angry red; at the same time, her attitude of excitement changed into frustration. She wanted to know more than anything what Mister thought about her morning breakdown drama. M could not wait any longer, so she ditched out of class forty minutes earlier than she was supposed to leave.

M stormed through the front door like a hurricane in full force. She whirled right past her housemates and into her room. She did not know if Mister wrote her back yet or not, and she was not about to let her roommates keep her from him. She expected a response. M got out a group hello as she blurred past them. Her brute hurricane force faded into an excited torrent of torment while waiting for her slow computer to get into her e-mail account.

For those moments of wait, M's hopes were filled with self-generated expectations. Then when she looked at her inbox, her hope was obliterated. The sole e-mail in her inbox was the confirmation e-mail to activate her new phone. No messages from Mister made M feel empty inside with nothing to look forward to. Yet again Mister was at the helm of her torture. It was hard for M to accept she was losing control, but that was exactly what was happening. M was emotionally tied up in knots, not knowing what Mister thought. To regain her lost composure and his lost attention, she wrote him a quick good-night note. Nothing spectacular, just ordinary. "Sweet dreams, Mister! Xoxoxo, M."

The rest of Mister's afternoon and night went as smooth as butter. He made two more sales, and one strong possibility remained on the table. Mister's emotional state had been in total chaos ever since his lucid dream was dreamed up a week ago. His newly rekindled friendship with D and making new friends with S and M had Mister squirming in his pants.

He drove home, walked in the front door, let Rocket in, and said hello to Alex.

"What's up, A? Do you know how the Yankees did?"

"They won again. Three games in a row. But now they go to Boston. You know that saga."

"Fuck the Red Sox. They are going to lose to the Yankee blue and white."

"I know, huh! How is that girl you have been seeing?"

"It is going slow, Mister. Slower than I would like. She is a good girl though, and I like that about her."

"I know you like that. I am that way too. Well, sort of, kind of. I like the innocent girl-next-door mentality, but I also like her to be a strong tease. The kind of woman that knows when to take me in her hand and make me beg."

"I would be happy just to find a good woman with a good heart that wants to be with me. But it seems that they are all taken by men that don't deserve and appreciate what they have. It is terribly sad."

He and Alex talked for several minutes more about the right woman before Mister went back to his room with rocket following.

He felt bad that he did not write M back sooner, but his day was stacked with appointments and emotional conflicts that monopolized his time. Mister knew she deserved to hear back from him at once, especially with the care and attention she put into her last e-mail, but sleep won out. Before he could write to M, Mister fell asleep lying facedown on the bed with Rocket by his side. Not even an act of God could disturb his somnia this cold spring night.

CHAPTER 19

• • • • • • • • ● ● • • • • • •

Mister's Enigma

The sound of Mister's alarm going off shockingly woke him up from a comatose state of dreamland delight. He rolled over and shut down the nasty-sounding alarm as fast as he could. He would rather lie in bed dreaming of S, M, and D than get up and go anywhere. Unfortunately, he had a full day of sales possibilities beckoning his attention that would not allow him to stay in bed any longer. Mister was mainly motivated by success, which kept him moving forward. He knew that one day he would be free of the torment, and finally, that day had come. Mister wanted to ride the success for all that it was worth.

Whenever Mister woke up, so did Rocket. That was a given. The doggie door was always open so that Rocket could go outside whenever he wanted. Even though he treated Rocket like his only child, he was still a dog. Rocket had his own space on the side of the house with his very own temperature-controlled doghouse to keep him protected from the outside elements while Mister was out working hard for his steak bones. This morning was no different. After Mister let Rocket outside, he walked down the hallway to get some refrigerated coffee. He microwaved it, then poured it into his richly dressed silver-accented travel mug and took it back with him to the bathroom to sip on. Mister projected success in everything he did. His sharply dressed appearance showed off his non-ordinary sales success; he was the company's senior sales representative, only sharing responsibilities with D. He stripped off his boxers and cotton T-shirt, trading them in for a naked dance in the steamy hot shower of melodic melodies. As the man named Mister stepped into the shower a dirty boy and walked out a clean man, he resumed his dominant role as the company's leading sales representative with commanding authority.

Unintentionally, Mister found himself thinking solely about M. And with the hot shower water cascading over his body, steamy images of M filled up his head. Mister could not explain his feelings for her just yet, but he knew that they were more than what he expected to have for a woman that he had not yet met. It could be her feistiness, or maybe it was her innocence that left him wanting more. Whatever it was, he was intrigued. Not even his ex-fiancée could ever make him feel that emotionally alive like M made him feel. His shower-time feelings for M were not made of lust more than they came from plausible victory. He liked a challenge, and M was that.

As the dimly lit bathroom became brighter and lighter with morning maturity, the foggy steam remained. Mister opened the glass door, grabbed the towel off the nearby brass J-hook, and towel-dried himself off while standing erect behind the glass shower walls. Tying the towel around his waist, he strutted into the closet and picked out an outfit to wear. Mister's routine schedule usually took thirty-five minutes flat from rolling out of bed to walking out of the house. And once again, he was right on the mark. With travel mug in hand, he pushed his way out the front door and right into the Humvee. He started it up, put it in gear, and pulled around the horseshoe-shaped driveway. Before he got completely out of the driveway, the ringing phone startled him. Mister never missed a call as he was always tethered to the highways and byways of the world in some fashion or another. He snickered in a devious manner after he saw it was M but continued to pull out into oncoming traffic to keep ahead of his schedule.

Mister,

Where did you go? Did I scare you away? I hope not. That is not my intention. If you are working a ton, I can understand that. But can you blame me for wondering where you went? Okay, vulnerability time; I have a huge crush on you. I do not know how or why it happened so fast, but this is different for sure.

    You can answer me if you want, or not, but I have questions that I want answers to. I want to know more about the man that calls himself Mister. I have never met a man before with such a unique name. It is kind of sexy. When I hear the name Mister, I think of a man covered up in a dark cloak to conceal his identity. He has a charming confidence that is exemplified in every action he makes. Strong character depth tends to excite others around him, yet his deep personality and strong sexual desire is simply concealed. That is what I know so far. How close am I to being right? Even though I know all of that, I still want to know more. Believe me when I say that I want to know. Enlighten, Mister. Please let me into your blacked-out world of erotic genius.

    Why did you pick me out of the thousands of girls on the website? What are you wanting out of this? Am I the only one you are talking to? How did you get this incredible with words? Those are the kinds of questions I want answers to. If you answer them, I will strongly consider tossing you my soaking-wet thong to see what kind of reaction this girl can get.

M

Mister found himself smack dab in the middle of a moral dilemma over S, M, and D. He was confused about which one to pick. Not to mention his moralistic past kept interjecting itself into his new guiltless future. The one thing Mister knew was his lust-filled ideas kept clogging up his thought process.

Should I tell her my truths or delicately skirt around them? What will she think of me if I let her into my world? Could she handle it? What will I do if she can't?

Luckily, Mister had extra time to think about his near future while driving to his first sales call of the day. Thoughts about the three ladies melted his mind into mush, and right then, Mister knew that his next moves had to be meticulously right. He got along with each of them equally well, but M was his favorite. Mister loved giving his attention away but needed it reciprocated. His past girlfriends never gave him the required reciprocation he demanded, hence his strong attraction towards M. He liked that she kept up his intensity in her responses, which kept him strongly turned on.

Mister made it to his first appointment with less than ten minutes to spare. He always used those pre-appointment minutes to get into character, trading in loose worldly thoughts for strict pompous business mojo.

Shortly after he dreamed up the lucid wet dream, Mister walked into an open window of confidence and success. His closing percentages for the month were 90 percent favorable. With every signed contract, Mister's pocketbook grew. Not only was he closing nine out of every ten appointments, he also got half of those to buy the extended service agreements, including the one he just signed and sold. Mister's passion and integrity bled out of him in every appointment he ran. That kind of intensity earned him long lunches, like the one he was about to take. He walked across the busy street to the nearby park and headed to the wooden-planked bridge to watch the koi fish swimming by while planning his next moves. With the sun straight up in the sky warming everything in sight, sounds of koi splashing around mesmerized Mister calm. As he watched people walk, jog, and bike ride by, Mister was hypnotized into an open-eyed daydream.

Up until now, Mister had only been an enigma to M, but now that she demanded to know more, he did not know what to say. He did not know if M caught onto the truths, he already foretold in previous e-mailed messages or not, but he hoped she did. Mister did not tell any fallacies of falling in love, nor did he say he was prince charming there to sweep her off her feet. Rather he told M of finding a well-deserving woman to go on a long-lasting sexual journey with him. A quest so hot and so great that it would deeply connect them together forever. Before the dream, he did not think that could be possible, but now he knew it was more than plausible. He needed to find his sexual soul mate for survival. He did not know when or where she would be found, but he had no other choice but to look. He strictly wanted something unique, something undefined, yet well defined in its own way. As he stood on top of the bridge, he recalled being set free from all his tormented past. Mister also remembered making that solemn promise to himself and to the world that he would never be tormented like that again. He loved the new Mister so much more than the old one. His lost confidence was back. It showed in everything he now did. It was that unlimited confidence that made this the right time to find her, his Miss.

A sudden burst of clarity came to Mister, and in that instant, he knew that he needed to write M back. He stopped standing on the well-traveled bridge and walked over to the closest available park bench. The table that he walked to held memories for him and D. They had several mentoring meetings at that table. If that table could talk, it would tell stories of secret kissing, hot word sharing, a lot of what-if scenarios, and encouragement. The table was one hundred yards off to the right of the dirt bike path, sitting under a tall oak tree. There was lots of brushy shrubbery that secluded it from the kids' playground. As Mister took a seat at the partially shaded bench, he wrote M back something truthfully vulnerable.

M,

You caught me off guard with that last e-mail full of questions. I was getting lost in our flirty e-mails of naughty fantasy and fun, but then when reality hit me square in the face, I did not know how to respond. That is the honest-to-God truth. So forgive me. Even though I am still recovering from the shock and awe of your campaign, I wanted to answer most of your questions while keeping somewhat of a mysterious cloak loosely wrapped around me for my protection. I will do my best to keep you intrigued, if you can use your imagination to imagine the rest. For better or worse, that is me.

Humbly, I consider myself to have above-average intelligence. But like everyone else, I have insecurities, so much so that I let myself be a victim to my own life tragedies. I have lived for decades with self-inflicted torment and ridicule beyond my better judgment. I felt powerless over things that happened to me. I let them get me down, and then I stopped them from happening to me by putting myself in my own self-built jail. That was until I dreamed up an interesting déjà-vu-like lucid wet dream weeks ago. And now I am a changed man. I am not holding myself hostage anymore. I am emotionally free to do whatever I want. Though I will always be emotionally sensitive. I wear my emotions on my sleeves, and sometimes that's a bad thing to wear, but that is who I am. To be completely honest with you about my personals ad, the woman I am looking for will want and need to captivate my attention just as much as I will keep hers. I just want to say that I am not looking for a wife. Of course, if the perfect woman comes along, I won't deny myself seeing her dressed in white. You shouldn't judge me solely on my ad. That is just a small part of who I am. I am more complex than that. My dream set me free from a lot of my past darkness that once plagued my soul, and for that, I am grateful for it happening. If it were not for my lucid dream weeks ago, we would not have ever crossed paths. That much I know.

It was the way you expressed your fears and wants and needs in your personals ad that caught my attention more than anything else. It wasn't the usual bullshit that everyone shoveled in their profiles. It read just as an unfolding story that has yet to be completed. Being that you wrote it in the third-party perspective turned me on even more. It was the overall feeling that you made me get. It showed me your creativity, and that's exactly what I want in a woman. You earned my attention when you showed me that you are someone that is not afraid to share herself with the world while coveting so much. It is completely refreshing to know that a woman like you exists. The way you let me see deep inside of you without really letting me see in. I like it!

For the first few sentences of your ad, I got this feeling that your entire soul rested in my hands. To be honest, it made me hard with envy. I know that you probably did not want anyone to read between the lines, but I saw what you wanted me to see. It was right after I read your ad that I knew I had to respond. Right from the get-go, I knew that I had to write you something extra special to grab you out of your world and bring you into mine. I can only assume that you are straddling both of our worlds now. That's when I had to figure out a way to keep such a passionate woman intrigued, and then I came up with my second e-mail. That is when I decided to write you a mysterious fantasy instead of the usual get-to-know-me dossier. It made me feel sexually erotic to write you what I did. It turned me on then, and it still turns me on now. I am more sensitive to things that other guys wouldn't be as sensitive to. If I have learned anything, it is that my sensitivity and niceness usually brings people closer to me, but then it also pushes them away later on too. I have no idea why most women are turned on by the bad boys more than the good guys. In my opinion, nice guys finish last. It is not something that I want to believe, but it is the inevitable truth. The bad guys ruin good girls. It's not fair. I can only imagine it has something to do with the testosterone and estrogen dance of attraction, but it is still wrong.

So, M, I can confidently say that you're helping me be emotionally free, and for that, I can only say thank you. I hope we can keep each other entertained for a long while. What do you think?

Mister

Mister finished his Q&A session while sitting on the park bench under the brilliant blue sky. Soft wind blowing and kids playing in the background made Mister contemplate sending it to her. The things he wrote were not the usual boring ones, rather stuff that could make or break a friendship. He reread it a few times to make sure that was what he wanted to write, for he knew that once it was sent it could not be taken back. It was a nearby fire engine's ear-piercing siren that broke his concentration, reminding him about his two-o'clock. He made the final decision to send it, then sped down the road like his hair was on fire. His short drive over to his two-o'clock allowed Mister to vividly think back through past relationships and remember his shortcomings. His torment was gone, yet it made a guest appearance to remind him of things that once were. He got to his next appointment and ran it like the leading salesman he was.

M's day passed slower than she wanted it to. She wanted life stagnation to change, yet she could not let go of the comfortable rut she was stuck in. Mister was someone that could very easily cave it in with a sledgehammer. M unknowingly gave him the opportunity to do it when she bought her fancy new smartphone. She liked his naughtiness and found it imperative to keep up with it in real time. Her usual office hustle and bustle was replaced with a calm before the storm due to an off-site executive board meeting. Then in mid-thought of goal planning, sounds of her vibrating phone buzzing against her hard desk startled her excitement back to life. New messages arrived; two junk spam messages and an e-mail from Mister. She giggled, then gave herself an imaginary pat on the back for buying the new phone when she did.

M contemplated reading it while she sat in her cubicle area. She imagined all kinds of things about his e-mail that equated to electronically charged protons excitedly dancing out of control. M expected Mister to ignore her questions, but when she saw answers to them, she smiled big time.

M's desire to have Mister grew exponentially while reading more about who he was. She could not hide the giddy smirk on her blushing face, and for the fourth day in a row, she was sexually hot and wet because of him. She felt everything good, yet she could not believe it. Mister's addictive attention grew so strong too fast, it made her question everything. She wanted to see if he was truly real or not and the only effective way to measure that was silence. She did not know how he would react to silent treatment, but it was something she needed to find out for herself.

CHAPTER 20

Silent Treatment

M needed to test her feelings for Mister without being as obvious as a "meet me" e-mail. She did not know how he would truly react to the silent treatment, but she took the risk and went for it. A few days to see if she could get him out of her mind was in order. While giving him the silent treatment, she focused on work, school, and everything she had been doing before Mister happened. M wanted to go further than just entry-level management, so she studied the inner workings of the company while trying to complete her end of the month reports due in a few days. Work and school kept her mind partially off Mister. Even though she was not in contact with him, she thought about his lingering ideas more than ever. He was intense, and she liked that. But M did not want or need any more disappointment. The second day of silent treatment was M's most challenging. Kodi heard it in M's voice and saw it in her actions. Kodi thought that a nice girls' night out to dinner might help M.

"M, I see your mind is somewhere else. It has been like that for a few days now. Did he already break your heart? Do you want to have dinner and talk about it with me tonight?"

"No, Kodi, he did not break my heart. I am giving him the silent treatment. And yes, let's do dinner. I am trying not to think about him right now."

Kodi did not ask any questions, but she walked off with naughty intentions beginning to formulate in her head. She was not about to let Mister have M without a fight. There was a part of Kodi that wanted M to be hers.

As it ticktocked past 5:00 PM, they were both already out in the parking garage getting into M's car. A steakhouse six blocks down the street was where they went. On the drive over, Kodi kept trying to get information out of M about her silent treatment.

"So why are you giving him the silent treatment? Did he say something wrong to piss you off?"

"No, Kodi, it was nothing like that. It's me. I want to see if I could stop thinking about him and sort out my true feelings. And no, he has not asked me out on a date yet, but I want to be prepared to answer him when he does. Does that make sense?"

Just as M parked in the steakhouse parking lot, she stopped talking and looked over at Kodi with a naughty smirk that spelled everything out for Kodi. Before they stepped out of the car, Kodi wanted to confirm her suspicions.

"I see! You like him a lot, don't you? M, you better not let him break your heart. Remember last time? Months of crying and trying to guess what you did wrong. You can't put out on the first date either, or I will kill you. I swear!"

They were greeted by a familiar-faced hostess. She laughed and flirted with them before sitting them down. Kodi frequented the steakhouse more than M did only because she had friends that worked there. On their way over to the table, the girls turned many heads at the bar as they were led passed the bar to a table off to the left side. Kodi made it her favorite table to sit at; requesting that spot was a given. It had bench seats and a perfect view of the entire bar scene. They ordered up a bottle of red wine and an appetizer dish. A cute buxom waitress delivered their bottle of wine and glasses to them with a first-class smile. Once again, Kodi took the liberty to flirt with the waitress while M watched. Kodi got away with saying soft-core sexual innuendoes designed to get everyone's attention at the table, especially M's. Kodi wanted to make M jealous, but M was not thinking about Kodi like that. As the waitress poured chilled red wine into their empty wine glasses, Kodi kept M blushing with more of her bold flirtations.

"I like your pants. Umm, I like the bra too. Where did you get it from? I like that lace color. Is that a front-clasping one? I have been looking for those lately. I like how easy they come off."

Kodi sassy-giggled to get a rise out of M.

"I ordered it off the internet. It came from France. They have a ton of cute things on their website. You should check it out. But you better not show up here wearing the same outfits as I am. Because if you do, I will take you in the back and spank your ass hard with a ruler."

The waitress topped off the girls' glasses, smiled, then swayed her hips away. Kodi watched the waitress walk away, and M watched Kodi ogle at her thick bottom.

"Kodi, I thought I was your one and only girl crush?"

The window was open, and Kodi did not hesitate to climb in headfirst.

"You know, M, I would rather have you all to myself. Why do you keep turning me down and putting me off? Why?"

Kodi smiled, and M blushed. Their schoolgirl giggles were evidently flirtatious as they sipped on wine like future lovers might. In the forefront of Kodi's mind was getting M to make out with her. Kodi wanted to make a more-direct pass at M, but Kodi felt it was not the right time to make any serious moves just yet. That did not stop Kodi from exercising her God-given flirtatiousness while impatiently waiting for the alcoholic wine buzz to get to M.

"I have never really kissed a girl before, Kodi. Sure, we kissed at the bars on a few occasions just to tease the boys, but those were my first girl kisses. Ever! At first, I was like, 'Oh my god,' but then I figured you were just trying to be a slutty tease, so I went along with it. To be honest, the kisses were kinda sexy. They might have even made me really wet too. Even though I liked the kisses, I never really thought about letting it go any further. Then when you told me about your girl-on-girl experiences, I did not know how to be. But I admit it intrigues me, though it never goes further than wonder."

"Really, M?"

"Yes, really, Kodi. I have never fooled around with another woman, except for kissing you. Don't hate me."

"How could I hate you, M. You are adorable. Look what you did to me, M. I am extremely turned on and wet. No fair! I want to kiss you now. What do you think about that?"

M made a weird funny face while crisscrossing her eyes and legs to disarm the moment. Kodi gave it her best shot at escalating the sexual tension much further than just talk.

"I have an idea, M! How about we take the next bottle of wine back to my house, strip down to our underwear, and make out? I won't tell anyone. I swear."

"Kodi, stop that! You are such a tease. You can't tease me any more like that tonight. Please?"

Kodi backed down on her bedding M, at least for the night, but Kodi kept flirting with M while consuming the rest of the red wine and cheese sticks. M nudged their time over before Kodi could physically move closer than she ready for. M drove Kodi back to her car so they could go home separately. Of course, Kodi tried one last time to get a good-night kiss. This time, M let Kodi kiss her on the lips, but she purposely withheld the tongue for good reason.

"I had a really fucking good time, M. But I will go home without you. Unless . . ."

M was turned on by the entire night. She was just as horny as Kodi was, but she was not about to let her know that.

"Kodi!"

M never answered Kodi's direct line of questioning, and Kodi took that as a positive possibility.

M's next two days went by fast as lightning. Kodi kept trying to get M's attention, but M kept skirting around the situation. There was a part of her that wanted to taste Kodi's swollen mound of goodness, but she wanted Mister more. She redirected her pent-up energies, substituting them with work. Every lonely morning of the silent treatment, M woke up and satisfied her quest for balance with guilt-less morning-time orgasms with Mr. Showerhead. She went through her morning rituals just like before, pre-Mister. She wanted him to be out of her mind, but that did not happen. She missed his constant intensity, yet she was not about to surrender just yet. Every next morning while primping in front of the bathroom mirror, M fantasized about what Mister would look like in her bed, and in the shower, and between her legs.

I want his cologne to linger in my nose, and every breath I take, I want his scent to make me quiver. I want him to live inside of me. I want him to see all that I see and feel all that I feel.

Instead of being weak and surrendering, she stayed strong. M tried to replace him with work and school. Though it only halfway worked. Between getting adjusted to her new manager role and fending off Kodi's sexual advances, time passed by faster than slow.

For the lack of having a better epicenter, Mister concentrated all his efforts on selling the shit out of everything his company offered. Recent sales performance and elevated confidence levels made his attempts successful. He made sale after sale, shooting his average up to 900 percent. All but one appointment was sold, and every sale included the extended warranty. The extended warranty add-ons were where Mister made his high bonuses. He always outperformed D in that department. After all, he was the company's warranty king. D did not mind letting him keep that title all to himself while she outsold him.

Going on the second day of silence was the hardest for Mister to deal with. He needed an emotional pick-me-up from second-guessing what he did wrong to M. He felt alone and rejected without M being there to mind-fuck. But when he turned his interests back to D, teasing her for that instant ego boost, made all the difference in his world. Flirting with D and stoking fire under S was on his agenda. But still, moments of pre–lucid wet dream vividly flashed across his melancholy psyche with diminishing accuracy.

That second-day afternoon, Mister walked into D's office and pushed almost all her sexually repressed buttons over a ten-minute visit. He flirted with her intensely and teased her wet. He complimented her and her outfit and new hairdo. He made D hot again. He looked at her with charm in his hazel eyes, and that spoke too directly to D's every last need. He ogled her the way he used to. D purposely fueled his ogling curiosity with her legs-parted-open show, an up-the-skirt view that brought back memories of their first encounter. Mister left D's office with a hard-on and a smile so big that it was his new North Star.

Mister's confidence levels excelled even more while M gave him the silent treatment. A little part of Mister was scared that she would not ever write back, but bigger parts of him hoped she would. Yet still he let her have space, but inside, he was dying a slow death.

While Mister waited for M to write back, he continued to write S and give lavish attention to D at work. He gave S the attention he was giving M. He felt that S could be some sort of seductress. He liked her boldness and innuendoes; they were strong and to the point but still had his doubts.

After he saw D that morning, his suspicions of D being S was stronger than ever before. There were things that S said that were similar to things D would say. S was flirtatious just like D was, and he felt that she was too comfortable and confident not to somehow know him more than she led on. If Mister was presented with the mathematical problem to define Q in the problem $S + Q$, his best guessed answer would have equaled D. In fact, in a recent e-mail, S explicitly told him not to cum on her desk. He was not 100 percent sure that D was S, but he was more than determined to find out.

Right after Mister saw D walk past his office, he pulled out his cellphone and wrote S to instigate a reaction.

S,

I am thinking about you more than ever. Where did you go? Did I hit a nerve? Maybe I guessed, right? Do we already know each other? I cannot handle not knowing what you are thinking. Reveal yourself to me. Please? Tell me something so that I do not keep wondering. But if we do not know each other, then show me a picture. Please? I will do almost anything you want, if only you would just show me your picture. I will not judge you just on your looks. I swear, that is not me at all. Show me your picture, please, or lose me forever!

If you promise me that you will not let me get away without revealing yourself to me, I promise not to cum on your desk. Instead, I would cum all over your fucking face and in your mouth and down your throat and make you swallow it. Swallow it or share it with me. You choose. I can handle your innuendoes if you can handle mine. I wish that you could lie next to me. That would simply be amazing. Hmm, I wonder, could we quiver, and would we come together? Hmm . . .

Mister

Mister did not know how S would take his challenging e-mail, but he hoped to learn who S was. M purposely withheld herself from Mister's equations hoping that every day that she was silent, he would be lost in a hazy fog of disbelief, as she would be too. But the thick fog around Mister kept him sedated enough to outlast her silent treatment. The fourth day of the silent treatment was almost done and over with, and M could not handle his loss anymore. She craved his attention badly, but somehow, M knew that Mister would appreciate her deliberate silence. He once admitted to her that he liked to be teased exactly like that.

While sitting in her room all alone at seventeen minutes past 10:00 PM, she decided to put an end to the silence.

CHAPTER 21

Broken Silence

Mister,

I tried to break free from your seductive grip, but I could not do it. I made myself mad at you for no good reason. It was nothing that you did more than it was my own inability to get you out of my head. I wanted you to disappear. But dammit, you did not, and now the only thing I can do is give you a chance. I know, I know, it took you a lot of coaxing, but here I am. Woo-hoo! Just now, I had an epiphany that makes me want to toss you the key to my chastity belt. There is only one key in existence, so you cannot lose it. And for sure, you can't use it to break my heart. Those are the only two rules that come with taking possession of the key. For now, I will keep possession of it until you come and take it from me. Right now, though, you need to help me write my second attempt at fantasy telling, for I want to keep being Mister's naughty indulgence.

Here on planet Earth, there exists an innocent, gorgeous brunette with sweeping dramatic curves that out-dramatize Lombard Street. She was sensually hot yet too shy to ever let anyone see that part of her personality. Though she wanted to be naughtier than shy, no one ever showed her how to let out that kind of statement. She had all the makings of being a headlining star in someone's lucid wet dream come true.

There also exists a risqué debonair gentleman that takes with him every bland word in the *Webster's Dictionary* everywhere he goes. He changes their blandness into sweet erotic seduction with every word he speaks. He has looked everywhere for his innocent sex starlet, but unsuccessful in finding her.

Then one day, miraculous events brought them together. Their meeting was by chance, yet fate was the only catalyst. Miss Brunette contemplated asking the Mister Risqué Gentleman to dinner, but her contemplations stopped short of going through with it. Miss Innocent Brunette clung to some of her old-fashioned values, but they never impeded her ability to be a hard-prick tease. On more than one occasion since his risquéness knocked on her white-painted front door, she has wondered what it would be like to be Mister's Miss.

Miss Innocent Brunette hesitated moving forward due to his fast insertion into her life. She felt like it was her responsibility to slow it down and verify their validity, opting to give him the silent treatment. She did it for her own reasons. Then when she could not take her own kind of torture anymore, she ended it. She used the only form of communication that they had established to communicate to him exactly what she wanted. She knew that she had to say something profoundly great to accurately convey her feelings without fear. She chose to sink herself into her own version of Mister's intense hedonistic play land. Her breaths were slow and deep, and her eyes were closed when she blindly stumbled into a place she had never been before.

The room was lukewarm, but internally, she was stuck in a steamy sauna set on high. As the temperature dropped below sixty-five degrees, her long-sleeved pajamas kept her warm. She fell asleep with sizzling-hot wordplay of Mister's banging around her thoughts. Happy smiles of joy came and went as she deeply fell to sleep. Miss Innocent Brunette slept through the night being herself but awoke being Mister's Miss.

Positive trembling energy flowed out of her while chameleonizing into Mister's Miss. Mister was her new addiction. His aftereffects were stronger than the most potent narcotic in existence. She was intoxicated and lost in all time and space, not having one fucking clue as to what day it was. What she did care about was her feelings about Mr. Risquéness. She wants to tell him all her secrets, yet she digressed.

She sat on the edge of her bed, staring out of the close-by window, thinking about this man named Mister. She virtually sees him standing outside of her bedroom window even though he is not. She subconsciously feels his strong omnipresence pressing against her erect nipples even though they had not touched. Mister's Miss opens the window to see what it is that he wants. Right away, his sexy voice and light-scented cologne stimulate her hot pussy wet. He sees his vivacious brunette trying to hide her giddiness while flashing her the biggest smile he has ever had. His gleaming smiles immediately give her goose bumps inside and out. She feels everything he sees. He sees everything she feels. He knows her every thought before she can think it up. No matter how mundane or sultry they are, all her thoughts are about him. He reads her empty pages like a well-written novel. She hypothetically thinks up things she wants to say to him.

"I need you to come and help me do something naughty to myself. I have this strong pent-up excitement that I want to share with you, for I want to repay you in spades for making me engorged with a desire I have yet to feel. Thank you, Mister, for wanting me. I admit I blush every time I think about the pleasure you could give me. I owe you more than I can give, but dammit, I do not know how to hand it over to you. Help me surrender because I cannot get by with the norm anymore. Where I would usually be content with one before-work orgasm, I now crave more. I would have you before and after my morning showers every day if you would let me."

Miss Innocent Brunette purposely erased her old fantasies and replaced them with new imaginary ones of Mister slowly pushing in and pulling out of her delicate lady parts. The visions that she sees of her and Mister are so vividly real that she is mystically connected.

"I smell your smell and taste your taste just as if you had orgasmed in my mouth. Those are my new fantasies that I now think up while I selfishly touch myself."

Miss Innocent Brunette does not know if she deserves to be Mister's Miss, but she wanted to find out. Every emotion is more powerful than the last she felt for him. It was only after silly boy Mister penetrated her mind on multilayered platforms that she did not want to ever be the girl next door that hides inside anymore. Where she once let all the neighborhood boys spy on her through the open window for cheap thrills, she now needed to be the one that was thrilled. Her life used to be daunting, and now it is titillating. She did not know that kind of change was needed, but now that she let Mister corrupt her innocence, she realized how much she needed his kind of change.

"Mister, you make me feel like I am off in someone else's fantasy looking in. No matter if you are across town or across the world, every second that passes I can feel your throbbing cock deep inside of me. The images you paint for me make me shiver up and quiver down with every stroke of your soiled paintbrush on my pristine canvas. Everywhere I turn, there you are. You pay attention to me. I like that, and I want more."

Miss Innocent Brunette was smart enough to know that their kind of connection they are making is a once-in-a-lifetime event, and she was not about to fuck it up. Mister's Miss is convinced that wherever he is at now, he can taste her tang on his palpable flavor palate.

"I know you can taste me, Mister! I just know you can. How do I taste? How do I smell? Answer me, Mister! Please?"

Now it is your turn to help me finish off my fantasy, of course, in your own words. Tell me and show me what I am missing. The good girl in me cannot help but think you are too good to be true. It's natural for any woman to feel this way about a man like you. Is it not? To me, you are a gentleman that feels as sexy as a slight breeze on a midsummer's night. But maybe you want to be free and not be had by another. Whatever you do, Mister, take me with you. Drive me somewhere. Take me anywhere, but don't leave me here on this whatchamacallit computer thingy. Take me offline. Make me blush and make me hot. Whatever you do, make me come so hard that I get lightheaded. Please, Mister! Please! Right now, this very second, I choose to give you the only key to my well-guarded chastity belt. Come and take it! I dare you, Mister. Come and get it from me. Take the tarnished metal key off me because I am under your spell.

M

M looked over at the bedside alarm clock then sighed when she learned that she was right on time. Before losing all her strong morning courage, she smiled, giggled, and sent off the e-mail to him. She closed her laptop and went into the kitchen to get coffee. She took the hot coffee with her back to the bathroom, then stripped off her pajamas and walked into the steamy shower with spectacular thoughts of everything good. M's morning-time orgasm with Mr. Showerhead was helped by Mister's pornographic words of encouragement. His words and her fantasies caused a deep river of strong currents that kept washing over her entire existence.

All morning, M had wondered if Mister read her seducible, incomplete charms or not. She wanted him to be erect no matter where he was at. She felt she deserved to know if he was.

It just ticked fifteen minutes past seven, and Mister was still asleep. He purposely set the alarm to go off at 8:00 AM since his first appointment was at 10:00 AM. Originally, he planned to go into the office specifically to get answers from D, but now that Mister was woken by an overzealous phone making noise, he felt an urgency to see. When he saw that it was a message was from M, he wasted no time to read it. From the confines of his cozy warm bed, blurry eyes, and all, Mister read her concoction of erotica. What M wrote caught Mister off guard more than it did anything else. His sexual urges came, yet Mister let his semi-erect cock go untouched as he fell back to sleep.

Twenty-eight minutes later, his alarm went off. With extra sleep, Mister sprung out of bed with jubilant spry. His shower was spectacular even though he was not naughty. He dressed and walked out the front door in his usual thirty-five-minute-flat routine.

While pondering what his next ramblings to M should be about, he gloated out the front door and drove into work. M's ego-stroking techniques made Mister completely forget about all his past torment, replacing it with feelings of confidence and joy that he deserved to experience.

"I do not want to push her away, but I also don't want to make her fall in love with me either. What can I write to keep her straddling the border of love and lust?"

Mister needed depth. He wanted her everything, and if he could not have everything, it would not work.

M kept busy with work, but still her panties stayed wet over Mister's naughty intentions. It was only three hours ago that M e-mailed Mister, yet she had expected to hear back from him before now. She just poured her body and soul out to him and nothing. Not even so much as a "I got your e-mail, and I will write more later" or a "Wow," but nothing was unacceptable. His absence was making her fucking nuts. She needed to hear something from him before she physically vaporized into the atmosphere. Her feelings for him were anything but ordinary, try extraordinary. At this point, M was hot on Mister's trail. She wanted him inside of her at all costs, but she did not know where he was at.

Mister was clueless to M's growing addiction for him, but maybe that was a good thing.

"What a dick he is. That fucking asshole! Fucker!"

M's oversexed impatience was taken out on her friends and coworkers alike. M even struck out at Kodi, but Kodi snapped back at her "Stop being so bitchy." M really did not mean to be snappy, but when she let herself get that emotionally involved, fear and rejection began settling in. Her frustrations turned to torment, which extended out her razor-sharp claws of protection.

"Did I say something to turn him off? Maybe he had to work, but the least he could have done was say something, anything."

Right after she bit off Kodi's head, M recognized herself losing control. So she put Mister out of her mind by taking a brisk walk around the office building to regain composure. With every footstep she took, negative energy was released and positivity helped to replenish her focus where it needed to be, work. Twelve of her fifteen-minute break was consumed with walking out the negativity. The walk worked. M got back to work a little bit out of breath and a lot bit calmer. She logged back into the work server and went right to work. She concentrated on getting more familiar with her new management role.

Not even one hour later, M's phone radically vibrated against her ticklish pelvic bone. Even though it was during work hours, M had high expectations that the interruption would be from Mister. She did not even look at who the e-mail was from before she ripped it off the hip-clip and began reading it.

"Ahh, man! Shit! What the hell!"

More bullshit junk mail was what she found.

"I do not need a fucking flexible garden hose right now. I need Mister! Dammit!"

M almost let her emotions get the best of her when she gripped the phone tight and went to throw it against the cubicle divider. But in mid-throw, she kept holding onto it, she just could not let her expensively new smartphone go. M needed Mister's undivided attention more than she needed a fucking flexible hose.

"Where the hell is that man?"

CHAPTER 22

• • • • • • • • ● • • • • • •

Chastity

Mister finished his second morning appointment and broke for an early lunch. He decided on the usual sandwich shop, ordering up a ham-and-cheese meal to go. He took it with him to his favorite shaded tree parking lot spot across the way. On that day, Mister did not have a lot of time to think up more naughty stories, so instead, he tried his best to conjure up more erotic convictions to tell M all about.

As Mister sat in the Humvee parked on the edge of suburbia and Main Street, he turned down the stereo volume on some very deep words of a powerful seventies song to match the melodic melodies with the outside volume of the close-by river to get in the mood. He let the melodic tranquility serenade him into writing M something she could not forget.

> M,
>
> Okay, so right now you have me frozen in thought. Serious! I wanted to write you back right after I read your e-mail, but I fell back asleep. Then I had to be at work to run two back to back sales meetings. And now I am taking an early lunch. So I really did not have any time to write you

back until just now. Sorry if you thought that I forgot about you; that is not the case at all.

Ever since I had my lucid wet dream weeks ago, my luck has changed for the better. For one, we connected. Secondly, my work sales have doubled, and thirdly, I have been selling the elusive extended warranty more than ever before. I have intentions of asking you out on a date sometime soon, but work success means a lot to me. I am enthralled with our back-and-forth banter more than you know, especially the last one you sent me. All that I can say is, "Wow." I cannot do much more commenting than that, at least not right now. You see, I need to be in that kind of creative mood to finish your fantasy off. But know, I will finish what you started. The way you wrote it makes me excited to know you. You are my new late-night inspiration. I wake up in the middle of the night completely hard with nothing else but sweet visions of you in my head. Like a naive young man, my hand finds the opening in my boxers and loosely constricts itself around my fully erect cock. It is hard and full of life, so much so I cannot resist playing with it until it squirts warm lava everywhere. I make my own wet dream come true in the middle of the night. That is what I have become good at. Now that I made myself just as vulnerable as you did in your last e-mail, where do we go from here?

Mister

It just ticked past noontime when Kodi knocked on M's cubicle wall. Just as M promised, they walked out of the building on their way to lunch. Usual topics of love, lust, life, and work were talked about. M stayed away from the topic of Mister, especially since there was not much else to tell. The restaurant was crowded with the usual lunchtime rush. With everyone chitchatting away, the restaurants elevated background noise was too distracting to talk about him in depth. Even the busy waitress did not have a lot of time to talk, just "Are you ready to order?" came out of her mouth. But even the background distractions would not deter Kodi from asking about her new man.

"M, how are things going between you and . . . what's his name? I sense from your earlier grumpiness that things have not been going as well as you would have liked. What is up with that?"

"I like him a lot. I told him a lot of personal things earlier this morning. I thought he would have said something to me about them, but he still has not written me back. And I got frustrated and became angry, then took it out on you. I am sorry. I did not mean to be rude or bitchy. Forgive me."

"Yes, M, I accept your apology. We are good friends. I will not let anyone come in between our friendship. Promise! Have you tried talking to him on the phone? Maybe hearing his voice would calm down your fears. Has he tried to ask you out yet?"

M and Mister were not exactly officially dating, so M did not have a whole lot to say about him on the record. But off the record was a very different story.

"No, we have not talked on the phone or met in person, nor have we set a date to meet. He has not officially asked me out yet, and I am okay with that. He is a nice guy who likes to talk. I like his attention he gives me. He's intelligent, and he most definitely likes teasing me. I like the way he teases me."

Kodi had mixed feelings about their progress. On one hand, she wanted M to be happy, and on the other hand, she wanted M all to herself. All along, Kodi has been planting seeds in the back of M's mind to play for the same team that she was playing for—not straight, not gay, but bisexual.

"Men! Maybe your next relationship should be with a girl?"

Immediately M thought back to the smokers' pit when M touched her thigh, and the other girls' night out at the steakhouse.

The remembrances caused M to blush and giggle. M's playful laughs gave Kodi a small ray of hope.

"Maybe I should do just that! I have never dated a woman before. Will you go out with me, Kodi?"

M was halfway joking, but Kodi was 100 percent serious.

"Hell yes! When?"

"Tell you what, Kodi, if it doesn't work out with Mister, I will date you next."

M was flushed with blush when she said what she said. Yet she was secretly wet with hidden excitement.

"Fuck Mister, date me now!"

M started figuring out Kodi's intentions were more than just playful, but for now, she brushed them off.

"Kodi . . . Really? You want to date me?"

"Yes, M, I do want to date you. But not as a girlfriend. I want to kiss you all over, and I want to taste you on my lips. And I want you to do the same things to me."

"I don't think I could ever do sexual things with another woman. Though they are nice things to think about happening, but . . ."

Kodi stopped her in midsentence.

"But nothing, M. Let me teach you. I will show you how to play with a woman. We could have a lot of girl fun. Just the two of us. No one ever has to know. A big girl secret we could keep to ourselves."

M sighed, smiled and sinisterly cackled with plausible thoughts of possibility.

"I am not saying no. I do not even know where we would begin."

"I do, M. I know exactly where we will begin."

M was too flustered to do anything else but try and change the topic of chitchat. She was extremely uncomfortable with talking to Kodi in such a busy place about private intimate things, although there was a part of M that was glad Kodi monopolized most of their lunchtime conversation with her frivolous flirtations just so she did not have to talk about Mister. So M let Kodi get away with the flirts; otherwise, she would have been spotlighted to talk about him. M narrowly escaped talking about her secret addiction, but on their drive back to work, Kodi kept prying. Kodi made a strong attempt to learn anything extra about her competition.

"Do you know if he is just teasing you, or is he leading you on?"

"He is a tease, Kodi. No doubt about that. I like the way he teases me."

They pulled into the parking lot with permanent reminders of their sensational lunch lingering all over their panties. M parked her car next to Kodi's while Kodi tried to get more details out of her.

"Is he cute? In what ways does he flirt with you?"

"Yes, he is cute. I saw his pictures on his personal profile page. He has the most seductive bedroom eyes that I have ever seen. I can't wait to see them in person. He likes to write me sexy notes and naughty fantasies of things he wants to do to me."

"Oh! Really? Interesting. Maybe he is too good to be true. Did you ever consider that?"

M revealed enough details about Mister to help Kodi figure out a plan to win M over. Kodi had a girl crush on M, and M knew it. Yet still, she made sure she did not go down a path with Kodi that she might not be able to recover from. For now, M kept those steamy details to herself.

After several minutes back at her desk, M hesitated to get into a rhythm; she would rather be somewhere alone and private with Mister having hot afternoon delights. But minutes after logging back into the work server, her phone buzzed three times in a row. M was not used to hearing that kind of alert. So when she looked at the phone, she saw that there was a new message from him. Despite just returning from lunch, she wanted to take another break, but M felt too guilty to take another one. Instead of breaking, M sat at her desk and multitasked incognito style, switching between server work and Mister's fine words of elegance. Every few minutes, M picked up the phone and read more of Mister's message, then put it down to work. It was hard for her to concentrate on anything but Mister, especially with his seductive charm staring her down. At least to the naked eye, she looked intently productive to anyone watching.

M's boss was the best boss M ever had. They got along well, except during their monthly cycles when mood swings and hormone flow amplified the usual cantankerous possibilities. If it were not for her boss standing up for her, M would have never been promoted. Although M was still getting used to her new position, the reports still had to flow no matter what. But when her boss caught on to M's recent distractions, she had to say something. Out of the corner of M's peripheral vision, she spotted her boss walking toward her cubicle. M quickly grabbed up her cell phone and put it in between her thighs out of sight. Her boss specifically walked over to M and flashed her a reprimanding smile, followed up with a sarcastic comment about her recent lack of productivity.

"Where did M go? Have you seen her? The M I once knew disappeared. Can you help me find her? Because I cannot find her anywhere. By the way, I am the boss, and you are?"

M embarrassingly blushed. She had been caught red-handed and didn't know what to say to her boss's playful yet serious sarcasm. M's pink cheeks said it all. Fortunately for M, her boss got this excited look over her face and said something just as condescending as her looks were.

"It must be a man, huh?"

With nothing else to hide but the obvious, M nodded with bubbly excitement.

"I am happy for you, but while you are here at work, I need you to be 100 percent focused on work. Our quarter ends in two weeks, and you must have the month-ending reports done. You cannot make me look bad. So don't let your distractions ruin us both. By the way, you look amazing the last few weeks. Don't let him go. But don't let him take us down either. You sink, I sink too."

She walked away, leaving M flustered and mad at herself. Her boss was a lonely divorced woman who had been frigid for much longer than M had been, and sometimes her frustrated frigidity showed. She always had a close tab on the team she managed, almost to the point of being a tight anal bitch, but she was also not that strict with rest of the company policies. Over the last ten months, M's boss took her under her wing. M thought she did something wrong, but her boss was secretly grooming her for a management position. Even with her boss's unofficial reprimand, M wanted to finish reading what Mister wrote. But for now, she was forced to wait it out. She pushed herself to finish part one of the monthly report before doing anything else. One hour and a half later is when M finished the first part of the report. M could now take a break without feeling guilty. Before walking out to the pit, M wanted to share with her boss the recent progress she made on the reports to ease any possible apprehensions.

As M hurriedly climbed out from behind the desk, she headed right to her boss's office. She did not want to spend too much time there because she has other grandiose ideas of going out to the pit and reading the rest of Mister's pornographic words without interruption. But when her boss smiled and gave her some last-minute pointers on what the board of directors wanted to see in the reports, it prolonged M's already delayed afternoon break another unbearable five minutes. It was the longest five minutes of M's natural life. When it was over, she left her boss's office, sped down the hallway, and burst out the glass doors on her way to read his mischievous note. She made it outside without anyone on her trail, but she knew a select few saw her heading for the pit. The thought of interruptions made M deviate to her parked car. She quietly closed the car door while hiding inside. Finally, she was alone and able to finish off his naughty words of intrigue in peace. M felt his grip tightening. His intensity was all new to M, but she dug it a lot. His devoted attention made M want to keep up with his intensity, not fall behind. She gave him a quick response to let him know she was very interested in what he said.

Mr. Mister,

I was beginning to wonder if you were giving me back the same silent treatment that I gave you. It was not like you to not write me back ASAP. But now that you have, I must tell you something about the key. Before you come and take it from me, you should know that I have worn it for over a year in total. I say that because I want you to know how sincere I am about the belt and giving you the key to it. I take wearing it extremely serious, so if you intend on taking the key from me, I need to hear you plead with me for it. Why should I give it to you? Grovel and beg me for it. I dare you to ask me to come to you so that you can take the belt off me yourself. How will you plead with me for the key? Will you nicely ask for it? Will you demand for me to hand it over? Will you get on your knees and beg for it? Will you barter for it? I'm eager to see what you will do to get the key from me. Don't make me wait any longer, Mister. I am melting like an ice-cream cone on a hot July day. Don't let me drip onto the sidewalk anymore; rather, let my sweet cream drip into your wide-open mouth so that you catch every last drip of me with your tongue.

Hugs and kisses,
M

M had sore fingers from pecking away on the small LCD screen, but she finished it up before her break was over. And with five minutes to spare, M priority e-mailed it to him first-class electronic mail style.

She pled out her bleeding soul to him, and now she wanted his reaction. M did not know where he was at, but she wanted him to be stiff from her exclusive offer to come and get the only key to her well-guarded chastity belt. What M did not know was that Mister was in an afternoon appointment. Her anxiousness grew with the passing of every minute ticktocking by. It was an uncomfortable self-consciousness feeling of vulnerability. She could not believe she allowed herself to tell him all of what she told him, but now that she was completely exposed, M felt sexier than ever.

Not more than twenty-one minutes into his meeting, Mister's phone blew up with e-mail notifications. They all came at once, but he had a bigger sale on the table, and he was not going to be distracted. He was a determined self-made businessman, and he would not stop until he had the right answer. When Mister wanted something, he went after it wholeheartedly, throwing all caution aside. In between the equipment contract signature and the warranty explanation, Mister nonchalantly picked up his phone and silenced it. He inked out the contract just as it neared 4:50 PM.

And now, all that she asked herself was, "What is next?"

CHAPTER 23

Playing Hard to Get

Mister walked out of the meeting with uncontrollable excitement from meeting a new client and having unread messages to read. On his walk back to the Humvee, Mister found out that he missed a call from D and had two unread e-mails. He listened to D's voice message first. Nothing special, just D wanting him to take one of her next-week appointments. He did not respond to her right away; rather, he had one e-mail that was much more pressing than the other. It was a message from M. After Mister was inside of the Humvee, he took his time to read her note before driving to the next appointment. He full well knew that reading it would make him late, but once he saw the words *chastity belt*, he could not put it down. He felt that it was a huge gesture from M to offer up the only key to her chastity belt. Knowing that gave Mister a huge nitrous jolt of ego boost. While gloating, he started the Humvee, stepped on the gas, and drove down the highway with sex in his head and reckless abandonment in his severe traffic-manipulation swerve. He dodged through rush-hour traffic, making it exactly on time without any minutes to spare.

Mister razzle-dazzled another client with another extended warranty sale. For the first time in forever, Mister felt his entire life perfectly coming together. The overwhelming success made him want to walk on rarified air, but his down-to-earth lifestyle kept him securely touching the ground.

Before driving home and ending another successful day, he took an eight-minute timeout from life. He sat completely still in the quiet Humvee cabin and reflected on every moment since having the lucid wet dream, then collected his thoughts and wrote M back.

My sexy M,

Our last e-mails have stirred up many raw emotions within me. I get the exact feelings I did when I met my first crush. I feel as though you are my blank canvas and I am the soft-bristled brush. My strokes are slow and deliberate. I smear bold colors of scarlet red, navy blue, and everything in between all over your pure-white canvas. The smeared on wet paint will soon dry to elegant perfection. Every painting I paint of us will be a new fantasy fulfilled. We will hang up the numerous paintings on the walls to the right and left because I will paint many more than just one. When I think about how alive my sexual feelings are for you right now, it makes me want to whisper anything and everything to you while I hold you close against my chest. You make me ache in horny disbelief.

Let me tell you in advance, my naughty Miss, you are indeed the woman who is at the center of my every temptation. The one and only. The high we are on now is just the beginning! Don't worry about these feelings fading away; I will not let them go. For now, the time will pass slowly as you will find yourself sitting in class or at work, wondering where I am at or what I might be doing. You are going to be sucked into watching the clock all day and night. You are going to notice every waking second that passes by. You will wonder if I am thinking about you or if I am pleasuring myself to the steamy memories we have yet to make. Know that tonight, this dark cold spring night, I will lie in bed with an erection for you. Already, I am having hot steamy thoughts of you running through my veins, and it is not even nightfall yet. How lucky am I?

Mister

M got so caught up in finishing work and going to night school that she saved it for bedtime. But when bedtime came and passed, his hot note of lust had to be saved for morning as she fell fast to sleep. When M awoke in the morning, she was ecstatically jubilant, for she knew there was an unread e-mail from Mister that beckoned her attention. Despite waking up eight minutes late, she was not about to let life commitments separate her from reading his inspirational thoughts of lust. His words were exactly what she wanted to read. She felt his sincerity, and that comforted her to know he could be vulnerable. She felt compelled to write back, purposely letting herself be late for work to write. She had no choice but to write what she wrote.

Mister,

Here I am! I had all intentions of writing you back yesterday, but when I got home from school last night, I passed out on my bed. I slept through the night and literally just woke up. I fell asleep thinking about you, and woke up to thoughts of us spooning with each other. Never fear, your sexy lady is here! I always like everything you write me, even when you write simple words such as *maybe, possibly,* and *could be*, it excites me! I like how you can excite me like that. It is everything that you think up and write out that is charming and shamelessly fucking dirty all at the same time. How do you do that?

I even had a nasty dream about you last night while I was in class. I got there early as I usually do. And when I laid my head on the desk, I fell asleep. I did not mean to nap, but I was tired. It was weird why I had that kind of dream. But then the slamming classroom door abruptly brought me back to reality. Thank goodness that no one knew what I dreamed about! I was more embarrassed to be caught up in a dream like that at school than being woken up by the door. Somehow, I just knew that you would appreciate knowing that, but don't let it go to your head, Mister. Maybe some time, I can share my dream with you, but for now, it will remain my secret.

On another note, you know, you should never make a girl wait for anything. It is not nice, especially if that girl has fears of rejection. Look what you are doing to me. What makes this whole thing between you and I crazier still is that I am used to being the innocent girl next door. But now you make me feel like the hot neighborhood girl that every boy wants to fuck but nobody can have. You came into my life like a category five hurricane, and you are still bouncing off me with full force. I was shy and naive, but now I cannot wait for us to meet just so you can lay your gentleman-like touches all over me. Speaking of us meeting, why have you not officially asked me out yet? I even taunted you to come and get my chastity belt key from me. I figured a smart man such as yourself would have taken full advantage of my invitation. I really am daring you to come and take it from me. I dare you, Mister. I double dare you!

M

M finished off the e-mail and rushed her butt right into the shower. She left her condominium without putting on any makeup, saving that for the ride over to work. Besides M putting on the finishing touches to her outward glamour, she reflected on her rapidly changing life.

How did I get here? Yes, I know, dummy. I ignored men altogether for two years, yet here I am talking to the captain of the men's charm team. But how did I let him get by my strong defenses unchallenged? I was doing just fine without anyone else for so long. But god, I love his attention! I want to look into his eyes and tell him everything that I know and want. I wanna smell his lightly-sprayed-on cologne on the smalls of his neck while he holds me tight in his arms. Why doesn't he ask me out? God! I want to meet him bad.

Although she liked his daily hot little game of "tease me wet," she wanted to do more than play it over the internet. M needed to see him write those words, "Will you go out with me M?" She needed the "When do we meet?" aspect solved; she could not take any more of his charming smoothness without feeling its payoff.

Despite arriving at work fifteen minutes late, M sat inside of her car in the underground parking garage trying to get out of Mister's realm and back into manager mode. She did not want to disappoint her boss any more than she already had, but she could not work under Mister's spell. When she felt that her mind was right, she opened the car door and got out. But now there was another problem for her to contend with. As soon as she stepped out of the car, a warm, damp breeze blew up her skirt. The tickly light air softly made love to her wet spot without consent. With every step toward work that M took, the more she knew what it felt like to be Marilyn Monroe. She felt daring and sexy with a touch of bubbly blonde innocence. Feeling that erotic at work gave M a naughty arrogance to her every step. She walked by little Miss Bitchy Bitch with commanding confidence. Her heels click-clacked down the hallway, helping to announce her tardiness. She walked by her boss's office, not expecting to be in any kind of trouble, yet she was.

"Good morning, sleepyhead. Do not make me regret getting you promoted. I worked hard for my position, and I don't want your lack of focus to affect us both. Let's not make this a reoccurring event, okay? Can I count on you to be 100 percent present between 8:00 AM and 5:00 PM?"

M felt embarrassed after she strutted into work with such arrogant disrespect.

"Yes, I will pledge my 110 percent effort while I am here. I am sorry for screwing up. It is the newness of someone new that I am caught up in. But from now on, you will have my commitment."

M's boss nodded and walked away, letting M sigh and well up on her own terms. M knew what she had done. It was not a state secret that she was caught up in Mister's world of sexual enticement deeper than deep. Although M was sorry for acting the way she had been carrying on, she was not sorry for wanting to daydream more about him even though she knew full well he wanted a sexual soul mate over a wife.

She knew she had been acting shameless for weeks, but she did not care what others thought of her puppy-dog crush on Mister. Whenever she thought about him, it brought back feelings of her very first boyfriend when she was still an unpenetrated virgin. It must have been the feeling of firsts that made Mister so worth the experience. First kisses, first hugs, first unstoppable heartbeats of passion. She felt those feelings happening all over again.

M's morning epiphany made her well aware that their entire friendship was being forged out of remnants that once made up her impenetrable chastity belt. Something else besides meeting Mister made M deliriously crazy next school semester. It began in two months. Contemplations of attending next semester made her rethink it, especially with Mister vying for a piece of her attention. One part of M needed a break from all the busyness, and the other part wanted to keep going. She was mentally drained to the point of needing a semester or two off since she had been going to school for eight semesters without a break. The two-week countdown of deciding had begun. She had thirteen days to meet him and sort it all out. The decision was harder for her to make than she originally thought. Mister made M seriously waver on taking a break. Even though most of their conversations have bordered on being a hot pornographic film, she felt like she could talk to him about anything; she was that comfortable with him. Right then, she postponed making any decisions about next semester before they met in person. That was how she wanted it.

Despite the recent reprimands making M moody, she quietly kept thinking about him at work. M felt the need to let him into her very private world of secrecy without rocking the boat. She needed his help to get out of her funk, hoping he would do it in VIP-red-carpet style. She did not need to hear his voice to be wrapped up in his kingdom. Fantasies and daydreams of his presence kept her longing for his touch. To her, reading his words were just as good as hearing them spoken. It was Mister's debonair panache that made her heart race and soul spasm. Mister's realistic accuracy was what did it for M. She did not know how he did it, but he kept her feeling his deep pelvic thrusts slipping in and sliding out of her all day long. Although it was his intensity that kept M in the naughty zone, it was her nonsexual thoughts about him that made her feel extraordinarily sexy.

Mister woke up refreshed but disappointed since he had not heard from M in over a day, and that was a big deal. Mister always kept her wondering when, where, or how he might get to her next. He did not know if she was giving him more silent treatment or something else happened. The emptiness made Mister feel like a sad puppy dog strolling the quiet 4:00 AM streets. He pathetically waited it out for the second time in their three-week-old friendship.

With his recent sales career revitalized, he had a stacked day of appointments that started at 9:00 sharp. On the drive, Mister's sexual prowess ached all over. Despite having a full schedule, Mister was not about to give up thinking about S, M, or D. Keeping up with all three women emotionally empowered Mister, yet it mentally wiped him out. Though he was not going to let his stellar sales streak stop either. The new sexual catalyst taking over Mister's life was something new that he wished he had long ago. He loved his new personality, and he was not about to give it up. But what he needed right now was a tiny pause to replenish his energy.

"I am not going to do anything this weekend except wash the Humvee, watch baseball, and play fetch with Rocket. That is it. Yes, that is exactly what I am going to do."

Part of that fast-paced day was his inability to take an hour lunch, only a fast twenty-five-minute eat and run would have to do. His ongoing sales mojo kept him selling, two sales so far, and two appointments still to go. On his way over to the next appointment, Mister stopped off at the grocery store to get a Fuji apple and a coffee drink to go. He brought them back to the Humvee and ate lunch alone.

While Mister ate lunch alone, so did M. Kodi was off doing her own thing with her boyfriend and M hated being the useless third-crowd member. M lived it up, not taking one second for granted. The peace and quiet without Kodi was priceless. Yet still, something bothered M, Mister's lack of fast responses as of late. He came on fast and strong, and now it appears he had backed off a tad. Out of curiosity, M rechecked her phone to make sure it was still working. She restarted the email app, and still no new messages came through. Zero! But then something caught her eye. She noticed a saved draft. She did not remember writing anyone a draft, so she opened it. At first, she was perplexed, then she majorly freaked out.

"Ahh, shit! Dammit! How could I forget to send it? No wonder why he has not written me back. Dammit, M!"

She sighed in disgust. In full panic mode, M added a few more sentences to the earlier e-mail before officially sending it off.

> PS. I am soooooo sorry, Mister. I just looked at my phone to see why you hadn't written me back yet. And that is when I found out that I never sent it to you. Somehow it got saved in my draft folder. I feel stupid! Ugh! I specifically wrote it earlier this morning, hoping you would get to read it before work. I woke up refreshed and in a great mood, and at 6:15 AM, I typed it up. Shit! I am sorry. I am a bad girl. Spank me! But only if you want. I deserve it!
>
> Hugs,
> M

This time she made sure it was sent. With the sun shining in through his open moon roof and the fresh air dancing across his scent glands, he enjoyed every moment of fast lunch. The Humvee's cabin was massively wide and deep with expansive headroom everywhere. When he originally bought the Humvee three years ago, its military life was already made over with a fresh coat of civilian love. The cabin is covered with plush black carpet, maroon colored leather seats and dark wood trim accentuating its new life outside of the military. It has speakers everywhere and LCD screens embedded in the front seat headrests with a brand-new navigation system that doubled as an in-dash TV. The only thing Mister had to upgrade was the satellite. He now has internet, satellite TV, and satellite radio that truly made the Humvee one bad-assed mobile crises center. All Mister does is sit back in the captain's chair and enjoy the powerful feeling that driving around in an American made military fighting machine brings. He bought it mostly for its rugged sex appeal, but the prestige of owning it toppled the prestige. He knew he babied it too much, but would not change a thing. He never let anyone drink inside, only Mister had those exclusive privileges. The interior smelled exactly the same as Mister did, no fragranced air fresheners, just the smell of his daily-worn, light-scented cologne. That was intentional, he disliked every air freshener he ever smelled.

Mister finished lunch with eight minutes to spare. With extra time left, he felt he needed to right her wronged earlier draft blunder, so he gave her an expedited concoction of words to smooth it all over.

Dearest M,

I am sitting in my Humvee in the middle of a parking lot close by my next appointment thinking about you. I would be lying if I did not say your delay made me think that you were giving me the silent treatment again, but I am glad that you are not. Personally, I do not get the whole silent treatment thing, but all is fair in love and war, or so I have read. Humph, I know I can have a dizzying effect on others around me. At least that is what I have heard. Others have told me I have this rare intensity for love, life, and passion. I do not mean to be that way; it is just who I am. I am sincerely passionately intense about everything in my life that I care about. Can you blame me for chasing after something that I want until I get it?

Today was one of those days that I should not be taking a break, but here I am doing it. I enjoy you more than I deserve. But I am always up for a good challenge. You challenged me, did you not? Something about a dare, then a double dare to come and get the key to your chastity belt. I accept! As of now, I am planning to take the key from you. I hope that you did not expect me to pass up a challenge like that. Fuck caution because I want that key.

Mister

M gloated down to the smokers' pit and sat there soaking up his charming eloquence while basking in the springtime sun. She tore into his e-mail at a high rate of speed. She did not care who was watching; she had to read it. His words inspired her giddy up and go to all-time highs. After she reread his every word three times over, her break ended, but not without his note giving M inspiration to do great things.

That late afternoon, M put her own finishing touches on the monthly report to show off her talents. She was not in management to be par; she wanted to be the hole in one on the eighteenth course. M finished the monthly report ahead of schedule. She wanted to show everyone around her that they were right in promoting her. She had something to prove to her boss. She stayed forty-five minutes over just to do the reports to her own satisfaction. At 5:45 PM, M e-mailed the reports to her boss with an attached note asking for feedback and approval. That day, M succeeded. She walked out of work a proud peacock, fanning out all her exotic feathers for everyone to see.

M drove home, barely able to drag herself in through the front door without passing out. She had the anchor of life grappling along the floor with every footstep she took down the hallway. M fell asleep far earlier than any previous night, not by choice but out of survival.

CHAPTER 24

• • • • • • • • • ● • • • • • •

Revelations

With the darkness of the night surrendering to daybreak, M soundly slept under the warm covers only to be disturbed by the sounding alarm clock. She responded to its loud rhetoric with a sleepy discombobulated open-handed slap. It had been nine hours since M laid her head down, which meant she woke up dazed, hungry, and lonely. First things first—writing Mister. And from the warm confines of her comfortable bed, she sent him a good-morning note that would wake him up in more ways than uno.

Mister Sexy,

You must be the city's luckiest guy because for the second time this week you get to read another perverted billet-doux written by my own fantasies. I wish I could roll over and take your flaccid cock into my mouth and have my warm wet lips softly suck you awake. The warmth and wetness of my hot mouth would instantaneously wake you up just in time to see my head bobbing in between the apex of your splendor. Without any words, your hands would find my head and stroke my hair as I let you orgasm in my mouth.

But for now, Mister, we will both have to dream about that kind of morning wake-up call. Won't we?

But right now, you need to tell me something. Tell me anything. Whatever you do, use your convincing charm to keep me obsessed. I dare you, Mister. Make me moist again, Mister! I beg you, please?

M

M claimed the day as her own at the very same time her tasteful note was sent out into the digital domain. She stood by and waited until after it was sent, then joined Mr. Showerhead under the water. M supplemented Mr. Showerhead's massaging pleasure with Mister's gyrating literary excellence to make it one hot threesome. Orgasms had. Shower done. Next stop, kitchen.

"Good morning, M. It is a pleasant surprise to see you so alert this early in the morning. Did you already get coffee, or do you need me to brew you a cup?"

One of M's roommates was in the kitchen, eating breakfast, where a quick conversation ensued.

"I was just coming to get some coffee and a bagel. I did not eat dinner with you girls last night, and now, I am hungrier than hungry. Yes, please, start me some Irish coffee."

"What happened to you last night? We saw you walk in, and then you were gone."

M giggled, then kept on, keeping on.

"School and work and Mister caught up to me. I was flat-out tired."

"Have you met him yet?"

"Not yet, but his personality is intense. I feel like I have already met him even though I have not. Sorry if I appeared to be rude last night. I did not mean to be."

"It's okay. We just watched more reality drama and talked about our pathetic love lives. You did not miss much."

"Oh good! Not to cut you short, because I like talking to you, but I need to eat this bagel super fast and take off to work."

M grabbed her bagel and coffee and took them with her back to her room so she could eat, drink, and get ready for work. Out the door she went, taking with her a soulful joy she has not had in forever. Her amazing start to a mediocre day gave her enough confidence to flash Miss BB a smug look that said, "Watch out," as she entered the building. On the way to her cubicle, M's boss stopped her mid-step with pleasantries.

"Good morning, M. I got that report. I want to talk to you about it. Come and see me after you get settled. You have some interesting inclusions."

"Yeah? I decided to jazz up the report a little more. Was that okay to do?"

"M, I liked the report, but I have some suggestions to talk to you about, so come see me in a few."

M felt good that her boss seemed to be accepting of her rogue changes. She was on time to work and already being productive. M turned on her computer, logged into the server, checked e-mails, then went to her boss's office to talk.

"Hi, M. I liked the report you put together. But it gives me more ideas of things we can do to include in future reports. Those are good ideas you have. Give me the weekend to figure this out. That way, I can plan a good strategy to run it by my bosses. 'Good job' was what I wanted to say."

"Thank you! In the months that you had me typing up the reports for you, I always thought about suggesting we include those other categories for more detailed accuracy, but then, I reminded myself I was not the boss." M did a two-second chuckle, then continued, "Okay then, I will wait for you to let me know when you want to talk again. So far, my next week schedule is free."

"Okay then, let's meet early next week to discuss this."

M went back to her cubicle and got back to work. While M pecked away at the keyboard, Miss BB was writing M a note to find out what the earlier rude look was for. When Miss BB's e-mail arrived, it caused M to panic and freak out in fear of companywide rumors.

Hiya, M,

Did I do something to piss you off? Because you gave me a rude glare this morning. Anyway, I am sorry if I did something to make you pissed. I don't like making people mad at me. Did you know I am dating Guy? He told me he saw a juicy love letter on your computer the other day. Does that mean you have a new boyfriend? I think that's cute, if it is. Don't worry, I won't tell anyone. Guy writes me cute notes like that all the time. Mum is the word. Just between you and I, your ex didn't deserve you anyway. But seriously, if you ever want to talk, I am always available.

Friends,
B

B just happened to also be the first initial of her true first name. Beatrice. She went by B. She never knew why the office called her Miss BB. B just thought it was her randomly assigned nickname. What she did not know could not hurt her.

Right away, M called up Kodi, asking her to meet in the break room. They met, and M told Kodi what Miss BB wrote. Kodi's first reaction was to be mad, but then she was pissed.

"Miss BB did the same thing to me before the last rumor of me fucking the stockroom guy in the bathroom. Fuck her. Just be two-faced like she is. Tell her you appreciate her friendship but also tell her that that guy broke it off with you to get her sympathy. Then never talk about him again or send him e-mails from the office. Because fuck her!"

"Good idea, Kodi. Did you really fuck that stockroom guy?"

"Of course, I did. But she did not see or hear anything to assume that we *actually* fucked. The only thing I can think of is that she saw how we acted with each other afterwards. Unless . . . I wonder if it could have been Guy. It would not surprise me. Men have big mouths when it comes to things like that." Kodi laughed and gave M the best advice she could.

"Thanks for the advice, Kodi. I will tell Miss BB that exact thing and see how it plays itself out. Hopefully she stops her shit because I do not want to be part of any rumors or assumptions."

Just when M got back to her desk, she typed a response to Miss BB.

> Thank you, B. I appreciate your friendship offer. As for that guy and me, we broke it off already. It is probably for the best, but I admit I am sad. Screw it. I am over him. You are right, he does not deserve me. Maybe we can talk later about men, but for now, I must get back to work.
>
> M

M sent the internal e-mail off, hoping it would downplay Miss Bitchy Bitch's drama-spreading capability. M put her head down and entered in the inventory counts. She worked until it was lunch break, and even then she exited out the backdoor, intentionally avoiding Miss BB. M picked up a lunchtime salad to go, then parked in the underground garage and ate it in her car. She was not expecting any interruptions in the car, yet one sought her out.

> Hello, Miss,
>
> I cannot get you out of my head either. I think it's about time that I start calling you my Miss. You will be the Miss to my Mister. That is if you want to be Mister's Miss. Do you want to be her? I went to bed last night and reread all our back-and-forths. And now, I must cop to an erection. Yes, you gave it to me. My goodness, girl, you are driving me crazy horny mad. I know I should be embarrassed, but I am not. You should take

that as a compliment. Ever since I started writing you, M, I have been getting the best sleep ever, although this morning was the exception. I was inadvertently woken up by my wake-up alarm from a deep, sound sleep. When I opened my eyes, I saw and felt the rays of light shining in through my window. At first, I was annoyed, but then the warmth made me feel loved by the entire universe. To be woken up by the sun and man's best friend licking his foot at the same time was a bittersweet way to wake up. Though someone seemed to be missing out of the equation. LOL! Hmm . . .

When my dogs wetted, doggie-breathed tongue licked across my forehead, it made me laugh. Although I would rather have your tongue waking me up. Speaking of that, I especially liked your last e-mail describing to me how you would someday like to wake me up. I admit that it is my fault for not asking you out yet. What is wrong with me? I need to figure that out PDQ, don't I?

Your classroom dream must have been crazy. Did you wake up to a class full of people staring at you or just a few? I bet when you woke up it confused the crap out of you; I know that I would be dazed and confused. You probably did not have much time to react. I wish that I could have been with you in the classroom because I would have been the one man paying close attention to your mannerisms. I am one of those people that can tune into someone's emotional state if I try hard enough. Some might call it a gift, but I sometimes call it a curse. I have been right eleven times in my life, all of them ending in incredible friendships, although none of those times ever led to a sizzling-hot romance. Maybe I was too much of a pussy to act on my feelings, or maybe I was completely wrong about the whole vibe. But what I do know, life is all about timing. If it is not right, it will not work out in the end. Anyway, I can't talk too much more right now, but I will write a lot more later. But do know that you are on my mind.

Sweet daydreams,
Mister

Mister knew he had to get back to work because he was slammed with appointments. It was good that Mister's next appointment was only ten minutes away. He arrived a few minutes early as he always tried to do. While he put on his sophisticated business face, his ringing phone interrupted his readiness drill. Mister was not too concerned with reading it right then, no matter who it was. He did not let the slight interruption get in the way of stepping into sales character. With rejuvenated sales mojo, Mister ran the meeting with sincere intensity.

Mister rolled down the sales highway on an untouchable cloud of invincibility. He kept selling every single one of his appointments with no end in sight. He soared high above the cloud because for the second time that day he made another big sale with extras. He normally sold two extended warranties in a whole month, let alone in one day. He rode on the energy cloud all day long, selling another. Only one indecision plagued his perfect sales record, but he did not let that upset his applecart.

A tired Mister drove into the horseshoe driveway, ready to be at home. All he could think about was it was Friday night. He let a call from D go to voice mail. He was not in the mood to chitchat with her unless it was about work. Seconds after D left him a voice message, Mister listened and returned her call. She had questions about extended warranties, and since Mister was the extended warranty guru, D frequently relied on his help. Of course, D answered right away, and Mister helped her the best he could.

"Hey, Mister, do you know if our warranty plan covers batteries and network fix issues even if the customer changes the internal computer network around?"

With a serious tone, she waited for answers.

"Yes, the extended warranty covers anything and everything imaginable. The only thing it does not cover is replacing customer's existing provided equipment. Anything else?"

There was half a minute of silence before D tried to put a feeler out there to see if Mister read her earlier e-mail that she typed up forty-five minutes ago.

"Did you recover from my come-on-my-desk comment, or do I need to whip up some more of that kind of talk to get you back as my friend?"

"D, I always like your kind of ego boosts. But you had better watch it, or you might just walk in one morning and find my sticky cream all over your keyboard."

D heard Mister's sinister cackle clearly come from deep in his soul. He made it that obvious. Though his answer told D that he had not yet read her earlier e-mail. D had hoped he read it but was now completely flustered with any other conversation. She politely ended the call and resumed her last sales appointment of the day.

Before getting out of the Humvee, Mister checked his unread e-mail from earlier. He did not see any e-mails from D, just S. When he saw it was from S, the hairs on the back of his neck stood straight up.

Mister,

I wanted to write you back sooner, but I was in thinking mode. The longer I waited, the more hope I kept holding out. Now that the wait is all over with, I wanted to truly say I am sorry. Yes, I am D, and S is me too. That day, I saw you writing out your ad, and I got it in my mind to play with you and see how far I could get. You know me, always pushing the edge but never going over it! I guess you must have seen me get out of my car the other morning. I could not see you sitting in your Humvee. Your dark-tinted windows prevented me from noticing. Thank you for the temporary mirror. LOL! I am glad I could make you hard while you watched me adjust myself before walking into work. I hope this won't ruin our rekindled friendship because I would hate to lose you as a friend. And if you do not know this by now, I have always had a secret crush on you. I know I am still married, and that is why I do not think it is fair to let you have me while I am still married. It would not be right for me to do that to him even though that bastard has not given me any kind of attention in a long time. He does have good intentions, so I like to tell myself. However, it pisses me off that he cannot see me as a sexual play toy anymore. I won't get started on that right now because this e-mail is not the right time to do that. The reason I am telling you this is that I think we could be good together, although I do not want to give you false hopes of any kind. I am not going to do that anymore, and I am sorry if I hurt you at all in the past. I felt like I had to bare my soul to you at some point, and that point is now. Though all I want to do is bare my naked self to you. I won't e-mail you as S anymore since you know that I really am D. I must admit it was fun being S for a few weeks. I liked it.

Kisses and hugs,

D

Mister slapped his hands together and chuckled to himself, trying to laugh off D's escapades. At first, he did not know if he should be mad at her or just let her get away with it but then decided to make her squirm for a while. Officially learning D pretended to be S was a little relief on one hand, but on the other hand, it messed with his head a little. Even though their past lent them many practical jokes toward each other, he liked the pretend S a little too much to not suffer a bruised ego.

For more than a few minutes, Mister sat inside of the Humvee a little sad but then thought about ways to handle D's flagrant violation. He was not about to end their friendship; he valued their friendly past more than he cared to admit. Both felt comfortable enough to let them be themselves around each other. A true kind of vulnerability that meant something to Mister. They shared a lot of dark sadness and very personal thoughts that always kept them tightly bound to each other. Though one thing he knew for sure was that he was not about to let her joke go unpunished.

Mister got out of the Humvee and walked into the house, greeting Alex along the way.

"Wow, I am glad this week is finally over. It was a long one. I need some whiskey and a good baseball game to watch to drown out the chaos."

"Ahh, man, I hear you on that one. I am just about to get ready for a date. We are going to the movies."

"Sounds like a fun night. Well then, I guess it will be me and Rocket watching the Yankees game. I could use the peace and quiet. For me, it's been one of those great weeks that I did not want to ever end. Busy but extremely productive and satisfying. Is it the same girl you have been hot-tubbing with?"

"In fact, yes, that's the one. She has a name though. It is Kelsey. She's a great girl. She even likes baseball but roots for the wrong team."

Alex smiled and started to walk down the hallway to get ready.

"Funny. I guess you will have to try and convert her." Mister chuckled in between sentences. "But if Kelsey is a good catch, don't release her. The good ones are hard to come by."

"I agree. I am trying not to pull a catch and release."

"Good job, A."

Alex departed, and Mister dug into the bag of Blue Diamond almonds and the bottle of Gentleman Jack all by himself. He stayed out in the family room to watch the game on the big-screen projector and surround sound. He watched the Yankees win, then retired to the bedroom. Mister needed a quiet weekend alone to adjust to his newfound surge of success. He shut the door and cut himself off from the rest of the world so that he could properly unwind. He had everything close by that he needed to exist in his own private world for the night.

With Rocket lying by his side, songs randomly shuffled through his four-thousand-song music collection. Mister dove deep into a peaceful realm of existence as he checked out of life for the night.

CHAPTER 25

Night School Dreams

Saturday came in with lightning speed. Both Mister and M had their own weekend plans already set. Nothing special, just the usual errand running and getting ready for next-week kinds of things.

Mister always had a date with the Humvee every midday Saturday. It was usually a half-day event to wash his big black beauty. This Saturday, he saved the wash job until after he reworked his up-and-coming work schedule. His plan was to meet M this week, but since his schedule was already planned, he had to rearrange some of it to make a lunch date possible. He figured setting aside two hours would be best to relieve any unnecessary "chicken with his head cut off" kind of rushing around. He wanted it to go smoothly perfect.

I think it will be best to spring it on her at the last minute. I do not want her to get cold feet and not go through with meeting me. That cannot happen. I could not handle the rejection. I hope she will say yes.

That was his diabolical plan to meet her in the flesh. He was not going to sit around and let her keep taunting him with dares and double dares. After all, Mister loved the challenge that came with the chase. He knew that her availability was not as flexible as his was, but he was not about to let her schedule prevent them from having an in the flesh soiree. He moved his schedule around some on a few days of that week to overcompensate for her inflexibility with his pliability. The timing had to be right, and the only way to find that out

233

was feel it out. It was a good thing that he had a few days to figure something out.

Brilliant orange sunrays shined in through her partially closed blinds perfectly. Last night's simple trade down from the Velvety Ones to drab flannels was intentional; her room was cooler more than any other night. The flannels and the penetrating sun kept her toasty warm through the night. When M should have been sleeping, she was awake. The harder she tried to put him out of her mind, the more that he showed up. It was one of those mornings that M wished Mister had been spooning against her backside. She would have lain in bed all day, never leaving his comfort, strength, or stamina. This was one morning that she could have used his lavish attention upon her body and soul. She yearned to hear him whisper, "Good morning, M," yet any words at all would have sufficed. His sensualistic words were chicken soup for her soul, making her feel as though she was already his princess. She got her sexy back in less than three weeks of knowing Mister. His constant words kept M warmer than the Velvety Ones ever could.

Instinctively, M's hands touched her flannel-covered breasts with soft playful pinches, specifically focused on massaging her light-brown areolas. Closing her eyes, she let her hands touch herself as her mind made up something sensually sexualized. M slipped into a naughty Saturday morning fantasy about being Mister's Miss.

I wake up to a lavish breakfast in bed prepared by his own hands. I turn over and see him patiently standing over me, watching me sleep. He has a portable table set up beside the bed that has homemade waffles, with an over-medium egg on top, along with a bowl of fresh fruit and homemade whipped cream. He has this devilish smile on his face as he sees me stirring awake. His plush, cotton-white robe is loosely wrapped around him, intentionally hiding his goodies from my eyesight. I stretch out on the bed while at the same time my Mister unties his robe at the waist and kneels one knee on the bed right close to my face. I roll my head over to him, and all I see is his big beautiful erection. His neatly trimmed man hair shows off his big package with stunning clarity. Once he sees my reaction, he takes it further by dabbing a spoon full of thick, sweet whipped cream onto the top of his dick with expectations. He puts his hands on his waist and waits for me to taste his superbly prepared cream . . .

Just when M's fantasy started to get good, she was interrupted by her annoying phones message alert. M grabbed for her phone to shush it up so she could get back to her fantasy. It was unfortunate that her steamy fantasy had prematurely come and gone. The junk e-mail interruption absolutely pissed her off. Despite the blown fantasy, M woke up knowing that she had a full day of errands, laundry, and grocery shopping with the girls waiting to be done.

That Saturday morning, M celebrated freedom from inventory, work, and school. It was one day she did not have to be anywhere to do any of those. Her last two weeks of voluntary inventory counts helped her company get accurate. For the last two years, M volunteered to work the inventory shift. Last year was fun since Kodi did it alongside M, but this year, M did it alone. She paid for it with limited sleep and two missed morning orgasms. Mainly, she volunteered her time to show off her dedicated faith in the company's year-over-year growth. She was proud to work there; it showed in everything extra she did on the company's behalf. But now that the inventory count was completed, M looked forward to getting back to simple normalcy.

Though M's private celebration party held in Mr. Showerhead's remembrance could not be first, it would not be last either. She sat up in bed and planned an aromatic candlelit, wine-sipping bubble bath. She added fragranced candles to the shopping list for her freedom party. M's plan was to grocery-shop then bubble-bath before pussycat theater began. And in between events, she planned on writing something special for Mister. M needed to figure out a way to coax Mister into meeting her so that she could decide about next semester's college plan. M knew she had to push all the right buttons and say all the right things to force his hand. Something unexpected, something hot, something to make his big prick erect. She wanted to lure him into her web and start using her exponential power of estrogen on him.

The game plan was to massage his bruised ego with her own thoughts and ideas. Since M knew she was not as good at writing, she had to conjure up something to get him out from behind the computer screen. With a little inspiration, she would later dazzle his pecker off. In the meantime, M put her hair up in a bun and got dressed to go out and grocery-shop. M's roommates waited for M because they knew her schedule was much more fucked than their schedules were. And since it was M's condominium, they gave her the due respect she deserved.

All three girls had booked this night for a girls' night-in party, an exclusive private party they conjured up weeks ago. Three sexy, semi-available, dressed-down friends hanging out with each other was something they all needed to partake in. Weeks ago, before M knew Mister existed, the girls planned a once-in-a-blue-moon movie night event. Pajamas, wine, and chic flicks would set the perfect tone for Pussycat Theater. They still had to pick out the movie, but everything else was figured out. M had invited Kodi, but she already had previous plans of entertainment. Even without Kodi being there, it would be an R-rated pajama shindig. However, right now it was grocery-shopping time. On their drive over to the supermarket, her two curious roommates started probing her about the new man that kept her in a fantastic mood.

"M, you have to tell us about him."

"Who are you referring to?"

"You know whom that I am talking about, M. Don't play dumb with us."

Both girls cackled simultaneously to let M know she could not hide him anymore.

"You can trust us. We will keep it just between us girls."

"Oh, all right, he is the most charming man ever. And no, neither of you can have him. He is mine. He pays attention to me. He listens, and he makes me horny all the time with his whimsical ways."

M's giggle made her roommates know there was more she was not telling.

As the three girls walked into the supermarket, they prepared to buy out the store. While they walked around and picked out the necessities of life, M thought about asking her girlfriends some "what should I do" questions.

"I was thinking about writing him a sexy love letter with more emphasis on the sexy part. Do you think I should? I keep changing my mind. I don't want to come off as a slut, or easy. What do you girls think?"

"Write him! What do you have to lose? If you want him that way, go for it. But you had better do it in first-class diva style. Grab his bull by the horns and don't let go."

As the girls walked out of produce into dairy, both of her roommates told M that she should do what she felt was right.

"He writes me dirty stories. They turn me on to read. He writes about things that shock me, but I like it. Is that weird or what? I want to write him one back, but . . . but I do not think the way he thinks. It's hard for me to get into that naughty kind of fuck-me zone all by myself. But I really want to write him something back that will make him come in his pants."

The gleam in M's eyes told her roommates that she was serious. The crazy dog-eyed stare that she got back from her roommates made her want to scribe him something ejaculatingly perfect.

"Go for it, M. Do it! Hit him where it counts."

They all stood in the checkout line giggling and carrying on. Then M drove home and left the grocery put-away to her roommates while she did laundry. She let her roomies figure out which movies they were going to internet-stream for pussycat theater. M did not care about what she saw, more than she cared about socializing. Movie night was not something she could always count on due to the girls never having the same schedules. With boyfriends darting in and out of all their lives, nothing was predictable. However, when they got together, it was always a smashing party in a box. Sometimes they broke out the fingernail polish and painted each other's nails; other times they talked about men, and still other times they laughed and got buzzed on wine. No matter what they talked about or did, it was always a kickass time that could not be topped.

M gathered the first load of laundry and marched it down to the washer. With every footstep she took, she felt tingly sensations through every erogenous zone. She stood in front of the washer and put clothes in the front loader while trying to keep her hands off herself. Hot, erotic feelings of needing to come culminated into a need to be massaged by eight pulsating water jets. M turned on the washer then beelined it for the shower. She kept the bathroom lights off and lit her newly purchased cucumber-scented candles while stepping in the shower for an early afternoon sex-fest with Mr. Showerhead. While fantasizing about Mister, she came hard more than once. It was then that she knew she had to tell him about her night school dream.

Mister,

I woke up to sexy thoughts of you, as I can only speak the truth. You make me crazy, Mister. I was going to e-mail you right when I woke up, but then I got caught up in doing chores and errands. We girls just got back from getting groceries, and now that shopping is done with, I can concentrate on bigger and better things. If your ears are burning, it's because I was just talking about you to my roommates. They cornered me into spilling the beans. Don't worry, I did not tell them the juicy stuff. If they knew what I know, they would feel how I feel, and we cannot have three ladies competing for your attention in the same house at the same time. Disasterrrr!

I woke up a little bit sad because I did not remember dreaming about you in my sleep. However, it was nice to get a break from your hypnotic control. Oops, did I just say that? Yes, okay, I confess. You have a strong hold on my emotions, and I do not know what to do about it. I do know what I want to do about it though. How many more double dares do I need to threaten you with before you do something about it? Huh, Mister? I still have this silly old tarnished key dangling around my neck. The problem is, I don't want to lug it around with me anymore. In fact, I think my chastity belt is starting to rust from the many nights of total saturation you made me have. You had better hope the key still works when you finally take it from me. I would hate for my rusty belt hole to be too frigid to work for you.

Mister, you do not have to be on bended knee, but you must be on bended knees when you come and take the key from me just as you have eluded to in all your naughty stories of erotic manipulation. I hope you know you are perverting the "innocent girl next door." There is no turning back for me now. I am in way too deep. I cannot ever forget your awe-inspiring words of erotic orgasm. They seep into me at all hours of the day and night. You, Mister, have made me read too much to want to ever go back to being the good girl next door. Only if it is embedded in one of our future fantasies. I feel as though you can see right through me. It's scary to know a man full of gentle persuasion can see into me like you can. That is dangerous! I do not know how I will feel when I give myself to you, but I know that I want to know. I like how you are okay with making me the center of attention. How can a man such as yourself be so willing to put my pleasure over his? I just do not get it. But maybe I shouldn't get it at all, yet I do.

I'm embarrassed to say that most of your e-mails made my stargazing lily bloom with sweet love nectar. Being honest, when you first e-mailed me, I treated you like every other response that I got. That is why I did not put too much effort into you then, but when you kept writing me with your indifferent thoughts and ideas, they got to me. The more you wrote, the more I want to talk with you. Your words always are sexy and sincere. I feel that sincerity, and that is the second biggest reason we are still talking. I really cannot turn away from you away even if I tried. Your persistence is hot. I like being chased after. It is an exciting rush. But will you still chase me after me when I am caught? You will have to keep me hot and bothered if you want me to stay. If you can do that, I will be your hot sex slave.

I never really told you about the numerous nights that I have used my unused vibrator. It's all because of you that I am like this now. I want to share with you one of the hottest nights of my entire life. I feel that you should get to know what you have done to me firsthand. In my innocent girl-next-door kind of mentality, enjoy.

We have been e-mailing each other back and forth for over two weeks now. I am finally set-tling into the idea of us touching each other skin on skin. I played hard to get because I knew you liked it. If you need any more realness than that, I purposely did not tell you what I did in the car before driving home the night when I dreamed of you in class. I was a bad girl that night when I indulged in my own selfish pleasure. I closed my eyes and cuddled up to my chrome-colored vibrating friend that had been hiding in my purse for over a year now. It was a naughty gift from Kodi. She gave it to me for my birthday. I never needed it until that night. Now, my once-unused vibrating egg has become my best friend. I like feeling it best when I wear a thong. My thong holds it tight up against my clitoris, not ever let-ting it escape from the perfect spot. However, if it ever moved out of the special spot, I could always put it back in place with a shove. Personally, I like feeling it after it's been turned on for a few minutes because of its warmth. I had to tell you about that vibrator because of what happened next.

Funny coincidence or not, that night, the professor talked about sharks. Something about the best businessmen are like sharks, and that was all it took for me to look at you as a great white. The professor continued, but I tuned out and went into daydream mode. I did not care if the professor looked over at me. But if he did, he would not have gotten me out of my dream. When I felt much moisture between my thighs, I knew I had to go somewhere other than class. I grabbed my notebook and backpack and walked out. Under the dark starry night, I speed-walked out to my car so that I could take care of myself. I kept thinking that you were chasing after me in the cold depths of the ocean just to eat me up. My crazy thoughts went everywhere naughty and nowhere good. Your keen smell of the surrounding territory makes you hone in on the scent of my sweet blood in the water. Your erect fin perks up and guides you right to me. Then I thought . . .

"Mister Shark, I want to be your sweet addiction. I know you must have me to survive, just as I must have you to go on."

You smell my excitement dancing in the water around you even though you have never smelled me before. Somehow, I know you want to gobble me up. I see your fin rise out of the water, and I get hot and bothered by the fear that you might eat me out—I mean, up. Shark or no shark, that night, I sat in my empty car in the middle of the college parking lot writing down the exact things I scribble down now.

You make me want to feel your touch while you lick my tight twat like it is the only piece of candy in the universe. Those are the very thoughts that stopped me writing and look around the parking lot to see if anyone was around. I looked around and did not care who saw me lower my seatback, unsnap and unzip my pants, and wiggle my hands deep into my panties. I wanted to e-mail you then, but by the time I would have gotten it written, my pleasure would have been over. So instead, I enjoyed my fantasy solo-style while envisioning you made pure carnivorous love to me.

You sat next to me in my passenger seat, watching me watch you. I felt myself up in the college parking lot while sending you an over dramatic e-mail, asking for help. I made up a dead-car-battery excuse to get you to come over and rescue me. You instantly write me back, making me feel your powerful shark-like exterior gently rub against my body. You fell for it, and I played out the damsel-in-distress screenplay with innocent sincerity. You investigated my sweet scent of sexual opulence with your gills. I hid my slow finger bang from passersby while keeping my fantasy of you going down on me alive. I let your past written words, thoughts, and ideas vibrantly overtake me.

As plain as day, I saw you swim back around toward me in hunt mode. Gracefully slow, you approached me with your dorsal fin breaking the surface. You converge on the scent of my fresh blood pooling all around me. In literal seconds, the huge shark dubbed Mister showed up outside of my car window. Appearing out of thin air, he looked in through my steam-covered window to see my pants pushed down mid-thigh and both of my hands under my thong. Mister Shark stood outside of my car door, intently watching my every gesture. The chilly dark night and partially steamed car windows concealed my public display of affection, yet you were left exposed.

As you peeped in, only metal and glass separated us, yet you kept watching me inch closer to climaxing. Instead of interrupting me, you actively participated in your own sneaky way. You pulled out your penis and massaged it. I cannot see it, but I know it is in your hand. My eyes intently watch you watch me. I imagined you grabbed my hanging hair and firmly pulled it downward to guide my head into your lap. Both of your hands guide my mouth up and down on your big prick. The good little cocksucker in me kept your wet and erect. You forced it down my throat so deep that I choked on it. You made me lose all control, allowing my inner slut to take over so that I could give you a first-class VIP masturbation show.

I rolled my window halfway down to let the steam dissolve so that you could get a better view. My nice gesture granted you two bonuses in one—cleared up visuals and sniffy smells of my intoxicating twat. The sudden burst of excitement penetrating your scent palate abruptly ended in a cataclysm of wow. A knee-buckling orgasm threw you off balance, forcing you to lean against my car for support. Once you smelt my tang, I knew you wanted more when you stuck your nose in through the open window to sniff it more. I could not deny you what you sought after.

Seeing you desire to have more of my scent made me ache all over. I placed my lips up to the window and let you kiss me. During our passionate kisses, I heard your hand banging against my car door. The banging sound made me want to orgasm again just because I wanted you that bad. I did not open my door, nor did I take your cock in my mouth. Instead, I pushed myself deeper into my seat and concentrated on my own selfish pleasure. I acted just the way you would have wanted me to, intentionally forcing you to stay outside and watch.

Instead of opening my car door and taking your erection into my mouth, I pushed myself deeper into the seat and concentrated on my own pleasure. I intentionally forced you to stay outside the car and watch my show of affection and desire.

To show you that I was not completely selfish, I shared my pussy-dipped fingers with you, giving you, your very own Miss Creamsicle delight. You raised my Creamsicle close to your nose and got high on its addictive properties before you sucked my fingers dry. I redipped them just so you could enjoy a second round of my Creamsicle delight. The rhythm of your dick quickly banging against my dirty car door made me well aware of your looming release. I stole my fingers out of your mouth and restrummed myself good. I imagined seeing your body bucking up against my car at the very same time I started my own quivering climax. We peacefully stayed in that moment and savored the pleasure high. I stopped being a tease when I reached over and unlocked the passenger side door. I did not have to say anything; everything was that obvious.

You treated my open invitation with urgency, running right over to the unlocked door without delay. You climbed in and shut the door. We used our eyes to communicate our wants. I looked over at you and smiled, then lifted my hips up out of the seat to reposition myself. In mid-air, I pulled my pants and panties off in one swift push. I purposely took off my sexually stained thong and tossed it over to you to enjoy. I fell back into my seat and kept on going. I had complete confidence that you would figure out what to do with my smelly thong once you had it in your hands. Just as I thought, I watched you bring my scented thong up to your nose and deeply inhale. My sexually-rained-on thong made you hard for the second time in five minutes. It excited me to see Mister smelling my perfume and pussy-infused panties as if they were his to keep.

With no panties on, you watched me reach into my purse, pull out an egg-shaped vibrator, put it directly on top of my naked clitoris and turn it on. Hum and buzz it went! My partially naked body iridescently glowed in the dark from the amber-colored overhead parking-lot lights that reflected down on me. It was so fucking sexual and so fucking hot how I stayed in the orgasm zone for as long as I did. I was tired when I got to my car, and now I was not. My naughty alone time lifted me up out of tiredness and delivered me into an indescribable realm of uncontrollable awakenment. It was so wrong to be getting off in the middle of the school parking lot, but I was doing it, and I did not care who saw.

The second orgasm was just as intense as the first one was. That night in my car, I was a good girl gone bad. I was out of breath and sweaty. I already came twice, but I needed another. So when I looked over at you in my passenger seat and our eyes met, we instantly were in each other's souls. You looked so fucking sexy sitting there in my car with your erect cock out, so sexy that I spat into the palm of my right hand and reached over to help you out. You released him to me, and I gripped your shaft with tight conviction. I rubbed myself, and I stroked you at the same time. But then after twenty-one ups and downs, I deliberately stopped so that I could concentrate on my third. At least I gave my saliva for lubrication and fragrance thong for sniffy inspiration. It took you less than two minutes to cum all over the front of your clean, button down polo.

It excited me to see you shoot your warm semen all over your freshly laundered shirt. That was my visual cue to get off again. So I quivered and came with two fingers deep inside of my vagina. When you came, I came too. We looked at each other with jubilant joy, then you took my thong and vanished into the darkness of the night.

Even though you were not there, Mister, you were there. I cannot speculate on what would have happened if you were inside of my car that night, but I could guess that I would have climbed on top of you, put you inside of me myself, and rocked up and rolled down on you until we both climaxed together. Look what you have done to me. You are a bad boy, but I like it.

Thank you for helping me open up to all things possible. We need to meet in the flesh sometime soon. Don't we?

XoXoXoXo,
M

M could not wait for him to get her lusty letter. She knew he would be excited after reading it, but just how excited, she did not know. M sent it to him, then took a later weekend afternoon bubble bath. The bubbles were plentiful, and the flickering candlelight set the perfect ambience. Turning down the lights, M romantically enjoyed her bubble bath in the soft glow. She stayed under the bubbles for a good part of an hour. No music, no TV, just the sounds of the bubbles popping and fizzling away played a soothing melody that touched her soul. Then . . .

"M, we are going to start making dinner. Come and join us when you can."

Her two roommates started the party without her. But minutes after M heard the pussycat theater announcer, she walked into the kitchen and found the girls already sipping on the first of three mediocre-priced wines. M picked out a glass, poured it full, and joined the party. She walked in on story sharing of men, work, and life. It did not take long for the girls to settle the bet.

"We were just talking about you. We wondered where you disappeared too. It made us wonder if you decided to take our advice and write him a good fuck me story. So . . . did you?"

M had prepared herself for any question except for that one.

"I took a bubble bath. And yes, I might have written him something sexy. But I am not exactly confessing to anything."

M giggled.

"You owe me twenty dollars."

"I know. I did not think she would go through with it. Okay you win. Damn you, M!"

Her two roommates had a twenty-dollar bet about whether M would write him a story or not. Obviously, one guessed right.

Nonetheless, the girls had their girls' night in while being buzzed on wine and giggles. It was a well-worth-it event that all three of them needed. They took a six-hour guilt-free vacation from emotions, men, and life, though M could not help but constantly wonder what Mister was doing across town.

CHAPTER 26

Calm before the Storm

Mister was across the way, over one town, and down two blocks, sleeping. He had comatosely slept through the night and morning without having another lucid wet dream. His nocturnal rest gave him a manly appetite; that was all he knew. Oddly enough, the house was silent. It was like Alex never came home.

"Oh boy, did Alex get lucky? I bet he did. Now it is my turn. Isn't it?"

Despite Alex's disappearing act, Mister went to the kitchen and brewed fresh coffee and made three eggs over-easy style. Still no Alex, so Mister finished breakfast and went outside, opened the garage, and took out all the things needed to clean his Humvee. Mister and Alex loosely scheduled vehicle clean out for every Saturday morning. Mister thought he was going to be the only one washing anything that morning, but before the garage door stopped opening, Alex pulled up and parked. Mister turned around and saw Alex smiling and waving from behind the windshield. Right then, Mister knew Alex got some.

"You did get lucky, didn't you?"

Alex's chuckle told Mister the correct answer.

"Maybe."

Alex snickered, then continued.

"I slept there, but then she kicked me out because she had to work. Let me go inside and get some breakfast, then I will be out."

Mister laughed, then uncoiled the water hose, and turned the water on. He started the Humvee was job without Alex. He could not help but wonder what it would be like to meet M in person. He had thought it forty-nine thousand times up until that moment.

"How do I ask her out? What if she says no? What if we perfectly get along? What then? I really hope we get along. I want her bad. She had better show up if I ask her to. But what if she doesn't show up at all?"

Alex walked out of the house, interrupting Mister's morning thoughts. Together, they cleaned their cars and talked about baseball, leaving girls out of the equation. After baseball talk and car-washing, Alex took a restroom break, then came back, and resumed washing. Their ping-ponged banter had been halted by Mister's lack of enthusiasm.

"What is up with you, Mister? You usually have more to say. Is everything okay?"

"Yeah, A. I am more than okay. Just thinking about life is all. Ya know?"

"Yes, Mister, I know the feeling. I have been thinking a lot about that too. I do not know what to do with mine. I do know what I want to do, but I don't have the means to do it. Right now, I feel restless but excited about the possibilities."

"I know the feeling. Been there, done that. Are you losing interest in going to school? That happened to me. I took a semester off, and it helped me get refocused. Though you cannot take off more than one semester; otherwise, you won't ever go back. True fact!"

"Hmm. I have been thinking about that a lot. I like Kelcey. She is a great girl, and we get along well. She makes me want to get a full-time job and stop school. I feel so immature when I tell people that I am in school. Working part-time does not do it for me anymore."

"Oh yeah, Alex? I know exactly what you are saying. When you start feeling like that, you need something to change. Can you get a job in a museum or something? What kind of jobs does one seek out with psychology knowledge besides being a shrink?"

"I have applied for several jobs. I just wish I had the BA degree. I am two semesters away. I hate being so close yet so far away. I wanted to get into the counseling field. I like helping others solve problems. I sent out my résumé to fifteen places last week. Maybe someone can hire me as their apprentice or something like that. I would not mind having on-the-job training."

"Oh, nice, Alex. At least you have an idea of what you want to do. I say go for it."

Despite Mister appearing to be engaged in Alex's future, all sorts of places and times, plans and ideas to meet M overruled his mental capacity. His mind was in overdrive, trying to plan out their first date. Mister knew he had to win her affections over at all costs. He was not going to take no for an answer, but with M being completely silent, he was more than concerned. Complete silence. Not even the usual junk e-mail made his phone ring. He expected quiet since it was the weekend, but not that quiet. Since it was M's turn to write, Mister remained silent. Then finally, Saturday, mid-afternoon, he got alerted. He put down the Windex and traded it in for his ringing and buzzing phone. His hands and clothes were already dirty from washing the Humvee, and now, his mind was made filthy from the way M told of her night-school parking-lot pleasure. Her words of sensual delight doused him with sexual depravity. Every next sentence made his penis grow and grow big. He felt the blood rushing into his best friend at a rapid rate so fast that it made his khaki shorts bulge.

"Hey, A, I need a bathroom break. I will be right back."

Mister left the Windex bottle sitting on the floor of the Humvee right next to the dirty rag while he speed-walked right into the bathroom to take care of himself. He did not have to pee; he had to come. How could he not want to shoot his semen all over the sink while reading her perverted words? He got off to the idea that he perverted M's sturdy mind of innocence, making her innocent thoughts be just as naughty as his were. His knee-buckling orgasm ended as fast as it started.

He strutted passed Alex back to where he was before M's midday dirty e-mail of lust. It took him all of eighteen minutes to finish washing the Humvee. He put everything away, rolled up the hose, and walked inside with a different agenda.

M,

OMG is all I can say! Yes. Oh. My. God, M! Your fantasy makes me a stumbling drunk, and I did not have to consume any alcohol to be this high. I was in the middle of washing the Humvee when I had to stop and take a jerk-off break because of you. Really, I did! I could not help but want to make love to myself after reading your NC-17-rated words. An intense orgasm made me shake and shiver all over. My hands were dirty from washing off the Humvee, but I did not care when I grabbed the nearby silky hand lotion, squirted it in the palm of my hand, and rubbed it in to my manhood. It did not take me long to get it slick enough to make it feel silky smooth. I did not have to do a whole lot to orgasm either. I thought about you and me the entire time I fucked myself. You made me want to watch myself climax in the bathroom mirror. The first burst of creamy come landed on the mirror. There was a lot of built-up pressure that caused such an outburst like that. It felt amazing to shoot it that far. I wanted to share my midday break with you. It is only fair that you get to know what I did. Isn't it? I must now get back to washing the Hummer, then food-shop.

I will write you more later.

Mister

M was told to expect another e-mail later on, but exacts where not known. It made her feel good that he constantly kept in contact. Even though the e-mail was not as long as his others were, it showed

M that she was on his mind. Their private pussycat theater party did not stop until just after 2:00 AM, but M had a fun girls' night in with the women on Spruce Way.

Mister spent Sunday watching preseason baseball and talking with Alex. The chitter-chatter of Sunday was centered on the up-and-coming baseball season. Mister did weeding out in the front-yard flower bed between games while Alex mowed the lawn. Once upon a time, all the gardening was left up to his late mom. He took over her coveted role of keeping all the entrusted rose bush's budding. Out of Mister's quiet Sunday in suburbia, flourished determination.

M woke up Sunday in a great mood. Although she wondered when Mister's next note would come. Even though M wanted to lie in bed all day thinking about him, she rolled out of bed with sleep in her eyes. While rubbing her eyes, she heard her roommates talking through the closed door. At first, she could not make out what they were saying, but when she opened the door, she heard them talking about fantasies of Prince Charming while cleaning up the kitchen. She quickly poured herself some already brewed coffee and joined in on their on-going conversation.

"Not all men are bad. You just have to find the right one, is all."

They giggled and chatted more about their ideal princes.

"Mine has to be tall, handsome, and a gentleman. I want him to open the door for me and kiss me good-night every night with passionate meaning," said M.

"Mine has to be dominate, yet he will know when to shut up and let me have my way," said her oldest roommate.

"Mine has to make a lot of money. And he needs to spoil me with presents and gifts and kisses whenever I want them," said her youngest roommate.

Each gave their ideal Prince Charming qualities in succession. It was as if they just put their order in for the man of their dreams, hoping that he would show up on their bedroom porch.

The three girls spent most of the day doing a thorough spring cleaning of the condo while trading gossip and relationship war stories. M worked herself into a late-afternoon nap, only waking up to the smells of cooking fajitas. Her roommates made something simple yet delicious. They continued their girl talk while sitting around the TV, catching up on their prerecorded programs as they finished off the last bottle of wine in the house. The magenta-colored alcohol seduced M to sleep. She had waited all day for an e-mail from Mister that never came.

The only remaining responsibilities that Mister had was making Sunday dinner for Alex and Rocket. He served up the usual Sunday steak dinner while watching baseball highlights on ESPN. Mister chuckled to himself while remembering what he did last weekend. In looking back, he could not believe that he stuck himself into a seventy-two-hour sexual blender of splendor. Although he was still partially inside of the blender, at least he was not comatose anymore. As he cooked dinner and thought up new things to write M, he shared guy talk with Alex while listening to the ballgame in the background. It became one of those super awesome mid-spring nights worth remembering.

M did not know it yet, but Mister was in the middle of creating new fantasies to tease her with. He needed to make M's nipples hard with excitement and panties stained with wetness. But that wasn't happening tonight. Instead of writing her something, he wrote her nothing. As he lay sprawled out on his bed, he knew with complete surety that this was the week that they would meet in the flesh. At fifty minutes past 11:00 PM, Mister crashed through the wide-open gates of dreamland.

• • • • • • • • • ● • • • • • •

Building It Up

The weekend passed, and Mister woke up to a new work week. He was up ten minutes earlier than his alarm sounded. Mister's jazzed excitement for the up-and-coming meet-and-greet with M was what made him want to be awake more than it was work deadlines. For the second time ever, Mister truly felt absolute positivity about his life as a collective whole; possibilities of meeting M inspired that. Over the weekend, Mister decided that they should meet offline sooner than soon, as in that up-and-coming week, and that was his job to make happen.

With end-of-the-month forecasted reports due, Mister planned to be at work by seven to intentionally take advantage of the unoccupied office. Mr. Tsar never worried about getting the reports on time despite Mister's procrastination methods. It was clockwork how he walked out the door in his usual thirty-five-minute-flat get-ready-for-work routine. On his drive to work, he watched the dark morning blue sky slowly turned lighter, then light. He thought about everything that had happened since having his dream. Feelings of happiness, freedom, and growth were felt strong deep inside of his spirit. He parked his rig far out in the parking lot and walked into work with joyful glee. He turned off the alarm and turned on the essential lights while walking down the dark hallway. A quick pit stop at the break room was necessary due to the unwritten office rule of first one there started the coffeepots a-brewing. As he walked passed D's empty office, he had strong urges to unload his liquid orgasm all over her desk. Luckily, they were just ideas, at least for the time being.

Mister walked into his dark office six minutes past seven. He sat down, turned on his desk lamp, and started report writing. It was one of those once-in-a-blue-moon kind of days that he had abundant energy and excitement riffling through his veins. Mister was never in the office that early, but he liked how it felt to have the entire office to himself. The office was tranquilly quiet, which allowed him to hear some raindrops faintly falling. Even though he could not see the rain from where he sat, he was attracted to its erotic sound. The seductive lull of the rain catapulted him into another daydream. He did not go into work to dream, yet daydream he did. Fantasies of M were as vividly real as real could be.

M appeared outside of his office window in the pouring down rain. She was dressed in a casualized, cottonized, sky-blue, shoe-top length, button down frock. The coming-down rain drenched her hair wet in the most sensualized way a man could ever imagine. The raindrops soaked into her dress, making it cling to her curves like Saran wrap. She smiled, then pressed her front side against the glass and puckered him a lucid wet kiss.

Still shallow in the dream, Mister was compelled to walk over to the office window and peer out at the falling rain. He stood in front of the window and converged on the drops with tunnel vision. High-up clouds kept the sky a dark-grayish blue with serious threats of a major torrential downpour in its mist. For now, the rain was a steady constant. With every droplet of water splattering against something hard, sensual echoes triple-amplified through his head. Dark clouds mixed with occasional bolts of lightning turned his G-rated fantasy into an NC-17 fabrication about M.

Right before his daydreaming eyes, the office window vanished into thin air, and she walked in. She dripped with rain and spoke with shy innocence.

"My, my, Mister. There you are. Are you going to stand there or help me dry off? Towel, please! No towel? All righty then, you better help me out of my dress before I get cold! Slip it over my head and throw it on your desk if you want."

Mister was too stupefied by how his window disappeared in an instant to speak. Instead, he invaded her personal space with a masculine hand grab for the hem of her skirt. At first, he tugged on it, then lifted it slowly. Mister treated his office guest as a peepshow treat.

Even though Mister and M had not known each other for very long, he was 150 fucking percent powerless over her naive personality. No matter what he did or did not do, he could not get M out of his head. She was there at every twisted turn. All their conversations were unexpectedly sexual from the beginning which made for a fast, tight intimate bond from the get-go. What mattered most was day after day, night after night, he kept her turned on by being himself. He made damn good efforts to convey his intimate sentiments to M any way he could.

She giggled, then put her hands at her sides and perpendicularly opened them to stop her dress from going up any further. Her stoppage made him look at her face-to-face to find out why.

His lust quickly turned downright dirty as the rain pounded the ground harder. Although he should have been writing the forecasted sales reports, he put work on hold and let the daydream play itself out.

She reached for and grabbed his tie, using it for a dog leash to yank him over to his desk. She forcefully pushed him down into the chair, hiked her left leg up, rested her bare foot on his armrest, and locked eyes with him in an erotic stare-down contest. He felt her wetness drip onto his pants and business dress shirt when she moved in close and removed his tie so that she could use it to tie his hands together behind his chairback.

Even though they had not yet met, Mister's daydreamed impression was too realistic to dismiss. His fast morning roller-coaster ride of emotions came to a screeching halt when D delicately meandered into his office without any kind of announcement. When D spoke in her high-pitched, energetic "good morning" voice, his daydream burst.

Despite being in dream mode, he nonchalantly returned her hello with a "Hey." It was not her perky hello that woke him up more than it was her appearance. The more he looked, the faster he got back to reality. Mister was stunned to see D at work before 8:30 AM due to dropping the kids off at school. Yet there she was standing in his doorway, looking just as sassy as ever.

"I'm sorry, D. I was daydreaming, and I did not hear you come in. For the record, I wasn't trying to ignore you."

"It's okay, Mister. I see how you are. Kidding! I could tell you were deep in thought, so I am sorry for being the interruption."

D felt awkward, especially since that was their first face-to-face since she admitted she was S, but she was not about to let that ruin her mood.

"You must be busy with the forecasts. But since I saw your lights on, I wanted to say hi. If you need anything, I will be down the hallway and to the left."

D walked out of his office just as quietly as she entered it. But minutes later, his office became a parade of who's who. Both Tsars came in to say hello five minutes apart from each other, then the installation manager stopped in for a chitchat about hiring more installers to handle the new workload. Now that his daydream was totally lost in translation, he sat back down and picked up where he left off. Though his concentration was weak at best, he kept pushing through the rhetoric to finish the reports with time to spare. He printed them out and picked them up, then walked them over to Mr. Tsar's office and hand-delivered them.

"Here are the reports. We are making sales history this month and set a three-month record for extended warranty sales. You will like this report."

"Will this sales productivity stay consistent for the coming quarter?"

"Max, I am fairly certain we can maintain it for at least the next quarter."

Max smiled and quietly clapped his hands then gave Mister a fist-bump.

"Good job! You and D keep up the great work. If we can keep up those performance levels going, we can open a satellite office. That is on my future to-do plans. Thank you for the reports, Mister, and have a great day."

Mister walked out with a skip to his step and a smile that made his day. He had one hour to kill before having to leave for his eleven-thirty appointment, so he took his overjoyed happiness down to D's office and made a guest appearance. He wanted to tell D the good news about the sales report, and Mr. Tsar's thoughts of the company's future, but he was still hurt over her playing S ordeal. He should not have been in D's office, but he was there with mixed feelings. When he entered her office, the first thing he noticed was the smell of her perfectly selected perfume. The mixture of her perfume scent and body chemistry played well together in a melody meant just for him to hear. Not everyone could match perfume with their body chemistry as well as she could, but it appears D knew that secret. With D sitting behind her paper-covered desk, Mister intentionally cleared his throat then broke the great news to D in a flirtatiously flashy way.

"You're looking better than a juicy bowl of ripe cherries on a warm Sunday morning. Are you trying to earn brownie points by working early?"

His opening comments mellowed D out of her worried state of mind, settling her into friend mode. Even though his feelings were still hurt over the S thing, Mister kept his personal feelings out of the mix while telling D about the good sales news.

"We did it, D! We did it!"

D looked up at him with confusion.

"Come again? What did we do?"

"I just did the sales quota reports, and it was our best quarter ever."

"Oh, wow! Awesome. So how do you plan on celebrating that feat with me, Mister?"

Her smile lit up his brilliant mind, flooding his brain with all kinds of sexual thoughts, mostly centered on her desk. Of course, Mister was not about to tell D his real thoughts, but he almost succumbed to her charm.

"How about you get me another one of those full-body massages with a happy ending? That would be a good way to celebrate success. Unless you want to give it to me? Or maybe we can get tandem massages with happy endings? Your treat."

"Does that mean you're not mad at me anymore about my pretending to be S?"

"Oh, I am still mad about that, D. You are going to have to make that up to me in a much bigger way than a massage."

"I really am sorry for trying to run a game on you like that, but it was fun. Wasn't it?" She giggled like a remorseful schoolgirl. "Tell me how I can make it up to you, and I will do it. Anything, just name it."

"Let me get back to you on that. As for our friendship, I will not let S ruin us. I admit you really had me going for the first few e-mails. You gave it away when you used your "don't cum on my desk" comment. That and your overly aggressive innuendoes made me think I was talking to someone I already knew. A stranger does not say some of the things you did unless they know they could get away with it. You obviously knew you could get away with what you said, and that gave you away. But it took me a while to figure it all out. When I added everything up and I still could not get the correct answer, I knew there was more to who S was. Then a few more e-mails later, I put it all together. I cannot lie; you majorly bummed me out. My only wish is that you would have given us a better chance to get together. I am mad at you for that. You can call me selfish if you want, but things would have been much different if only you would have accepted my advances. But instead, you now have competition, full-blown competition at that, D. Right now, you still have a chance, but I do not know for how much longer."

Mister was honestly brutal with D for a purpose—to sincerely tell her what she would miss.

"Humph! Full-blown competition, eh? Really? Good for you, Mister. You deserve someone good. I am not ready to end my marriage yet, but I am almost there. I just need to make it right within me first. I know you understand me better than anyone, but I feel like I should keep telling you that. You are a great man, and I am sure you will make someone very happy even if it is not me. But if it is me, I promise that every fucking day you wake up next to me, Mister, I will take your soft cock into my hot mouth and suck it off. Soft and slow is the way I would do it until you cum in my mouth. Every morning without fail."

D also wanted Mister to know what he would miss.

"On that note, D, I need to go before I end up cumming all over your desk, pants, and hands."

Mister did not give D any sort of chance to respond as he sarcastically smirked, then walked off, ending their conversation with a playful snicker to his evil laugh. The way he left D's office gave her future ideas of what might come next.

He walked back to his office, sat down in his leather chair, and gloated over the victory. He knew he had gotten under D's skin. He wanted her to feel bad, and bad was exactly how he made her feel. Mister's gloating was short-lived. He knew he needed to write something to M before he left the office to keep her intrigued. He quickly typed out a good-morning flirt to M.

Good morning,

I am sorry about last night. Ha ha! I am already apologizing for things from the night before. I will not make that a habit. Anyway, I got caught up in doing weekend chores and watching baseball with my roommate. I did not purposely try to avoid you; I needed to relax, and that was how I did it. I have so many things I want to say and write to you. Don't be upset with me because I am honestly thinking about you. But for now, I can only say hi. I will write a ton more later.

XoXoXo,
Mister

Without hesitation, Mister sent the e-mail to M then prepared for the rest of his day with due diligence. He brought with him the keys of success everywhere he went.

M was at work, working away before her boss got it. M greeted her boss with a "good morning," which made her boss pleasantly smile.

"Give me fifteen minutes then come and see me so that we can talk about how we can make the reports better."

"Okay! I will see you in fifteen."

Her boss went to her office, then prepared to meet M. Luckily, M's phone rang minutes after her boss left. Instead of reading it right away, she saved it for the first morning break. Just before break time, M walked into her boss's office with a notepad and her mind willingly ready to share her ideas on how to make the monthly reports better.

"I guess M came back. Where so ever did you find her? I thought she was lost forever."

"M always has been here. She was just distracted for a minute. Although she is still preoccupied, M promises not to ever let it affect her work again. She does not want to let you or the company down."

That morning, M and her boss came to an understanding. They both knew what was expected of the other. Then they hatched plans and ideas on how to make the reports more comprehensive. One hour twenty minutes later, M walked out of her boss's glass-walled office, heading outside to the pit for a fifteen-minute break. When M passed by the front desk, Miss BB grinned like she knew something that M did not, but M did not let Miss BB's catty grin affect her excited mood in the least bit.

M read Mister's e-mail with expectations, but after she read its short amount of words, disappointment ensued. When what she wanted was another round of sexy stories fueled by his naughty perversion, all she got was a jazzless note saying hi. M picked herself up from the disappointment, then walked back into work while flashing Miss BB a sarcastic glare aimed right at her forehead. As M walked down the hallway, she prepared not to write him back for a long while; his jazzless note messed with her head that much.

CHAPTER 28

The Catch

Mister had been on an epic roll ever since his lucid wet dream was dreamed. Though it was more than just the dream that produced those results. M's extra shove of confidence also gave him superhero abilities. Mister knew he made the right decision in holding out hope for his past torment to be gone. He could almost touch the light at the end of the tunnel; it was that close.

His two sales appointments were poor distractions that barely kept him away from the main event. Nonetheless, he made a sale with one appointment remaining. In between making follow-up phone calls and shuffling through new prospects, Mister broke for lunch. He drove to the sandwich place where he got root beer and a salad to go. He chose the usual close-by park to eat. Parking under the aged oaks, he opened the sunroof and let the cooler air take him somewhere special.

The crisp rain-flavored air that mixed well with the rushing river kept Mister's overwhelmed mind entertained. After eating, he spent ten minutes concentrating on nailing out the finer details of their lunchtime date. He knew the when and where only in his head. The back-and-forth made him want everything to be perfect right down to the first *hello*, yet unsurety kept Mister sharpening and resharpening the details. He spent his entire lunchtime conjuring up the right way to ask her out.

My sweet Miss,

Sorry that my last email was not a long story of sexual tease. I wanted it to be, but I got caught up with life and work. Please forgive my lack of focus. I know you deserve to get more attention than I have given you over the last few days, and for that, I am sorry. I have had a ton of things going on ever since I dreamed that dream, but I am so glad I dreamed it. Its happening gave me emotional freedom from a tumultuous past of self-tormented locked-up seclusion. So when you levied your many ways of hot and bother against me, I was shocked, then stunned, and now, I'm ready to do something about it. That is the truth! M, I quadruple dare you to go on this hot erotic adventure with me. Together, you and me, let's make this thing real and take it offline. Answer, Mister, because he wants to know!

Mister

M received his second e-mail of the day just as she took her afternoon break. She did not need any explanations; rather, she only needed him. After reading his last e-mail, M wanted Mister to lay his gentlemanlike ways upon her womanhood. It made her feel like she mattered to him, and for that, she gave him an unfiltered response.

Mister,

I cannot comment on anything else but the obvious. We infamously get along, and that is all I need to know to answer you. But before I answer, I need to tell you about some things that are on my mind. Things that might be obvious, but hopefully not.

Thank you. Thank you for showing me there is more to life than work and school. I was too busy protecting my heart that I forgot about the other part of me. Firstly, you make me like the "us" possibilities more than I had planned. Secondly, I never imagined that I would find someone as interesting as you are. Thirdly, you give me a whirlwind of hope that amazes me. And lastly, it is your charm and intellect that constantly make me quiver whenever I think about us being together. What else can a girl ask for besides having her very own Mister to play with? You make me feel risqué, and I like it.

So yes, you were right when you suggested that I had both of my hands inside my pants. You, Mister, are a bad influence, sir. Whatever you do, don't stop! Still want to meet?

M

He got her e-mail just before walking into his last Monday appointment. Mister strutted into the business meeting with an extra ego charge to his step all because of M's interest. He knew she did not have to tell him all those things, yet she did, and that made his head spin with dizzy delight.

Despite having ultra-high confidence, he could not close the deal, but there was still opportunity. It was his second no-sale in three weeks, but he did not let it bother him, shedding it off like an unneeded fur coat. Sure, it was a hiccup, but his good fortune was unstoppable. He blew off the no-sale by writing M a third e-mail in just as many hours, for he knew the time had come.

Dearest Miss,

Three e-mails from me in one day. I know, crazy, right? Well then, I had better make this one count. All righty then! This is not a long love letter or an erotic sex story; instead, it is me asking you a direct question that requires a direct answer.

I want to see you, I need to see you, and I demand to see you. I will not take no for an answer. So tomorrow, Tuesday, early afternoon, we meet. Meet me for coffee, hugs, and flirts? What do you say?

Mister

M pulled out her handy-dandy smartphone and read his overdue question with expectant excitement. She could have answered him two weeks prior, but he never asked. The entire time, they played their version of a sexualized "duck, duck, goose" game that erotically made each other squirm in their undies. She exceptionally played the game well, for she knew he liked, wanted, and deserved to be teased hard. Even though M wanted to respond right away, she deliberately stalled her response until after she got home.

M prominently walked into her condominium with arrogance oozing out of her every stride, acting like she owned the whole damn complex. She was not even remotely bothered by her roommate's favorite weeknight reality-drama engrossment. She let them binge-watch their favorite reality dramas without much more than a fast hello before sneaking off to her room. M grabbed her laptop from the bed, put it on the desk, and got onto the internet in preparation of writing him back.

Before sitting down and answering his direct question, she tried on three of her sexiest outfits to do a dry run for their face-to-face unification. M picked out three outfits and tried them on. She modeled them in the mirror with dips and dashes to pick out the right look. While twirling around in front of the full-length mirror at 11:05 PM, M paid close attention to how her skirt fluttered and boots elevated her ass. She wanted her bold appearance to break his heart and willpower all at the same time. After trying on all three outfits, she picked the one that would make him drool the most.

M chose the virgin-white skirt ensemble to wear. She knew it would be hard to keep the white clean, but she also knew that her chastity belt innuendoes explicitly dictated the color. She got the idea that her black-and-white-striped V-neck vest and calf-length, side-zipped boots would make his mind explode with thoughts of "sexy," but she unequivocally knew his heart would instantly palpitate from imagining the visuals of her steal-made chastity belt being on. What she did not know was if the chrome-colored sturdy-posted heels or the lace-top stockings would strike the kill shot. Whichever it was, she knew she would have to come prepared to play-out any hand Mister dealt.

Before sitting down to write him her answer to his question, M put on the blue Velvety Ones to keep her confidence strong enough to properly answer him with a resounding *yes*. Seconds after the crushed velvet touched her skin, she felt its naughty effects. What started with searing intensity shooting out of her nipples ended with a glistening, well-lubricated pussy ready for climax.

Mister,

I thought you would never ask. I was beginning to wonder if you were a wet dream, but obviously, you are not. I am glad for that. So you want to meet me, do you? And you won't take no for an answer? Hmm . . . Then how can I answer you, if you already answered for me? However, just in case you need to hear it from my innocent lips, YES. YES! YES, let's meet. I will meet you tomorrow. Tomorrow for lunch, we will meet. But one thing. You never told me where. So what I propose is meeting at Café Puséé. It is the newest coffee place in town. Kodi and I checked it out last week, and it was very Italianesque. It has glass windows everywhere, and it has all the coffee and caffeine you could ever want. The atmosphere is swanky, and they play jazzy kinds of music to quench everyone's thirst for stimulation. You can even get on the internet and work there if you wanted. Although I think working there is discouraged more than it is promoted. Let's meet there. I will see you at 1:30 PM.

M

After her response, M got into bed and touched herself all over. With the room dark, her hands glided over the soft velvet as she felt herself up. With every naughty touch she took, her confidence and sexiness tri-folded into a slow solo bedtime finger-bang job.

Mister had been anxious ever since he asked her, and still no conclusion. The wait was miserably sexy. He wondered when or if she would write back. Then as time changed to 11:02 PM, his anxiousness turned into nervousness as the room's silence was interrupted by a vibrating phone. Pins and needles pricked his emotions while deciding if he should read her e-mail then or wait until morning.

All kinds of thoughts ranged from "I do not deserve her" to "What will I do if she says no?" to "Will the new Mister be able to be sustainable?" plagued his every thought. Even though he moved on and put the past torment out of his mind, his past still weakened his character. Despite all of it, he bravely opened her message and read it aloud.

Immediately, Mister knew her answer, and that instantly made him erect. Seeing her *yes* gave him godlike strength. Right at once, her three yeses in succession literally drowned out all past insecurities, helping him to blast through the end of the dimly lit tunnel into a new realm of probability. Minutes after he read her definitive answer to his solo question, he passed out on the loveseat with Rocket lying at the foot of the bed.

He woke up with a Tuesday morning woodie. The erection reminded him to look extra spiffy for their lunch date. Even though he had two appointments before their date, he positively knew that he had to dazzle her panties off with his appearance and personality. It was a good thing that he did not have much time to think about their date because he would have missed the two beforehand sales. He gave himself a forty-five-minute break between his second appointment and their date to rid out any of his shrewd businessman mentality, trading it in for his red-hot Romeo effect.

M had all damn day to think about Mister and their date. From the time M woke up, she was thoroughly excited in every way known to womankind. Her priority was getting off with Mr. Showerhead so that she could calm her fears and nervousness while extending her overnight Velvety Ones confidence boost. She let the showerhead get herself off twice before getting out of the shower. The first orgasm was necessary to get her mind clear, and the second one was necessary to stay confident in her decision to see him.

M's workday passed by as slow as falling molasses. All day long, she focused on Mister's searing-hot words of sexual mystique during her few daydreams of how it would all go down. M did not know if he would be sweet and gentle or naughty and perverted. Nevertheless, M had mentally prepared for both.

It approached zero hour. Both were excited to meet each other for the first time. In Mister's mind, he already knew exactly how it was going to go, whereas M could only conjure up and speculate possibilities. Mister planned to lead their naughty little midday soiree, expecting M to follow his lead. The crowds were restless, and the day was gorgeous in every way conceivable. Together, there would be enough kindling to start a five-alarm fire.

The subtle breeze and bright sunlight jazzed up the springtime landscape with vibrant new blossoms at the same time their nervous adrenaline began pumping through their veins. Neither knew what the other's plan was, but they both planned to be early for their date. Mister's plan was to get there early to get the perfect table while M's plan was to do makeup touchups and talk herself into being Mister's Miss.

Mister arrived at Café Puséé first. He did not see anything out of the ordinary after walking in. His casual stroll into the café revealed an elegant medium-sized Italianesque coffeehouse. He was shocked to see how much it resembled the one in his fantasy. Upon closer inspection, Café Puséé had an undeniable eroticism feel to it. It was more of a feeling than a look, yet its sexually sensualized interior let Mister know it was the right place for their first face-to-face.

Without knowing Mister's daydreams or fantasies, M picked out a place that almost matched his imaginary vision to a tee without knowing. Some four days ago, Mister daydreamed of a fantasy in his Humvee that looked and felt the same as Café Puséé. It was not a perfect match, but it was close enough to chill him to the core. It was spaciously spread-out with ample seating everywhere. Its many windows and several skylights were strategically placed to highlight the center water fountain. The water feature added a romantically erotic ambience that spoke the sensual language of love and lust. The floor was made from stamped concrete, reminiscent of the streets in Italy, and the walls were painted and textured just as a small romantic café in Italy might be decorated.

Mister gave himself a self-guided tour around the café to get a feel for its ambience. In minutes, he spotted the best seat in the house. It was a smaller private booth on the left of the shop that looked, sounded, and felt right. The table was occupied with three teenage girls and a motherly figure that looked like they were about to leave. So Mister inconspicuously waited it out by nonchalantly walking around the café. Then finally, they had left, and the table was his. He cleaned up the left-behind crumpled up napkins, bread-crumbs, and empty porcelain cups like it was his job. The table was in earshot of the babbling water feature. Its trickling water was very reminiscent of an Italianesque shop. He liked that the booth was far enough away from prying ears yet close enough to hear the cascading water. Even the incoming sunrays made the spot the sexiest place to sit. Café Puséé was the perfect place for two new lovers to meet for the very first time. Mister demanded the spot to be perfect in every way, for he had a new lover coming to see him.

He used the remaining fifteen minutes to prepare for M's arrival. As soon as he settled in at the best table in the house, Mister excitedly sat there counting down the seconds before he would see his Miss for the very first time. Testosterone freely pumped through his veins, including the thick one in his pants. His emotions were on an up-and-down roller coaster coasting through his soul one note at a time. Only eight minutes before she would arrive.

Then the glass-front French-styled door opened. Even though it was eight minutes earlier than their one-thirty date, she sashayed in through the door with her ruffle-edged skirt fluttering abound. Her glistening lips shimmered and heels clickety-clacked as she made her way inside. His Miss was eight minutes early, and Mister was a frazzled fucking mess.

ABOUT THE AUTHOR

C. Robins became an erotic fiction writer to survive a loveless, unappreciated marriage. After years of romantic starvation and built-up passion ever raging through his bloodstream, he chose to pour out his feelings through positive writings of friendship, lust, and pleasure. C. Robins turned his sadness and rejection into *Mister's Miss*. He is a natural tease that wants to share his lyricism and unique writing style with anyone and everyone that seek out a deep erotic journey. The words, scenes, and scenarios that C. Robbins writes about serve him with the cathartic healing that he needs to adapt and overcome. He writes the *Mister's Miss* series for everyone that is, has, or will be stuck in a less-than-desirable relationship. May his healing be your entertainment.

CPSIA information can be obtained
at www.ICGtesting.com
Printed in the USA
LVHW031257120620
657937LV00003B/610